# CONTENTS

# MURDER

# IN PARADISE

## A LEILANI KEALOHA
## HAWAIIAN THRILLER

### BOOK 1

BY

## CHUCK MORGAN

Printed in the United States of America

First printing 2025

**ISBN 978-1-968179-10-6 (eBook)**

**ISBN 978-1-968179-11-3 (Paperback)**

**ISBN 978-1-968179-12-0 (Hardback)**

LIBRARY OF CONGRESS CONTROL NUMBER

**2025914341**

# DEDICATION

To all those readers who still believe in the power of family over adversity. This story is for you.

# CHAPTER ONE

## *Body in the Banyon Grove*

Detective Leilani Kealoha parked her department-issued Explorer past the last legal turnoff before the banyan preserve. The sun was above the Koʻolau ridge, but the humidity already pressed against her skin, seeping through the starched polyester of her blouse. She unclipped the badge from the visor and looped it through her belt, giving herself the momentary satisfaction of its weight, a subtle reminder that she belonged here, despite what some would say about her blood or her badge. She pulled the rover radio from its charger under the dash and hooked it to her belt.

She ducked under the fluttering yellow tape. HPD CRIME SCENE DO NOT CROSS, strung between the spiked posts of last night's emergency barricade. The tape had already sagged in the tropical damp, curling in on itself, but still enough to keep back the small knot of activists at the trailhead. They clustered with battered cardboard signs: PROTECT SACRED SITES; AʻOLE DEVELOPMENT; and in stenciled red, KAPU. A few teenagers shot her the stink-eye from behind their camera phones, which made her smile. She recognized one as a cousin from her mother's side, hālau connection, two generations back. She gave them all a nod as she passed. "Mōhala ka pua," she murmured. The blossom unfolds. Let them know she'd seen them, and that they'd been seen by her.

The banyan grove itself was sacred, officially listed as historic on some state registry, but more importantly it was revered by the older families and the practitioners. Generations of ceremonies, untold burials in the roots. Leilani had spent childhood afternoons here, learning chants and picking up fallen leaves as offerings, long before she learned how to dust for prints or take blood samples. It hurt to think about how a sacred place could become the backdrop for something this profane.

She pulled out her phone and fired off a quick voice memo to the sergeant: "Kealoha on scene, 8:22. Perimeter secure. Crowd under control." Not exactly accurate, but better to sound in command. She thumbed open the evidence kit from her trunk and started down the uneven path, eyes scanning the trampled undergrowth for anything the uniforms might've missed.

The body of Sonny Alana sprawled at the foot

of the oldest tree, its branches fanning up in a living vault, aerial roots draping to the loamy floor like church organ pipes. Leilani experienced a pang of recognition, the way one recognizes a ruined altar. Sonny's tan slacks were dark at the knees and thighs, stained with wet earth. His blue aloha shirt was twisted under one armpit, torn where it had snagged on the root cluster. His eyes were still open, fixed on a patch of sky through the canopy. His mouth was agape, lips stretched in a grimace, a gloss of drying saliva crusted at the chin.

She knelt beside the body, careful not to let her shadow fall across the face. She catalogued everything: abrasions along the knuckles and forearms, consistent with defensive wounds; fresh crescent cuts on the palms; dirt pressed deep in the nail beds. He had fought hard and lost. The throat, already swelling purple, told the rest. The neck had collapsed in on itself, the angle too steep for anything but violence.

The preliminary photos had been taken last night, judging from the cold flash scarring in the image preview. Leilani switched the setting to manual and moved in for closeups: hands, face, the fresh bruising on the inside of the right elbow. She circled the body once, twice, stopping at the marks scuffed into the bark behind the head. Parallel lines, possibly fingernails, running vertical up the trunk. To the untrained eye it might look like animal damage, but she recognized panic—the desperate upward clawing of someone being dragged down.

She bagged a leaf flecked with blood, tweezed it into the smallest envelope, sealed it and set it in the evidence box. Moving carefully, she used the tape lift on a patch of fabric near Sonny's ribs, where a few dark hairs clung stubbornly to the cotton. Every movement became deliberate, ritualistic; she worked through the checklist from memory, letting her hands find the work while her mind trailed the possibilities.

Behind her, the chanting began: a half-sung, half-shouted oli, calling for justice for the 'āina. The crowd at the perimeter had grown. More signs, more faces. The line of police tape was a membrane, thin and arbitrary. She heard the rhythm and breath of the chant as a living pulse. Leilani forced herself to focus.

At the base of the tree, three offering bowls were arranged in a perfect crescent. One held a bundle of ti leaves tied with a purple cord. The second held a scattering of salt and limu kala. The third, closest to the body, was filled with kukui nuts and a single wrinkled lilikoi. Around them, on small rocks, were pieces of black tapa marked with red pigment: more kapu, more warnings.

She snapped images of each offering and used

a gloved finger to nudge a scrap of paper hidden under the ti leaf. The handwriting was bold, in permanent marker: "We are not afraid. We will not move." The threat and / or promise was left ambiguous.

Her phone buzzed. "Detective, you need anything?" A patrolman, one of the rookies, barely old enough to remember Sonny from his days as a councilman, or from his recent TV stints lambasting the police. Leilani shook her head, not looking up from the body. "Keep the protesters off the tape. And if anyone tries to get a shot, block it. This is sacred ground."

She heard the rookie relay the order in an awkward staccato and the chorus of protest from the crowd. Another sound: the soft click of a digital camera. Leilani turned. A woman in a black tank top, mirrored sunglasses, held her ground near the clearing, snapping methodically, unbothered by the uniform blocking her. She recognized the woman from the morning's social feeds—a local freelancer, live-streaming already.

Leilani sighed. She ran down the checklist: document, collect, preserve. The forensics van would arrive in half an hour, followed by the meat wagon. In the meantime, she scoured the dirt around the body, finding a crushed cigarette, lipstick print on the filter, and a set of fresh, wide boot prints. She used the casting kit to mold one perfect track. She flagged the spot for the techs.

Somewhere past the tree line, a generator started up, a low droning pulse. She guessed the news crews were already setting up their satellite dishes, getting ready for the ten o'clock update. She hated how a body could become content, how quickly the transformation occurred.

A hundred yards away, the protesters' chanting gave way to the sounds of drumming. She sensed it in her chest, a slow, syncopated thunder. It reminded her of funerals, and of the year she spent as a junior cop breaking up drum circles in Kaka'ako after midnight. Always the same: elders chanting, kids circling, someone eventually getting mouthy or drunk. But this morning, the energy was heavier, weighted with something deeper than performance.

She squatted by Sonny's feet, looking up at the vault of banyan roots. Strips of faded cloth and lei left over from past ceremonies drifted in the humid breeze. Above her, half a dozen Mynah birds argued over a spot on the highest branch. She sensed the sweat building under her collar, and something else, a memory. Her mother, reciting a proverb. "He ali'i ka 'āina, he kauwā ke kanaka." The land is the chief; man is its servant. This place had mana. The stench of death thickening the air.

Leilani wiped her brow with the back of her

glove and exhaled. With a practiced motion, she reached into the evidence kit and pulled out the metal calipers, measuring the length and width of the abrasions. Each number was logged onto the notepad methodically and coldly. She hated the feeling of reducing a man's life to data points, but this was the job. If she did it right, the dead would have their say.

"Detective Kealoha?" The voice was soft, careful. She turned to see an older officer, his uniform crisp but eyes shadowed by a long night. "They found something near the lower trailhead. Looks like another offering, but it might be more."

She nodded, stood up, dusted herself off. "Lead the way."

As she left the body, she was aware of the activists watching her. She did not look over her shoulder, did not break stride. Let them see her as they would—the cop, the Hawaiian, the stranger, the daughter of this place. It did not matter. The facts of the case would follow her, like the roots of the banyan, winding deep beneath the surface, impossible to untangle.

At the base of the lower trailhead, the ground sloped steeply, muddy and treacherous. Another patrolman pointed to a cluster of stones along the path. In the center, a wooden bowl, lacquered and old, filled with cracked eggs and a tangle of blonde hair. A hand-lettered card, tucked under the rim, NO REST UNTIL JUSTICE. She lifted the bowl in gloved hands and photographed every angle. Another message for the living or the dead.

She radioed the sergeant. "Sarge, we found additional evidence, symbolic, or ritual significance. Request ETA on forensics." The reply crackled back: "Fifteen minutes. You're trending."

Of course, she was.

Leilani climbed back up the path, taking the long route around the body to avoid further contaminating the scene. As she passed under the canopy, she took one last look at Sonny Alana, face up, arms flung wide, as if trying to embrace the sky. She experienced a wave of vertigo, as though the roots were tugging her downward, urging her to listen to what the dead would say if given voice.

She made a mental note to visit her mother that night, bring flowers, and to ask for wisdom. But first, the case. Always the case. She steadied herself, locked away the reverence, and started cataloguing evidence with renewed resolve. Whatever had happened here, whoever had dared to spill blood on this sacred ground, she would find them. And she would bring the full weight of the law and the ancestors down on their heads.

Makoa waited for her beneath the banyan's arched shadows, perched on a gnarled root that rose from the earth like a knotted, arthritic hand. He wore a faded navy work shirt and slacks, rubber slippers that were translucent at the heel. His face was lined with sun and salt, each wrinkle a tally mark for decades spent in this climate, but his eyes were sharp as a 'io's. When Leilani approached, he nodded but did not rise.

She noticed at once that his hands, broad, dark, speckled with scars, shook slightly as he smoothed his shirt across his thighs. Whether from age or nerves, she couldn't say, but she registered the detail and filed it away.

"Morning, Makoa," she said, standing outside the umbrella of roots. "I appreciate you staying."

He shrugged. "Not like they're going to let me get anything done now." His voice was raspy, a sandpaper drawl. He glanced past Leilani's shoulder, to where the protest crowd swelled and thinned at intervals, their numbers shifting with the rhythm of passing traffic and word-of-mouth updates.

"Can we sit?" Leilani gestured at a low bench formed by an ancient horizontal root. Makoa inclined his head and slid over, motioning her to join. The movement had a certain courtesy, old-school, local style, even here in the aftermath of murder.

She took out her notepad, kept it at her knee, pen uncapped but resting. "I'd like to ask about the man you found."

Makoa scratched the side of his jaw. "Sonny. Never thought I'd see him dead. I mean." He shook his head. "If you'd asked me last week, maybe. But not like this. Not here."

Leilani waited. The silence worked on him, drew him out.

"I get here early. Four, sometimes four-thirty. The sun's not up yet. There's always something, kids tagging the markers, people breaking bottles, or making a mess. I do my loop. Clean up and put out the offerings for the kumu." He swallowed, voice dropping. "Last night, someone knocked over three of the stone shrines, the ones up by the north fence. Poured paint on the petroglyph slabs. Not the first time, but this was deliberate. Mean. So, I come to fix."

He paused, eyes traveling up the massive trunk overhead, as if searching for answers among its thousand arms.

"I hear voices from the path, two, three people. Can't make out words, only the tone. Arguing, angry. I figure it's more vandalism. I wait a little, start up to chase them out. But by the time I get here." He pointed a trembling finger to where Sonny's body waited under a tarp. "Already too late. One man on the ground, not moving. Others gone."

Leilani jotted notes, but mostly she listened, letting his words fill the space. She'd learned early on that patience earned more than interrogation.

"You say you recognized Sonny?"

"Of course. Everyone knows Sonny. He is always here making speeches. You've seen his videos?" Makoa rolled his eyes, not unkindly. "Used to be about aloha ʻāina, but lately it's him versus the world. He fights the developers, he fights the cops, he fights the activists if they don't do it his way."

"You mentioned developers," Leilani prompted.

Makoa's face grew stony. "It's always the same. They come with fancy clothes and lawyers. Promise one thing, do another. They want to turn this land into condos or a golf course, like everywhere else. But this place..." He stopped, searching for the right English, switching to Hawaiian. "He wahi pana. Sacred spot."

She nodded. "And you think Sonny was killed because of that?"

Makoa gave her a look, not unkind but piercing. "You know how it goes, Detective. Place has mana—power. Not everyone respects. Some see dollar signs. Some get greedy, or scared, or both."

Leilani wrote the phrase on her pad. Mana, power.

The old man looked past her again, uneasy. "You see them?" He tipped his chin at the protesters, whose numbers had doubled in the last hour. "They're mad, but they're scared too. They know if we lose this, we lose more than trees. It's our entire history. Our bones."

She followed his gaze, watching the crowd shift and eddy. "Did you see anyone suspicious in the last few days? Unusual visitors, people out of place?"

Makoa thought for a long moment. "Not out of place, no. But..." He hesitated, checking again that their conversation was private. "The other day, I see the councilman, Sonny, arguing with a kid and two men in suits. Not police, not regular local. Mainland style. The kid, he was..." He fumbled for words, drew an outline in the air. "Small, but fierce. Couldn't hear what they said, but it was heated. Almost came to blows. The kid stormed off, the men left, and Sonny stood there, like he was waiting for another fight."

Leilani caught the way he said, kid. "You remember what the kid looked like?"

Makoa shrugged. "Long hair, skinny, wore one red hoodie. Mixed." He wrung his hands together and pressed his palms to his knees, grounding himself. "Reminded me of someone from before, but I can't remember."

Leilani ran her mind through the list of local youth leaders and troublemakers, none matching exactly. She made a note to check city cameras for the red hoodie. "Thank you," she said. "You did right calling it in."

"I no like trouble, Detective," Makoa said, voice softening. "I want to keep the place, pono. But sometimes, the old ways and the new ways." He let the words trail off, gesturing at the sacred grove, the police tape, the crowd with their iPhones and GoPros.

They sat in silence, broken by the rising chant from the trailhead. Leilani wanted to say something comforting, something that would matter, but came up short. Instead, she tore a card from her pad and wrote her cell number underneath her name.

"If you remember anything else, or if you feel threatened, you call me. Anytime."

Makoa took the card in both hands, studied it like a precious object. "Mahalo, Detective Kealoha." He said her name like it was a password. "You tell your mother I said hi, yeah?"

A smile tugged at her lips, unexpected and genuine. "I will."

They rose together, dusted off their hands, and parted ways under the watching banyan. Leilani turned her focus to the crime scene, but a new sense of gravity followed her, something heavier than the evidence kit at her hip.

As she moved to confer with the forensics team, she heard Makoa's voice float back on the breeze: "Be careful. Some spirits are not ready to rest."

The words carried, and they settle into the marrow of her bones. The case was only beginning, but already she sensed the past and the present colliding, roots tangled deep, refusing to let go.

Forensics swept the scene with practiced urgency, their muted conversation mixing with the distant thrum of protest and generator hum. Detective Kealoha walked a tight arc around the perimeter, cataloging each trace of violence, each ritual token, an archaeologist exhuming not only evidence, but the long-buried grudge of a community at war with itself.

She snapped a final set of photographs; boot prints at the north trailhead, a broken zip tie in the roots, a tiny gold cross left behind on the compacted earth. She bagged each item, labeled them in her sharp, methodical hand, and cross-checked her log against the collection list. The crime scene looked picked clean, as if the grove itself had conspired to keep what was necessary, what could not be denied.

As she zipped the last envelope into its folder, her phone vibrated, rattling against a nearby root. She fumbled the gloves off and answered with the clipped efficiency of someone too used to bad news.

"Detective Kealoha," she said, scanning the horizon.

"Good morning, Ms. Kealoha." The voice was unfamiliar, clipped, with a note of patience stretched thin. "This is Ms. Kamaka, Kai's homeroom teacher at Kahala Elementary. I'm calling about today's conference?"

Leilani blinked and looked down at her notepad as if the right words might wait there. "Conference?" she echoed, already picturing the pale pink slip at the bottom of her purse unread.

"Yes, parent-teacher conference," the voice replied. "We'd expected you at eight-thirty. Kai's been distracted this week, and we hoped to talk strategies for keeping him engaged."

Behind her, the forensic techs discussed trajectory analysis. Leilani thumbed the bridge of her nose, fighting the need to curse. "I'm sorry, Ms. Kamaka. Something came up at work. Can I call you after school?"

"Of course," said the teacher, polite but

unmistakably disappointed. "Please check your email—Kai left a note for you, too."

"I will. Thank you." She hung up, lingering over her son's name on the screen. "Kai Kealoha: missed conference." She typed a reminder for three, knowing she'd be lucky to get away by six. The sacrifice of her own childhood—surfing before homework, afternoons at grandma's hālau—had become the sacrifice of his, traded for the endless emergencies of adult life. She wondered what price she was paying for duty.

A movement at the tape caught her eye: the woman in the mirrored sunglasses, still snapping pictures, now flanked by two more teens with tripods and boom mics. "HPD, pack up!" Leilani called out, voice cutting through the sticky heat. "No more photos."

As the forensics team folded up their tarps, she signaled the meat wagon. Sonny's body, now bagged and tagged, was loaded with clinical reverence into the van. A few activists lowered their heads in a gesture that was neither prayer nor protest, but a moment of shared humanity for the dead.

The crime scene technician approached with a clipboard, eyes darting between Leilani's face and her badge. "Anything else before we clear, Detective?"

She ran through the sequence one last time:

footprints, blood spatter, the string of offerings. "Run the DNA on the hair and the cigarette filter. Get prints off the zip tie and the bowl. And check the red hoodie in the city cam feeds." She signed the clipboard with a practiced flourish.

The tech hesitated. He leaned in. "You want me to grab you a coffee? Or something to eat?" There was concern there, half buried under protocol.

Leilani almost laughed. "I'm good. Mahalo."

She watched as the crew packed up, the noise and mess of investigation gradually giving way to the low, persistent sound of the wind and the protest drumming. If she hustled, she'd make it to the station before lunch and still pick up Kai by three, as long as she didn't get called back here or somewhere worse.

She lingered a moment beneath the ancient canopy. Overhead, the banyan's limbs trembled in the rising heat, shadows stretching and folding, as if the tree were breathing in time with the living below. She wondered if Sonny's spirit had already left, or if it hovered on the roots, unwilling to quit the battlefield. The kapu signs, the offerings, the chanting at the trailhead. All of it was meant to keep the balance and to give the dead a clear path to the next place.

She drew herself up, dusted off the knees of her slacks, and headed for her Explorer. On the way, she passed Makoa, now kneeling by one of the repaired shrines, hands moving with the care of someone repairing a broken heirloom. He did not look up, but she knew he sensed her presence.

At the car, Leilani caught her reflection in the window, tired, salt streaks on her face, badge askew. She set her jaw, straightened the shield, and climbed in. The ancient AC wheezed, failed, and she rolled down the window. The morning air was thick with smoke and plumeria and the faint, persistent beat of protest drums.

As she pulled onto the highway, she looked once in the rearview mirror—caught herself split down the middle, detective, and mother, daughter, and stranger. The banyan grove receding in the glass looked almost peaceful now, a green island untouched by violence. But she knew the wounds ran deep, and that she carried them with her everywhere.

# CHAPTER TWO

## *Pressure from Above*

The murder board was nothing more than a rolling whiteboard, the wheels crusted with black gum and the surface permanently shadowed by ten years of dry-erase ghosts. Detective Kealoha stood beside it, spine straight, evidence photos clipped up in ordered lines. The first shot, Sonny Alana, face turned skyward under the cathedral of the banyan, anchored the narrative. Blood evidence, boot casts, the offerings at the roots: every image annotated in Leilani's clean, angular print. It was she suspected, a futile display of order in the face of everything that was not.

The room's air-conditioning cycled through bursts of chemical chill, stirring the musk of old coffee and mildew embedded in the acoustic tiles. Three senior officers sat in padded chairs along one wall, each with a different attitude toward Leilani's report. Closest was Lieutenant Uyeda, biceps bulging against the seams of his short-sleeve uniform; he looked like he'd have preferred to be interrogating a suspect rather than sitting through a slideshow. Next to him, Captain Ishimaru, thin and unsmiling, hands steepled in silent critique. And at the head of the table, the chief, Commissioner Nate Lau, squat and compact, with the face of a man who'd survived two marriages and five city councils and considered them equally hazardous.

"So, we found the vic here," Leilani said, tapping the laser pointer on the photo of Sonny's sprawled body. "Lividity consistent with time of death around midnight. No signs of sexual assault, but clear evidence of asphyxiation. The markings on the neck," She flipped to a closeup, the purpling unmistakable. "Don't match a cord or zip tie. Most likely a strong right hand, probably male. Trace evidence under the nails, skin, and blood. Still waiting on the lab for DNA, but prelim suggests it's not a simple brawl."

Commissioner Lau held up a meaty palm. "And the protest crowd?"

The pointer rested on her hip. "The crowd was organized, not random, and assembled before dawn. Someone sent out a blast on social media. The offering bowls and warning cards were planted after the murder. Almost staged."

Uyeda grunted. "Could be a setup. Political hit."

"Or revenge," Ishimaru added.

Leilani resisted the desire to correct. Instead, she advanced to the next evidence photo, an aerial shot of the banyan grove, crime scene tape glowing bright yellow in the morning haze. "The location wasn't random, either. The banyan is a recognized wahi pana, sacred to at least three families. Two of them have land claims pending with the city. Alana was fighting both sides—developers and cultural groups."

Lau's lips pinched into a tired smile. "So everyone had a motive."

Leilani nodded. "And none of the witnesses are talking. Makoa, the caretaker, gave us the basics but won't name names. The kids in the protest camp clam up the second a uniform walks in. This wasn't some tweaker gone wild; it's layered."

She clicked off the pointer. The city's new station had cost two million and was already too small for its staff; the briefing room was little more than a glassed-in fishbowl with blinds that never quite closed. Outside, she could see the blue flicker of squad lights and, beyond them, a growing cluster of protest signs. IWI KUPUNA NOT FOR SALE; KAPU MEANS NO; WHOSE LAND, WHOSE LAW?

"Detective," Lau said, his tone dropping to the register of a parent discussing curfew. "I'm getting calls every hour. The mayor's office. News crews. The Hawaiian Affairs rep is demanding a joint statement with us and the prosecutor. And that protest out there? It doubled in the last thirty minutes."

Leilani didn't look away. "With all due respect, sir, that's not my problem."

A flicker of something, approval maybe, crossed Uyeda's face. Ishimaru was impassive as always.

Lau folded his hands, slow and deliberate. "I appreciate your devotion to the science, Detective. But we're running out of time. Every day this sits unsolved is another black eye. If you have a suspect, I need it now."

"There are three possibilities," Leilani said. "The family feud angle, the development lobbyists or a radical faction from the protest itself. None fit cleanly. The only person who might have seen something is Makoa, and he's not talking until he gets a visit from his aumakua in a dream or whatever."

Uyeda snorted. "Send a squad with some poke and see if his ancestors get hungry."

Leilani let that pass. "The best lead is a witness statement, red hoodie, young, seen arguing with the vic about three hours before time of death. No prints at the scene, but we're running the city cams for facial rec."

Lau rapped a blunt finger on the table. "I want this wrapped by Friday. The longer we drag our heels, the more it looks like we're hiding something. That's three days, Detective."

Leilani's jaw worked, but her voice was steady. "You want a conviction, or you want the truth?"

Uyeda, ever the practical one, jumped in. "Both, if possible. Preferably in that order."

"Three days," Lau said, again. "If you need more uniforms, you get them. But no more midnight strolls through the banyan. The media's already running the angle that HPD's trampling on sacred ground."

Leilani didn't flinch, but inside, the deadline dropped like a stone. She gathered her folders with careful precision, tapping them into alignment as if that would bring the case into clarity. "You'll have a preliminary suspect by the end of day tomorrow. If I need to call in cultural liaisons or bring in someone from the governor's office, I'll do it."

Ishimaru spoke, gaze fixed on the tabletop. "Be careful with those activists, Detective. Some of them are tied to mainland groups. They want a confrontation, and we don't want to give them a martyr."

"That body under the banyan is already a martyr," Leilani said. "We have to figure out for whom."

Lau stood, signaling an end to the meeting. The men followed, and Leilani lingered, letting the door shut behind their retreating forms. She allowed herself a single, slow exhale. There was relief, but it was laced with dread. Three days to solve a murder. Three days to avoid becoming the next target, either of the killer, or of the system that wanted her to make the problem go away.

She packed up the photos, double checked the digital files, and swept her sleeve over the whiteboard, erasing the outline but not the memory. Outside, the low drumbeat of protest was getting closer, more insistent. She watched it through the streaked glass, wondered how many of those faces belonged to people who would never trust her, no matter what she found.

As she walked down the station corridor, the fluorescent lights hummed overhead, washing everything in the blue-white pallor of perpetual morning. The murder, the protests, the political crossfire, it all ran together, as unyielding as the root network under the banyan. Leilani let her thoughts spiral briefly. She snapped herself back into focus. There was no time for fear or for doubt. All she had was three days, and the facts.

She slipped her badge and gun off her belt as she entered her cubicle, tossing them onto the desk next to a half-drunk coffee and her phone, already blinking with new messages. She scrolled through, ignoring the news alerts, and tapped out a quick line to her son: "Late tonight. Study hard. I love you." She glanced at the screen a moment longer than necessary, opening the folder marked Sonny Alana: Evidence.

In three days, she would either have a suspect, or she'd be on the chopping block with the rest of them.

The neon blue of the screen reflected off the glass behind her, giving her face a second, ghostly outline. She squared her shoulders and began to dig.

The bullpen emptied after ten. The rhythm of desk drawers slamming and badge chains rattling was replaced by the tick of the wall clock. Leilani sat hunched over a desk covered with reports and evidence envelopes, her desk lamp throwing a tight halo onto the stacks. Outside, the city's sodium vapor lamps cast a perpetual dusk over the street, but the station was a sealed terrarium of cold, recycled air, and the faintest trace of last week's microwaved kalua pork.

She started with the homicide file, layered in the witness interviews, typed, printed, and annotated in multiple colors. Her fingertips shone with graphite dust, the side of her hand already stained blue from the pen she favored for corrections. Three times she caught herself rereading the same paragraph, her mind refusing to move forward until the facts fell into place.

She pivoted to the desktop computer, the screen's LED glow outlining every sleepless hour she'd accrued since the start of the case. In the search bar, she entered Keanu Alana, the victim's son, and hit return. Results spooled out, at first predictable, school records, social media, a string of youth sports reports. Deeper in the database came the arrest logs, trespassing, resisting arrest, multiple counts of disrupting lawful assembly. The pattern told its own story. Every charge dropped, every encounter occurring at or near one of the island's sacred sites slated for development.

Leilani kept reading, her eyes burning. "Aina Defenders," she mouthed, scrolling through a series of scanned flyers and group photos. There, in a grainy cellphone shot, was Keanu, shoulders squared, jaw set, arms locked with two girls in matching black T-shirts, all three blocking the path to a bulldozer. Someone had captioned the photo online.

Land protectors hold the line against destruction.

There was nothing ambiguous about the way Keanu glared into the camera, part pride, part defiance.

Leilani printed the image, pushed up from her

chair and tacked it to her own mini murder board, a battered cork rectangle half filled with mugshots, topo maps, and yellow Post-its. Next to Keanu's face, she added the protest group's name in big, red letters, underlined twice.

She cycled through more files, emails between the victim and a local councilwoman, witness statements that contradicted each other, a police report documenting threats spray painted at the previous development site. The only consistency was the intensity. Everyone had something to lose, and none of them were shy about saying so.

Her head throbbed in time with the clock. She massaged the back of her neck, finding the pressure point with practiced fingers, and closed her eyes longer than planned. When she opened them, the screen had timed out, and her own reflection hovered faintly, superimposed over the login prompt. She startled, snorting softly. Sleep was a luxury she couldn't afford.

As she resumed, a soft clatter came from the end of the corridor. The janitor, an older man with shoulders curved from decades of pushing a mop, approached with a rolling bin. He stopped at her desk, eyes flicking over the evidence board, and offered a nod of recognition.

"Hard night, Detective?" he asked, voice hoarse but kind.

She offered a thin smile. "Aren't they all?"

He lifted her trash can with both hands, not wanting to spill the overstuffed contents. "You want coffee? I put a new pot in the kitchen."

She almost laughed. "You're a lifesaver, Tommy. Mahalo."

He grinned, exposing a gold-capped canine, and moved on. The scent of bleach and floor polish followed in his wake, a reminder that the graveyard shift had its caretakers.

Refueled by caffeine, Leilani combed through another run of case notes, this time chasing the connections between the victim, the protesters and the corporate interests who'd spent six years trying to break the community's resistance. She scribbled timelines on legal pads, marked intersections in bold, and drew lines from Keanu's photo to several other faces. The first was a young woman named Malie, rumored to be his girlfriend and the social media engine behind the protests. There was an attorney specializing in indigenous rights and a retired construction exec who'd run for city council on a pro-development ticket.

The pattern crystallized like the first hint of salt on her tongue. Every incident, every protest, led to the same handful of sites, all of them sacred ground, all of them caught in legal limbo. And at the center, sometimes as ringleader, sometimes as target, was Sonny Alana.

She pulled up the public records search again, this time focusing on the luxury resort project nearest the banyan preserve. It had its own file, thick as a bible, containing environmental impact statements, injunctions, heated letters to the editor. The most recent clipping, a week old, showed Keanu at the front of a protest line, shouting into a bullhorn. Next to him, a developer's rep in an expensive aloha shirt grimaced at the media, two bodyguards bracketing him like parentheses.

Leilani circled the photo with a red marker, connecting it to the others with a length of string. The murder was an escalation, someone's last resort, or the inevitable endpoint.

She leaned back, flexing her hands, and scanned the board. Her eyelids drooped, the words and images threatening to blend. She blinked hard, and in that moment, the answer appeared closer, like she could almost touch it.

She logged her findings, scrawling a note to herself on the yellow pad.

Check the financial links between the developer, the councilwoman, and the protest group!

Underlined, exclamation point.

The next time she looked at the clock, it was two-thirty. The bullpen was dead silent except for the sound of the vending machine, and the red LED on the coffee pot gleaming from the kitchenette window.

She stood, stretched, and padded over to the break room, where Tommy had left the carafe half-full, a battered mug sitting beside it. She poured a cup, added two sugars, and let the warmth sink into her bones. The window over the sink looked out at the darkened city, the protest still visible as a knot of determined lights. She carried their expectations, and most of them would never see her as anything but a traitor to her own.

She returned to her desk, reset the search, and started in on the cross-references. No matter how tired she became, she would outlast the silence, and the dark. That was the job.

At the next lull, she pinned the newly printed clipping to the center of the board, circling the faces with the certainty that, come morning, she'd have to talk to every one of them; witnesses, suspects, or both.

Outside, the sun hadn't lightened the horizon. Leilani prepared for another day of fighting her way towards the truth, one inch at a time.

The break room was lit by the flickering panel above the vending machines. On the counter, a tray of stale malasadas sagged beside the microwave, the powdered sugar gone transparent from humidity. Leilani perched on a molded plastic chair; elbows braced on the Formica tabletop. The silence made her aware of every sound inside her own body—pulse in her ears, the uneven drag of her breath. The hour was too late for anyone but the night custodians and the lost.

She thumbed open her phone and scrolled to her mother's number, the favorite contact. The need to call had been there all night, but now, at three-forty-five, did the courage and the loneliness catch up to each other.

It rang once, twice. On the third, Naalei answered, voice threaded with sleep but quick to warm. "Lei," she said, using the old nickname, "Are you okay?"

"Hi, Mom." Her own voice sounded raw, scratchy. "Sorry it's so late or early. I." She trailed off, picking at a paper napkin. "Is Kai awake?"

A rustle, as if Naalei had turned on a lamp. "No, sweetheart. He tried so hard to wait up, but your son has his limits. He's snoring away on the couch, holding his little volcano project like it's a security blanket."

The image stung somewhere behind her eyes. Leilani closed them and let herself feel it. "He wanted help painting the lava tubes. I told him I'd be back by seven last night."

"I know, honey. I know." A pause. "You do what you must. I promised him we'd finish it together before school. He can wait. He's proud of you, you know."

Leilani tried to laugh, but it caught. "Yeah. I wish I could be there more often. Some days it's like the job's eating me alive."

"That's what jobs are for." A familiar edge of teasing in Naalei's tone. "To make us wish for the things we already have."

Leilani rested her forehead on the crook of her arm, the phone cradled in her other hand. She said nothing. The vending machine cycled on with a mechanical thunk, and a single fluorescent bulb over the sink snapped to life, buzzing like a faraway wasp.

"I'm working a case," she said. "Big one. Everyone's watching. They want it solved yesterday, and there's a lot at stake. Not for the department, but for the community."

Naalei let the silence linger. When she spoke, her voice was soft but flinty. "This the murder at the sacred grove?"

"Yeah. The victim's a community leader. Lot of history there. His family, the developers, the protesters, and everyone has something to lose. I keep peeling back layers and finding more secrets."

"That's the thing about old places, Lei. Secrets and roots run together. You can't pull one without shaking the other."

Leilani smiled. "That sounds like something Grandma would say."

"She said it to me, and her mother said it to her. Some things we never learn new. We remember."

A breath. "Do you think," Leilani began. "Do you think I'm doing the right thing? Some days, I'm not sure who I'm fighting for."

A sleepy sigh from the other end. "You're fighting for us, baby. For the ones who can't fight, and for the ones who don't know they're losing. Remember, the law is only as strong as the person who lives by it. But your heart, that's stronger."

Tears welled, sudden and uninvited. Leilani blinked them away, relieved that no one else was here to see. "Thanks, Mom."

"You eat something?"

Leilani laughed, this time for real. "You're worse than the guys at the station."

"That's because they'll never love you enough, and I always will. Now tell me, how's your case?"

She gave a sanitized version for maternal ears, the push and pull of interviews, the facts, and half-facts, the way nothing ever fit together as neatly as it did in training. She left out the blood, the contorted neck, the cloudy eyes of a man who died afraid. But she painted a picture of community unrest, of politics mingling with pain, and the impossible expectations of her bosses.

When she paused, Naalei filled in the quiet. "When you see people angry, look for what they're afraid of. When you see them silent, listen to what they're ashamed of. You know this, Leilani."

"Yeah," she whispered. "I do."

"I believe in you," her mother said. "So does your son. Get some sleep tonight, huh?"

"I will. Kiss Kai for me."

"Of course. And Lei?"

"Yeah, Mom?"

"Take care of yourself, too."

The call ended with a gentle click, and Leilani let her head rest on the cool surface of the table. Her breath slowed until her heartbeat evened out.

She glanced at her phone; the wallpaper showed a picture of Kai, hair wet and wild, catching a wave. His face split into pure glee. She traced the side of the screen with her thumb, locked it, and stood.

The vending machine hummed on, unchanged, but the world seemed lighter. She squared her shoulders, dumped her paper cup, and headed back to her desk. There was work to do, and not much time. But at least she'd remembered why.

Outside, the night pressed in, blue and bottomless. Leilani resumed the hunt, her mother's words running like a thread through every knot of the case.

# CHAPTER THREE

## *Radical Connections*

The office for the Koʻolau ʻĀina Defenders was easy to miss; a converted storefront in a strip mall whose other tenants included a payday lender and an abandoned vape shop. The faded awning read ONLY KĀKOʻO— SUPPORT LOCAL, its letters sun-blistered and half-peeling. Leilani let her eyes adjust to the dimness inside. The air smelled of burned soy and printer toner, every surface crowded with cardboard boxes, tracts, and battered Tupperware.

A folding table served as the front desk, behind which a woman sorted stacks of manila flyers into plastic bins. She was short, forty-something, and wore a tank top advertising an old protest march. Her hair was pulled into a graying bun with eyes behind thick, functional glasses. At the sound of Leilani's entrance, she glanced up, assessed the visitor, and called, "We're not taking donations today, but you can leave your name."

Leilani flashed the shield clipped to her belt as she crossed to the table. "Detective Kealoha, HPD. I'm here to speak with your director."

The woman's expression folded in on itself, lips pressed together, her gaze darting behind Leilani to the street beyond. "We already did an interview with the other officer. He said."

"This is a follow-up," Leilani interrupted. "Not the same as a statement. Please." She kept her tone steady, projecting nothing but procedural fatigue.

The woman nodded, let out a breath, and gestured toward the back. "Down the hall, last door. You want coffee?" she asked, the offer already half-withdrawn.

Leilani moved past, cataloguing every step. The floor was worn linoleum, spattered with footprints and mud. The walls were lined with posters from past battles. Mauna Kea standoffs, anti-GMO rallies, and anti-eviction vigils. Some had been annotated in Sharpie, tallying arrests, listing victories and betrayals.

In the hallway, Leilani passed two open doors. In the first was a couple of college kids hunched over battered laptops, headphones clamped on and faces washed blue in the screen-glow. In the second, a mural in progress, the plywood covered in handprints and a spray-painted map of Oahu, bisected by a red slash labeled *No Further.*

She knocked on the last door, which was already half open. "Come," said a voice.

The office was no larger than a closet, but the director had made the most of the vertical. File crates and ring binders towered in precarious stacks. On the desk, an old HP laptop perched atop a shoebox, flanked by two crumbling mugs filled with colored pens. The director herself sat in an armless office chair, both knees pulled up to her chest. She wore black jeans and a long-sleeved rash guard, with beaded bracelets stacked up one forearm. Her hair, short and severe, was dyed the color of eggplant. She did not offer her name.

"I know you," she said, peering over her knees at Leilani. "You used to come to marches with your auntie Naalei. The Kahoʻolawe occupation. You remember that?"

Leilani kept her smile neutral. "She was my mother. But yes. I was the one holding the ice packs for the sunburned uncles."

The director's eyes narrowed, flashing with a tiny flicker of recognition. "Leilani. Of course. Didn't think you'd end up on this side of things."

"It's not about sides," Leilani said. "I need to ask about Sonny Alana."

A shift in posture: the director's legs

uncrossed, feet planted. "You're not the first to come looking. We already told the other detective everything we know."

Leilani produced her notepad, uncapped the pen, and set both on her lap. "Let's do it again."

The director considered this and gave a resigned shrug. "Shoot."

"You said in your statement that Sonny was working with your group, but also that he had, let's call it strategic differences with the other organizers."

"That's fair," the director said, tone clipped. "He was passionate, but sometimes it got in the way of teamwork. He'd go off script. Make a media scene when we wanted quiet. He meant well, but he wasn't always easy."

Leilani made a note and looked up. "Did he ever threaten anyone?"

"Not with anything worse than a bad Tweet," the director said, rolling her eyes. "He was a pain in the ass, not a violent guy."

"You sure about that?"

The director's lips compressed into a line, hands twisting at the hem of her sleeve. "Look, I'm not going to trash a dead man. He fought hard, but he fought with words. He pissed off some of the old guard, but nothing out of the ordinary. Not in this work."

Leilani flipped to a fresh page. "How about direct action? There's talk of splits in the group over protest tactics."

The director let out a breath. "You think one of us took him out? Is that where this is going?"

"I think someone wanted to make a statement. The body, the offerings, the way it was staged. If it wasn't you or your crew, maybe it was someone trying to frame you."

The director's gaze flicked to the wall behind Leilani. "We don't kill our own. And we don't do it on sacred ground."

"Sometimes things get out of hand."

The director said nothing, but her jaw flexed hard enough that the muscle stood out in relief.

After a moment, Leilani continued. "Who was he arguing with last week? Reports said there was a confrontation at the North Shore hearing."

"Everyone was arguing at the hearing," the director said, a flash of amusement crossing her features. "Developers, activists, the media. Sonny called out two council reps in public: Takahashi and Duarte. He told them to their faces they were selling out. There was shoving in the hall, but it was all theater. Nothing you don't see at every zoning fight."

"You ever see him lose his temper? Off camera?"

The director picked at a bead on her bracelet. "He yelled sometimes. Got into it with a few of the young guys, but that's how it is. They'd make up over lunch after."

A silence fell, the hum of the building's old fridge audible through the wall. Leilani let it stretch, watching the director's body language; the way her hands fidgeted, the way her eyes kept returning to something over Leilani's shoulder.

She followed the gaze. On the wall, a large topo map of Oahu dominated the space. Pushpins in various shades, yellow, red, and black, dotted the island. Next to it, a bulletin board crammed with sign-up sheets, volunteer rosters and copies of city council agendas. A cluster of pins encircled the area where Sonny was found.

Leilani turned back. "What's the significance of the pins?"

The director hesitated. "Yellow for sites we're protecting, black for ones we lost, red for the ones still in play. It helps us keep track."

"And the banyan preserve?"

"That's been red for two years. Developers keep trying to force it through. Even after the injunction, they send their guys out. Security, private contractors, sometimes police. They play hardball."

Leilani jotted a note. "Has anyone ever threatened Sonny directly? Phone, email, in person?"

"Every activist gets threats. Death, rape, lawsuits, you name it. Most of it's trolling." She reached for her laptop, typed and angled the screen so Leilani could see. "These are the recent ones. Sonny was cc'ed on all of them."

Leilani scanned the emails: subject lines ranging from crude slurs to promises of final warning. None looked credible, but there was a vehemence to the language that set her teeth on edge.

"Anything stand out to you?" she asked.

The director shrugged. "Not unless you can arrest half the Facebook users in the state. We flag the bad ones, but nothing ever comes of it."

Leilani nodded, closed the notepad, and stood. "If you think of anything else, here's my card." She placed it on the desk, careful to make it visible.

The director took it, but held on to it with both hands, turning it over as if looking for some hidden message. "Detective Kealoha," she said, her voice softer. "If you're looking for a monster in this story, check the people trying to buy the island out from under us."

Leilani didn't reply. She let the silence speak

for her. She backed out of the office, glancing again at the wall of pins.

As she stepped back into the hallway, the din of the activists at their computers resumed, punctuated by a laser printer spitting out page after page. She passed the woman at the front desk, who watched her leave with an expression that blended fear, suspicion, and the faintest flicker of hope.

Outside, the heat was already up, the light bright enough to sting her eyes. Leilani paused by her car, let the memory of the conversation settle. She slid behind the wheel and scribbled a few more notes before the details could fade.

She looked once more at the strip mall, the faces at the window watching her go. They saw her as the enemy, at best, a pawn, at worst, a traitor. Maybe both were true. But the facts had to lead somewhere, and she intended to follow them all the way down.

She checked her phone. No new messages from the station, but three missed calls from her mother. She pressed "call back," started the engine, and let the evidence rattle around in her head as she drove. The banyan grove was calling, and somewhere in the tangle of roots and bones, the truth waited to be exhumed.

She returned to the Ko'olau 'Āina Defender's office an hour before lunch, knowing the routine would be different, more people, less privacy, but also more opportunities to read the room. The parking lot was already full: battered Hondas, two food trucks in the back lot, a city bus parked askew at the curb, with *Free Mauna Kea* banners taped across its windows.

Inside, the atmosphere was less bunker, more ant colony. Three women crowded around a color printer, collating flyers for a *Save the Springs* demonstration. A young man argued with someone on Zoom, fingers stabbing at the screen. The smell of coffee was sharper, tinged now with a smoky undernote that made her think of hibachi pits and campaign tents.

The director, Leilani caught her name now, stitched on a canvas tote by the door. PAULA was mid-sentence with a volunteer, her arms crossed defensively over a folder. She saw Leilani, her expression flattening from friendly to wary.

"Detective," Paula said. "You're back. Did you forget something?"

"I need a look at your calendar for last week," Leilani said. "Group meetings, special actions, anything that involved the North Shore."

Paula hesitated, pointing at a side table stacked with binders. "Knock yourself out. The monthly is in the green. Weeklies are orange. We're not a secret society." She added this with a forced smile.

Leilani nodded. "Can I see the map?"

Paula shifted, blocking the narrow hallway with her body. "Sure," she said, but didn't move to make space.

Leilani sidestepped her, letting her shoulder brush against the wall. Up close, the map was more elaborate: each colored pin linked to a photo, a taped-up printout, or a Post-it note. Red pins clustered around the east side of the island, but the sacred banyan preserve stood out. A single pin marked with a tiny black skull sticker. Above it, in a child's handwriting, was a Post-it that read, *NEVER GIVE UP*.

"You track threats?" Leilani asked, tapping the skull.

Paula gave a small shrug. "Mostly to remind us who's got the most to lose. It's not literal. If it were, there'd be more skulls."

Leilani let her finger drift over the adjacent pins. Some were marked with miniature construction helmets, others with hand-drawn Hawaiian flags. The network of pushpins and strings reminded her of the murder board back at the station. Order emerging from chaos, but just.

She turned, gesturing at the file binders. "Mind if I sit?"

Paula nodded, pulled up a metal chair and

hovered nearby. "Do you mind if I watch?"

Leilani made a show of not minding as Paula's presence hovered. The green binder was heavy, the pockets stretched with clippings and bulletins. She leafed through, scanning for Sonny's name. It came up repeatedly on printed sign-in sheets, in email chains about urgent site defense, and in clipped articles with his quotes circled in highlighter. He'd been the face of the movement at least as often as the director herself.

"What about this?" Leilani asked, pushing an agenda forward. "Last Thursday. There's a line about decisive action at the sacred grove. That the plan?"

Paula's mouth twitched. "Standard language. Every week, we talk about escalation. Usually it means organizing a march, a sit-in, or sending letters. Sonny was always for the big move, but he never acted alone."

"Who's the team?" Leilani pressed, indicating the sign-up beside the agenda.

"Anyone who shows up," Paula said evasively. "We're not a paramilitary group. It's whoever can take off work that day."

Leilani kept paging. In the orange binder, she found meeting minutes that were more raw, less edited for public consumption. Here, the tone shifted; references to stopping the bulldozers by any means, to night actions, to making a stand even if the cops have to drag us off. It was passionate, but also dangerous.

She read aloud a line: "If they touch the banyan, they'll know what it means to wake the ancestors." She looked up. "Who wrote that?"

Paula paled a shade. "Sonny. He was poetic like that. But it doesn't mean..."

A crash sounded from down the hall, as if an entire tray of mugs had been dropped. Both women jerked at the noise. A slammed file cabinet, somewhere out of sight. The tension in the office spiked, invisible but real. Leilani caught Paula's foot tapping double-time under the table.

"You ever worry your people might go too far?" Leilani said, voice soft.

"All the time," Paula answered. She gripped her chair. "But we keep each other honest. We're activists, not criminals."

Leilani set her pen down, measuring her next words. "So, what happened with Sonny? If you say he wouldn't have crossed the line, why is he dead under a sacred tree with his throat crushed?"

Paula's composure cracked. "That's what we're all asking. It doesn't make sense." Her voice sharpened. "He was reckless, but not suicidal. He'd never put himself in a position to get caught alone, unless."

"Unless?" Leilani pressed.

Paula's gaze flicked to the hallway, where a knot of volunteers pretended to work but were clearly eavesdropping. "Unless he trusted whoever he was meeting. Or it was family." The word landed with a certain bitterness.

Leilani took a breath. "Family?"

"Not literal. But around here, you're one of us, or you're the enemy. Sonny never made peace with that."

They sat in the office, listening to the copy machine rattle out more flyers.

"You think someone from the group did it?" Leilani asked.

Paula's eyes met hers, flat and unwavering. "No. I think someone wants you to think that."

Leilani closed the binder, slid it back to its place. "Thank you," she said, and meant it.

She stood to leave. At the door, she paused, looking again at the map, the single black skull, the red pins fanned outward like arteries.

"Who else has a copy of this?" she asked.

Paula shrugged. "No one. It's only for us."

Leilani nodded but filed the answer away as another maybe. She walked out into the main office, where the copier had fallen silent. Every head swiveled as she passed; the room united in its suspicion of authority.

At the exit, the front desk woman stopped her. "Detective," she said. "If you find who did this, will you actually arrest them, or make them go away?"

Leilani hesitated. "Depends on who it is."

"Doesn't it always," the woman replied, and returned to her sorting.

Outside, the sunlight had gone from gold to flat, a thick haze smearing the sky. Leilani made a call to the station, left a message for Uyeda. "Getting somewhere with the activist angle. Sonny had more enemies than friends. Will update later." She started the engine, the cool air needling the sweat on her arms.

She scrolled through the photos on her phone, snapped a shot of the map and the black skull, and another of the meeting minutes with Sonny's handwriting in the margin. She sent both to her own email, flagged for follow-up.

She stared at the dashboard, the sound of the engine filling her head. There was a connection forming, something ugly and inevitable. She noticed it in the tightening of her jaw, the slow curl of dread in her gut.

Leilani peeled out of the parking lot, her thoughts already racing ahead to what she'd find next.

She allowed the engine to idle for a minute before shifting back into detective mode. The day was half gone; the sun slamming through the windshield like a spotlight. She texted her mother.

*WORKING LATE AGAIN, WILL CALL.*

She scrolled the feed for new developments. Her inbox was already filled with media requests, half of them from reporters she recognized from her own school days, now hell-bent on turning every protest into a scandal.

She rubbed at her temple, scowling at the gnaw of hunger, and considered the lunch options within a two-mile radius. None seemed worth the risk of running into a local gossip with a camera phone, so she settled for a protein bar from the glove box and a half-empty cup of cold coffee.

She was halfway through the protein bar when someone tapped at her passenger side window. A thin shadow fell across the glass, young, male, the face hidden under a gray hoodie.

Leilani flicked the lock and rolled down the window a careful inch. "You lost, braddah?" she said, wary.

The boy thrust a manila envelope through the

gap. "For you. From the office," he mumbled, not meeting her gaze.

Leilani took the envelope. "Who sent you?"

But he'd already turned, disappearing in three long strides behind the food trucks and out of view.

She glanced down at the envelope, unmarked, thick, and sealed with a single strip of tape. The kind of package that might hold a subpoena, or a death threat, or an answer. She slit it open with her thumbnail, fanning the contents on the seat beside her.

Photographs. Glossy, black and white, the paper faintly chemical in the heat. The first image showed Sonny Alana, alive and upright, sitting at the picnic table of an outdoor café. Next, a closeup of Sonny locked in a tense conversation with a man whose face was unmistakable after all these years.

Leilani's throat closed, her body electrified with memory. The jawline, the scar under the eye, the shape of the hands. Her uncle, Edward Kealoha. Last seen by her at her father's funeral, in a pressed suit and with eyes that gave away nothing.

The subsequent photos were a sequence, Sonny and Edward arguing, hands gesturing, the energy between them fraying toward violence. A closeup, Sonny passing an envelope of his own across the table, Edward taking it, his mouth set in a bitter twist. In the background, a third man, blond, mainlander, cheap suit, watched the exchange, face obscured by the newspaper.

Her hands shook. She snapped herself out of it, counted the photos, eight, all time-stamped for three days before Sonny's death. She flipped them over, looking for writing, but the backs were blank.

She laid them out again, slower this time, her own reflection warping in the plastic dash. Why hadn't she heard about this meeting? Why hadn't her mother said anything, or why hadn't the investigation uncovered a family connection before now?

She looked up, scanning the street, but there was no sign of the courier. No surveillance van, no telltale click of a long lens. Only the relentless sun and the protein bar turning to dust in her mouth.

She dialed the precinct, got the day desk, and left a message for Uyeda. "Got new evidence, a suspect with ties to the victim. Will bring to station after follow-up." Her voice was as flat and steady as she could manage.

She gathered the photos into the envelope, tucking it under her thigh. The contact had been calculated, not random. Someone wanted her to see these, but not to talk about them. Not yet.

She started the car, letting the AC thrum, and gripped the wheel until the bones in her hand hurt. The next logical step was to track down Edward Kealoha, to see what had driven him into contact with Sonny, to figure out if family ties were now an advantage or a target on her back.

She sensed the old wound open: the one that came from growing up Hawaiian in a city that wanted you to forget your own name. The one that came from loving a family that never played by the rules. It was supposed to be a job, another crime to solve. But the past never stayed buried, not here, not anywhere. And now it was in her hands.

She shut her eyes. Opened them to the blinding light. There would be hell to pay for chasing this angle, for pulling at the root instead of trimming the leaf. But she'd already decided.

She placed the envelope on the dash. The path forward was ugly, but clear.

She pressed the gas and drove.

# CHAPTER FOUR

## *Family Ties Unraveled*

L eilani eased the Explorer onto the shoulder of Naio Drive, the crunch of gravel announcing her arrival. The Kealoha house stood three stories above the city, balanced on a slope with views that ran from Diamond Head all the way to the distant, shivering lights of Ewa Beach. A bougainvillea hedge bristled along the stone wall, thick with magenta and bees. Beyond that, a black basalt staircase zigzagged up to a broad, flagstone lanai. She clutched the envelope to her chest as she climbed, fingers wet with sweat despite the sunset cool.

The property was a study in overachievement. Tiki torches, wired for electric, not flame, framed the porch like sentinels, and the double doors were carved with pueo owls and unfurling ferns. At the threshold, a teak shoe rack offered guests a polite reminder, remove, or else. She noted the three sets of men's shoes, all size 11 or up, and an expensive pair of women's running sandals. Unfamiliar, probably not the housekeepers.

She rang the bell. Chimes echoed somewhere deep inside, a five-tone minor scale, the kind you heard in banks or government offices. Footsteps approached, measured but unhurried. When the door opened, Edward Kealoha filled the frame: six foot two, graying at the temples, his body still lean and dangerous under a linen camp shirt. His face lit with genuine pleasure as he registered Leilani's expression, and the warmth ebbed out of his eyes.

"Leilani girl," he said, voice pitched for family and not for visitors. "You finally come to see your old uncle?"

She nodded. "I need to talk. May I?"

Edward's smile faltered a fraction, but the host reflex was strong. "Of course. We were sitting down for supper. You hungry? Auntie's making laulau, real stuff, not grocery store."

She removed her shoes and placed them on the shoe rack. "I'm working. I won't stay long."

He stepped aside, motioning her into the entryway. The floor was polished concrete, inset with slivers of mother-of-pearl that caught the last rays through a line of clerestory windows. In the foyer, a Koa wood bench bore the family coat of arms. Three kalo leaves, a nod to some distant ali'i, or maybe a joke at colonizer expense.

On the wall, family photos from a hundred years, arranged in a tight, symmetrical grid. Her father's face appeared four times, always younger, always less at ease.

Edward led her into the living room. Floor-to-ceiling glass caught every ounce of the island's dying light, throwing gold across the surface of a baby grand piano and the raw-grain wooden slab of a custom-made dining table. The room was warm, but not lived in. The bookshelves appeared to be arranged by an interior decorator rather than a reader. Leilani scanned the shelves, law, local history and a scattering of trophy volumes with no signs of spine fatigue.

On the far wall, a series of framed commendations: Community Leadership, Rotary Club citizen of the Year, Outstanding Alumni, Mayor's Advisory Board. Beside them, an unframed certificate from the Hawaiian Sovereignty Council. The ink faded as if embarrassed to share the spotlight.

Edward gestured to the seating pit—low couches, faded surf mats, a glass coffee table littered with mail, and a green stone bowl of loose change. "Sit," he said. "You want a drink? I got water, kombucha, or you can try Auntie's tea. It's supposed to lower your blood pressure."

"I'm good." She laid the envelope carefully on her lap, as if it might explode.

He poured himself a glass of water from the pitcher on the counter, settled into the armchair across from her, legs crossed, toes flexed in the soft light. He regarded her with a look she recognized from old family dinners, equal parts fondness, caution and the sense that everything in the world was already old news.

"So," he said, after a beat. "You're working the Sonny thing, yeah?"

She slid the envelope across the glass, her finger resting on the tape. "I thought you might have something to say about it, Uncle."

He didn't touch the envelope at first. Instead, he stared through her, the way lawyers and uncles learned to do from years of outlasting other people's stories. "Not my kuleana, my responsibility," he said, using the old word for responsibility. "I know what everyone else knows. Shame, though. He was a stubborn bastard, but he believed in something."

"Open it," she said.

He did. He thumbed through the photos, one by one. Sonny at the café, Sonny and Edward in mid-argument, the envelope passing between them, the watching blond in the background. On the last one, his hand stilled, grip whitening.

He set the stack down and exhaled through his nose. "You've got a good source. They teach you that at the academy?"

"They taught us to dig."

He laughed. "You always were the stubborn one. As a little kid, you'd break your head on a coconut to see if it would crack." The smile evaporated. "Okay. What's the question?"

"Why were you meeting with him?" Her voice was neutral. "You told Mom you hadn't seen Sonny in years."

Edward massaged the bridge of his nose, the old scar at the base of his thumb ghosting white. "I didn't want to upset your mother. She worries too much, and there was nothing to tell."

"Nothing?" She gazed at the photos. "It looks heated. Looks like business."

"Lots of things look like business, Lei. Sometimes it's two old idiots arguing about the same things they argued about in high school." He uncrossed his legs and crossed them the other way, a contained fidget. "Sonny wanted help, that's all. He wanted me to write an op-ed or pull some strings at the city. Get the permit revoked for the development."

"Did you?"

"I listened," he said. "And I told him what I tell everyone. The world doesn't work that way. There's no magic fix. You got to fight clean, or not at all."

She stared him down, letting the silence grow.

"Was he blackmailing you?"

Edward looked genuinely surprised, almost amused. "With what? Old pictures from Farrington football? Your Auntie's secret laulau recipe?" He leaned forward. "I'm not in politics anymore. All I want is peace, Lei."

"That's not what it looks like, Uncle."

He perused the photos, fanned them out in his hands, and returned them to the envelope. "I can't help what people see. But you should know better." His voice was lower now, more dangerous. "We're family, Lei. You ask me direct; I tell you direct. I didn't kill Sonny. Didn't want him dead either."

"Did you know he'd die? Or that someone would make it look like us?" she asked.

Edward's mouth opened and closed. He wiped his hands on his pants and ran a finger along the table. "You're not asking the right questions. There's bigger fish in this pond, always have been. Sonny thought he could outswim them, but all he did was stir up the silt." He fixed her with a look. "You keep digging, Lei, you're going to find the same old bones."

She had an impulse to ask about her father, about all the things no one said at the funeral, or since, but forced it down. "Who's the third man?" she asked instead, tapping the photo of the blond watcher.

Edward shrugged. "Mainland guy. Some consultant from the developer's office. Sonny thought he could cut a side deal, leverage public outrage. But you know how it is. They smile and nod while they bulldoze you anyway."

A long silence. The last gold slipped out of the room, and with it, the temperature dropped a degree. From the kitchen, a faint clatter, someone clearing plates, or perhaps listening in.

Edward stood restless. He wandered to the sliding doors that opened onto the lanai, his silhouette black against the city's early lights. "You know why I never moved to the mainland?" he said, not turning back. "Over there, you're another face. Here, everyone remembers your grandfather, your mistakes, and your broken promises. You don't get to outrun yourself."

He returned, and the mask of the community leader was gone. He looked tired, truly tired, like a boxer who'd realized there was no bell for this round.

"Sonny came to me because he thought I could help. But I told him there are people you don't cross. You poke the old beasts, they bite back." He glanced at the study door. "This isn't about protesters or developers. There's someone else pulling strings. Could be for the fun of it."

"A name," she said.

"No names. Not yet. You ask the wrong person,

you get your badge revoked. Or worse, your family loses another member." The words came out sharper than he had meant.

She needed to push, but the warning in his eyes was sharp, unmistakable. Instead, she collected the envelope. She stood, smoothing the wrinkles from her slacks. "Thank you for your time, Uncle."

At the doorway, he put a hand on her shoulder. It was gentle, but it pressed her still. "Be careful, Lei. Some wounds in our family never healed. Don't open them all at once."

She nodded, picked up her shoes, but did not look back. The air on the porch was sweet with mock orange and the salt of night fog rolling in. She walked down the steps; the envelope tucked under her arm like a letter bomb; the words echoing behind her. Some wounds never healed.

It should have ended there. But as she reached the curb, the glass doors whispered open behind her and Edward's voice floated out, lower now, bereft of the family-room warmth.

"Lei, wait."

She stopped, toes cold against the rough stone, and turned. Edward's frame was outlined by the porch lights, his shadow cast long and sharp onto the concrete. He had shed the uncle persona; now he wore the air of someone who'd been called to the ring after the final bell.

"I shouldn't have snapped," he said, not quite apologetic. "Some things are better left in the dirt."

She said nothing, so he waved her back in, not as a host, but as someone compelled to show a crime scene before it could be swept clean.

Inside, the house seemed different. The kitchen lights were dimmed, the illumination coming from the city's haze through the glass wall. Edward motioned her toward the lanai, where a half-circle of chairs ringed a low fire table, unused and perfectly arranged. He didn't sit; instead, he paced, arms folded, his face caught by the shifting gold and blue of distant sirens.

"Are you interested in the old debts?" he said. "About why people like Sonny end up dead in places that were supposed to save them."

She didn't respond, so he continued. "Everyone here owes something to someone. No one gets land, or power, or peace, without paying the piper. Sometimes you don't know you're paying until someone comes to collect."

She followed him to the lanai, the city humming below. "And who's collecting now?"

He scoffed. "You know the name, or you wouldn't be here. There's always someone higher up, always a shadow over the shoulder. The families, the real ones, not the ones that show up at reunions, they still run things, even if you don't see their names on the buildings."

A chill set in, deeper than the trade wind, crawling under her badge and into her bones. "You're talking about the old syndicates."

She saw the age in his eyes, the bloodshot red at the corners. "I'm talking about the parts of us that never got colonized. The ones that remember how to hold a grudge for generations."

She let that sink in. "So why warn me off?"

"Because it won't matter. If you keep pushing, you'll get what you want, but it won't fix anything. The ground will swallow it whole, and you with it."

She pressed, leaning into the opening. "Give me the name."

He hesitated, his gaze flicking over her shoulder to the shadows inside. "The man Sonny was meeting; he's not the boss. He's a messenger. The real boss, nobody sees, not for twenty years. He lives off the grid, no photos, no emails, only runners and coded calls. They call him the Kahuna because he's got a hand in everything, but he's not what you'd expect. No tattoos, no criminal record. He could walk past you in the grocery store and you wouldn't blink."

She made a note in her phone, but Edward stopped her with a palm. "Don't write it down.

Remember it. They watch for patterns. You write, asking, connecting dots, and they'll see you coming before you see them."

They stood there quietly, listening to the noise of a basketball game from a neighbor's house and the low, endless rush of the H1. The city was a basin of secrets, and she was learning how to read its currents.

Leilani pivoted, let the conversation loop back. "You still haven't told me about the banyan."

He flinched, a visible crack. "That's not what you think, Lei. Everyone thinks it's about the tree, the burial ground, the protests. The real war is over who gets to tell the story."

She frowned. "So, it's PR?"

He laughed. "It's always PR. You change a story, you erase a people. And once the history's gone, the land is dirt to dig."

She thought of Makoa, and the activists, and all the old men who'd warned her about losing the narrative. "So why do you care if I dig?"

He hesitated long enough for her to notice it. "Because if you find the truth, they'll make an example. Sonny was a warning shot. Someone made it personal."

She looked for the threat in that, but it was all regret.

Edward turned away, arms folded so tight the

knuckles grew pale. "Some wounds in this family never closed, Leilani. You dig hard enough; you'll find your father at the bottom."

The name hung between them, taboo and radioactive. She remembered the funeral, the tight smiles, and the unspoken questions, the way everyone talked around the hole he'd left behind.

She tried to keep her voice level. "What do you mean, Uncle?"

"What I said."

They stood in the dark, a private orbit, neither willing to break the standoff.

She walked inside and stopped at the credenza, where an old cordless phone flashed with a message. Next to it sat a battered cigar box, the top layered with stickers from forgotten elections and labor unions. On the table, half-covered by a runner, was a framed photo she'd never seen before, her father and Edward, young, arms around each other, both in formal white, a woman's face torn away at the edge. Someone had tried to tape the corner back on, but the face was gone.

She gazed at it before looking at Edward, who loomed behind her.

He reached past her, not touching, and set a business card between them. The card was white, textured, and blank except for a simple, hand-drawn symbol, a triangle bisected by a single black line.

"If you see this," he said, his voice almost gone, "run. Don't call me. Don't call anyone."

She held the card. It was heavier than it looked.

"What is it?"

He ignored the question. Instead, he ushered her toward the entryway, the tension in his body now palpable. "I can't help you, Lei. Not anymore. Your father knew the cost of asking too many questions."

She slipped the card into her badge wallet, pressing it flat between her ID and the leather cover.

"Is this how you want it to end?" she said, pausing in the doorway. "With a threat and an empty house?"

He looked like he might cry. Instead, he straightened, wiped a hand over his jaw, and said, "That's the way any of us end, if we're lucky."

She let him close the door behind her and walked down the steps, the card burning a hole in her pocket. The moon was up, pale and useless, and the lights below twinkled like the promises of men who'd never been caught in a lie.

She climbed back into the Explorer, back straight, and contemplated the card for a long time. The symbol was sharp and inky, drawn with the precision of someone who never forgot a line.

She locked the doors and turned on the ignition, but she had no urge to go home.

She parked at the mouth of the cul-de-sac, the Explorer's engine shuddering to stillness as the sky shifted from deep blue to black. Her mother's house, high above, glowed soft and gold behind its wall of bougainvillea; movement coming from a single moth, battering itself against the porch light. Down the hill, a string of sodium lamps blinked on, each a pale island in the dusk.

Leilani pressed her forehead to the steering wheel. Her hands hurt, old blisters from rock climbing, new ones from ink and paper, all pulsing with the aftershock of what had passed. The card Edward had given her lay face up on the console, its symbol black and stark against the white.

She sat like that for several minutes, unmoving, her breath fogging the inside of the windshield. She wanted to go home, or to the station, or to the crime scene, but all her usual directions seemed wrong. She closed her eyes and saw the photo on Edward's table: her father's face, younger than she'd ever seen it, and next to it, a void where the woman's face had been. Her mother's silence was a living thing, whispering up from the floor mats.

She pulled her phone from the cup holder, thumb hovering over the contacts. She could call the station, feed the new evidence into the black hole of bureaucracy. Instead, she scrolled to Naalei's number. Her thumb trembled as she pressed the call button.

The phone rang once, twice, three times. She imagined her mother sitting on the porch, the night breeze riffling the hem of her muumuu, hands curled around a chipped mug.

On the fourth ring, Naalei answered, voice gentle but alert. "Lei?"

"Hi Mom." The words came out smaller than intended.

"Are you okay?"

Leilani hesitated. The old defenses the cops need to shield, to simplify, faltered in the face of that voice. "No," she said. "Not really."

Naalei's answer was immediate. "You want me to come get you?"

She almost laughed but realized she was close to crying. "No. I needed to talk."

There was a rustle, as if her mother was settling herself for a long conversation. "You had another fight with your uncle."

Leilani looked up at the house, the way its lights bled into the dark. "He told me things. About Dad. About the family. I don't know if I believe any of it."

"Your uncle wasn't always like this," Naalei said, soft and sad. "After your father died, he changed. He never stopped blaming himself."

Leilani let the memory roll over her, the way Edward had, as if she were the last living link to a man whose shadow he could never escape. "He said there were secrets. That Dad got too close to something, and that's why he's gone."

A long silence. "Come by tomorrow, Lei. There are things I never told you. I thought I was protecting you, but I could have been afraid."

Leilani nodded, remembering her mother couldn't see her. "Okay."

"You eat?" Naalei asked, the words familiar and absurdly comforting.

"No," Leilani admitted. "I haven't been hungry all day."

Her mother made a clucking sound. "Come for breakfast. I'll make eggs and rice. We'll talk."

The urge to confess everything, to dump the case, the photos, the symbol, was strong, but she held it back. "Thank you, Mom."

"I love you, baby."

"Love you, too."

The call ended, and the silence of the car pressed close. Outside, a dog barked somewhere distant, and the faint crash of surf filtered up from the shore. She let her head fall back against the headrest, stared up through the glass at the scattered stars, their light already years out of date.

She grabbed the card from the console and turned it over in her hand. The symbol was simple, but absolute; it had the feel of something ancient, coded language for a threat or a warning or a promise.

She slipped it into her wallet, right next to her ID, and the two artifacts seemed indistinguishable, both markers of identity, both tickets to a world she had never quite fit.

She started the engine; the Explorer rumbled back to life. In the rearview mirror, her mother's house was already dimming, the porch light flickering as if exhausted by its own history. She drove slowly, taking the long way down the hill, letting the rhythm of the turns and the hollow clatter of gravel soothe the tension in her jaw.

As she reached the main road, she glanced again at her phone. Two new messages from the station, both marked urgent, both probably more bodies to catalogue. She ignored them for the time being.

The car idled at the next intersection, hands on the wheel. The night was so clear she could make out the Milky Way stretched over the peaks, a bright, impossible scar.

She took a deep breath, filled her lungs with the salt and memory of the island, and pointed herself toward home.

Tomorrow, she would find out what her mother had to say. And she would know what kind of legacy she carried.

# CHAPTER FIVE

## *Echoes of the Past*

L eilani parked in front of her mother's house, the wheels crunching over the crushed coral, the familiar pitch, and sway of the Explorer betraying every pothole the city had never filled. She parked under the monkeypod tree, its limbs thick as a wrestler, and stepped out into the shadow, cool before sunrise burned off the night dew. The neighborhood had changed little. A new roofline here, a solar array there, but otherwise the same mesh of mango trees and tangle of morning-glory choking the fences.

She carried her badge, her gun secured in the lockbox mounted in the rear of the Explorer, a clean Tupperware and a bag from the grocery store down the hill. At the entry, she slipped off her shoes, as the script demanded, Nikes lined up against her mother's cracked leather slippers, a lone child's Croc left behind from some recent visit. The breeze was heavy with the scent of cooked rice and, underneath, the brackish undertone of a fish tank overdue for cleaning.

Inside, her mother was already up, already moving, mixing the scrambled eggs in the pan on the stove. She wore a faded muʻumuʻu, blue with a pattern of faded pikake, and her hair was pulled back in a bun that looked like it might outlast the century. On the counter, slabs of fresh opah sweated under a tent of wax paper, and a ceramic bowl nested with ogo, seaweed, waited by the sink. A row of potted herbs, basil, cilantro, two spindly mint plants, crowded the ledge above the sink, catching the first gold of daylight through the screens.

"Eh, Lei!" Naalei called, voice a little too bright, a little too rehearsed, as if trying to disguise her having been up since five.

Leilani leaned in for the obligatory hug, breathing in the sweat and floral powder of her mother's skin, the embrace tighter than it needed to be. When they parted, Naalei flicked her with a wet thumb. "You look tired. Working the entire night again?"

"Not the whole night," Leilani lied. She set her badge and phone on the windowsill, away from temptation, but the phone vibrated anyway. Three short buzzes in rapid succession. She ignored it, at least for now.

"Wash your hands," Naalei ordered, as if

Leilani were still a surly teenager. She complied, scrubbing at the ancient lava rock sink, which was as rough as sandpaper and always threatening to swallow her wedding band if she didn't pay attention.

"Breakfast?" her mother asked, but it was rhetorical. The bowl of rice was already there, along with the black lava salt, and two still warm buttered rolls wrapped in a paper napkin. She placed the egg pan on a hot pad.

Leilani poured two mugs of coffee from the old steel percolator; the handle patched with masking tape. She brought them to the table, sat, and placed a spoonful of eggs and rice on her plate. She watched her mother preparing the food for her evening meal. There was a rhythm to Naalei's hands, mashing, rolling, shaping the kalo into palm-sized rounds, eventually stacking them like poker chips on the board. She did this without looking, eyes instead tracking the sunrise or drifting to the small TV wedged above the fridge, where the morning news ran silent footage of last night's protest outside the city council offices.

Leilani poked at the food. She opened her phone. An email from the station, a reminder from the school district; Parent-Teacher Conference, 1:00 pm, Kahala Elementary. She closed the app, but the guilt lingered, a burn in her throat.

"You didn't bring Kai?" her mother asked.

"He stayed with Mrs. Kila last night. I'll pick him up before school."

"You know, it's good for him, being with other kids. But he misses you."

Leilani's reply was meant to be light, but it hit like a flat note: "Yeah, well, duty calls."

They ate in silence for a few minutes. Leilani ate fast, as if the next call might yank her away at any moment.

Finally, her mother asked, "So what's the news?" The question was pointed, not generic.

Leilani weighed her words. The protocols were clear: don't discuss open investigations, especially with family. But this was different— her mother was the network, the spider at the center of every rumor web from Kaimuki to the Windward side. If she didn't already know about the murder at the grove, she'd heard enough to fill in the blanks.

"Case got dumped on me," Leilani said, breaking a roll and buttering it one-handed. "Victim was a public figure, so everyone's watching."

"Ah," Naalei said. She scraped her thumb along the rim of the kalo bowl, flicking off the last of the mash. "That's the way of things now. Nobody gets to mourn in private."

Leilani nodded. She wanted to share, to spill everything, the witness who wouldn't talk, the activism, the strange symbolism at the scene, but bit it down. Instead, she asked, "How well did you know Sonny Alana?"

Her mother paused, registering the name as if she'd been waiting for it. "Sonny, yeah. He used to dance at the Lion's Club before he got into politics. He always had a big mouth." She started rolling the next ball of kalo, firmer now. "He did a lot for the community but also made a lot of enemies."

"Any names I should know?"

Naalei shrugged, but her fingers tensed. "He was always picking fights with the council. But it's not the politicians you gotta worry about. It's the ones who pay them. The old families. Developers, lawyers, the unions. People don't forget when you block their plans."

Leilani listened, the cop and the daughter sharing the same skull. "Did he ever come here? For meetings, or?" She left the question hanging.

Naalei's face closed, just a fraction. "Never at our house. But your father knew him. They fought together, sometimes against each other. All those marches, all those rallies, it's the same old people. Everyone wants to save something, or destroy something, or both."

At the mention of her father, Leilani

experienced a familiar ache, sharp and hot. She said nothing, focusing on her plate.

The conversation drifted to safer ground. Kai's new teacher, the rising price of rice, the upcoming funeral for a distant cousin, and that under it all, the groove of suspicion ran deep. Leilani checked her phone again, annoyed at her own lack of discipline. She put it in her pocket.

When they finished, Naalei stood and began clearing the plates. Leilani stood and moved to the sink. She washed the bowls, letting the scalding water numb her hands. As she worked, she caught her reflection in the steel of the faucet, hair pulled back and her eyes ringed with fatigue.

Her mother returned with the tray of haupia and tapped the top with a spoon. "Still needs to set," she pronounced, but scooped a test bite anyway. "You want some for the road?"

"I might be late tonight," Leilani warned.

Naalei's expression softened. "You always are."

They stood in the kitchen, the light now fully golden, the room warm and bright. Leilani was seventeen again, wondering who she would become, unsure if this version was the one she'd wanted.

Her mother wiped her hands on a tea towel. "Come here, Lei."

Leilani hesitated but let herself be held. For a few seconds, the case, the history, all of it faded, replaced by the simple animal comfort of being someone's child, if only in the kitchen, if only for a breath.

When they parted, her mother pressed a plastic-wrapped square of haupia into her hand. "For Kai," she said. "Or for you, if you get hungry."

Naalei cut a piece of haupia and plated it with two toothpicks, as if the dessert required surgical tools. "Sit," she said, "before it melts."

Leilani obeyed, perching on the vinyl seat.

"Tell me about Dad," Leilani said.

Her mother's face did not change, but the knife paused, the tip pressed into the cutting board. "What about him?"

"The protests. The resort fights. I need to know what happened. Not the after school special version, the real one."

Naalei made a noise halfway between a laugh and a grunt. She put the knife down, wiped her hands on the towel, and took the seat opposite. For a while, she looked at Leilani as if deciding which story to start with.

"Your father was a good man," she said, "but he could never do things halfway. When he believed in something, he'd put his whole life into it, even if it meant breaking his own heart. He grew up in a world where the people who looked like him were expected to keep quiet and make do. So, when he saw the land being sold off, the streams blocked, the old trails bulldozed for tourists, it was like something in him snapped. He said he was tired of being grateful for crumbs. He wanted the whole loaf, or at least to stop the theft."

Leilani kept her eyes fixed on the dessert, using the dull side of a toothpick to draw patterns in the condensation.

"He started small," her mother continued. "Meetings in church basements, late nights at the library, copying maps, and deeds by hand. He used code names for everyone, like in the old union days; Mongoose, Bluejay, Iron horse. It sounds silly now, but back in the day, every call gave the impression someone might be listening.

"And the developers?" Leilani asked.

"They tried to buy him off at first. Offered a job, offered a scholarship for you. But when he said no, the threats started. Dead fish in the mailbox, cut brake lines, and once a Molotov cocktail in the driveway." She paused, letting the details land. "But he never wavered. He said as long as he could walk to the sea and put his feet in the sand, he'd keep fighting."

Leilani took a piece of haupia, the coconut

jelly cold and sweet. "You think any of that's connected to what happened to Sonny Alana?"

Naalei's eyes sharpened, all pretense of the gentle mother evaporating. "That's why you're here, isn't it?"

Leilani said nothing.

"Listen to me," her mother said, reaching across the table. Her fingers closed over Leilani's, warm and firm. "The people who killed Sonny, if they are the same today, they don't forgive and they don't forget. They wear suits now, or they're on the city council, but they're still the same old blood. They hate anyone who stands between them and the money. Your father was lucky to last as long as he did."

Leilani's jaw tightened, the old frustration resurfacing. "But he died in a car accident."

"He died because he made enemies, Lei. Sometimes, the enemy doesn't have to pull the trigger. The universe does it for them." Her mother's voice dropped, almost to a whisper. "Your father knew it might end that way. He told me once that some stories don't finish. They get handed to the next one willing to speak up."

"I'm supposed to be impartial," Leilani said, her voice brittle. "The badge means I serve the law, not the old grudges."

"Badge or no badge," Naalei countered, her

hand still resting on her daughter's. "You're still part of this island, part of this story. Even if you pretend you're not."

The words burrowed deep. Leilani looked down, embarrassed to find her hand clutching the dessert so tight it had collapsed to mush.

"Why the haupia?" she said, desperate to shift the mood.

Her mother smiled, the storm breaking a little. "It's your father's recipe. He always said that no one could be sad eating coconut pudding. He'd make it after the hard meetings, the losses. It was his way of reminding us that life could still be sweet, if only for a minute."

They sat there, two generations of the same stubborn line, neither willing to let go. At length, Leilani rose, wiped her hands, and began washing the dessert plates, though there was hardly any mess left.

"The past and present are like waves on the same shore, Leilani," Naalei said, voice soft. "They look separate but come from the same ocean."

Leilani almost replied, almost let herself admit how badly she needed to hear it. Instead, she scrubbed harder. Her mother watching her, not with judgment but with a kind of resigned pride. She wondered how many other conversations like this had played out in kitchens like this one, across the island, all the way back to when the land was still whole.

After a while, Naalei stood and patted her shoulder. "Go on," she said. "You have work to do."

Leilani did not reply. She grabbed her bag, her badge, and a cold square of haupia. She kissed her mother's cheek, inhaled the familiar scent one more time, and left through the front door, past the shoes, into the searing light of early afternoon.

At the car, she paused, letting her eyes adjust. She looked back at the house, at the curtained window, where she knew her mother would stand for a few seconds before moving on to the next thing. It was an old ritual, and for once, Leilani didn't mind playing her part.

She slid into the Explorer, put the car in gear, and headed off, the next wave already forming behind her.

Kai's laughter bounced off the eaves and rattled every window on the lanai. He arrived home in the slipstream of a neighbor's moped, backpack trailing open and hair still wet from swimming class. He dropped his shoes at the back door in a spray of sand and flung himself into the kitchen, where he executed a perfect running slide on the tiles and collided with his grandmother's potted ginger.

"Careful, Kai," Leilani warned, but the scold was gentled by a smile.

He looked around and grinned like the sun was his. "Mom! Guess what! We made slime in science lab. I caught a gecko in the hall, and Mrs. Kila said I could keep it, but she's afraid of the tail coming off, so you have to help me make a tank."

Leilani kneeled and caught him mid-sentence, pressing a kiss to the top of his head. The saltwater and cafeteria pizza hit her in the face, but she didn't care.

"Slow down, scientist," she said. "Let your mouth catch up to your brain."

He pantomimed zipping his lips. "Did you bring my snack?"

She produced the square of haupia, still cold, and he popped it in his mouth whole, giving a thumbs-up as he chewed. Satisfied, he bounded off to his bedroom where a pile of half-finished LEGO projects awaited. Leilani followed, sitting cross-legged on the rug while he explained, at great volume and with much arm-flapping, the mechanics of his homemade catapult.

She half-listened, letting his voice fill the empty rooms inside her. It had been years since the house had seemed so full of life. The afternoon light slanted gold through the back windows, striping the old carpet and lighting up the battered surf trophies on the shelves. Her phone was silent; for the first time all week, she resisted the urge to check it.

After a while, Kai got restless. "Can we go outside, Mom? I want to try my new kite."

She didn't hesitate. "Grab your jacket. I'll race you to the plumeria tree."

They burst through the sliding door, down the steps, and out onto the backyard, which was a lumpy patchwork of crabgrass, black volcanic stones, and the occasional buried dog toy. Kai ran with the frenetic, vertical bounce of a ten-year-old, waving the kite above his head as if it might take off at any second.

Leilani jogged after him, her bare feet skidding on the cool, damp grass. She was a body in motion, not a cop, not a haunted daughter, but a woman who could run and laugh and shout her kid's name. The wind caught the kite, a crude diamond patched with duct tape and painted in Sharpie flames, and lifted it overhead. Kai's face broadened with surprise and pride. He let out a whoop, the kind that could reach the neighbor's lanai two houses over.

"Keep it steady!" Leilani called. She held the string, showing him how to brace against the pull, how to let out slack so the kite wouldn't nosedive.

He gripped the handle, his jaw set with determination. "It's flying, Mom! I made it myself!"

"You did," she said, almost winded. "You're a real engineer."

Kai looked up at the streak of blue and orange wobbling above the plumeria. "Is it true they find lost kites on the other side of the mountain, sometimes years later?"

"That's true," Leilani replied. "Sometimes they get caught in a tree, and sometimes they go all the way to Moloka'i if the wind is right. You never know where things end up."

He seemed to think about this, brow furrowed. "Is that what it's like when you're chasing bad guys? You never know where they'll end up?"

She smiled, both at the question and at herself for never having seen the parallel before. "Yeah, kind of. You follow the trail, but sometimes it leads somewhere you don't expect."

They played for a while, launching the kite, losing it, recovering it from the clutches of the guava hedge. Each failure was met with laughter, each success with a shriek. When the wind died, Kai flopped onto the grass, his chest heaving, the kite resting beside him like a fallen comrade.

"Come here," Leilani said. She grabbed a chunk of driftwood that had washed into the yard during the last rainstorm and handed it to him. "Tell me what you see."

Kai squinted, turning it over in his hands. "It's a stick," he said. He looked closer. "But it has holes and a line where something rubbed on it. Maybe it floated for a long time?"

"Good. Anything else?"

After sniffing it, he wrinkled his nose. "It's salty. And there's little red stuff. Maybe algae?"

"Maybe," she agreed. She turned the stick, showing him the faint groove at one end, where something had chewed it. "What do you think made this mark?"

He examined it. Shrugged. "A crab?"

"Could be," she said. "Could also be a fish with sharp teeth. You see how the line is kind of jagged, not smooth?"

He nodded, his face intent.

"That's what I do at work, Kai. I look for clues. I pay attention to the details, the things other people miss."

"Like a detective," he said, a little awed.

She ruffled his hair. "Exactly like that."

He considered this. "Did Grandpa do the same thing?"

She hesitated, surprised by the question's sharpness. "In his own way, yeah. He looked for what was wrong and tried to make it right."

Kai seemed satisfied. He lay in the grass,

squinting at the sky. "Do you think the people who hurt Sonny Alana are the same people who didn't want Grandpa to talk?"

Leilani blinked, startled by the question. "Who told you about Sonny?"

He shrugged, picking at a blade of grass. "Everybody at school is talking about it. Ms. Kila said he was a hero, but some kids say he was asking for it because he yelled at the police."

Leilani's heart twisted. "That's not how it works. No one ever deserves what happened to him."

Kai rolled onto his side, the thought clearly heavy. "Will you catch them?"

"I'm going to try," she said, and meant it.

They raced to the lanai. Sitting on the old picnic table was a tray loaded with fresh-cut pineapple, peeled lychees, and half-moon slices of apple banana. The table, part of their history, still bore the scars of years of careless carving, hearts, initials, and a faded tic-tac-toe grid from Leilani's own childhood.

"Fruit break!" Kai yelled, springing up to attack the tray. Leilani trailed after, sitting with her feet tucked under her and a wedge of pineapple juice running down her wrist.

They ate in companionable silence; the sunlight filtering through plumeria petals and making the world seem safe and simple. Kai asked questions about the clouds, if they meant rain, if they looked like dragons, if they could ever touch the moon. Leilani answered each one with care, surprised by how little she needed to pretend.

As the sun dipped behind the ridge, they lingered in the lavender dusk, the fruit tray empty, the air sweet and thick with the feel of another humid night. Leilani watched her son chase lizards through the grass, and she believed that there might be a way to keep them all safe.

When the first mosquitoes appeared, Leilani waved Kai inside.

They stood together, watching the last sliver of sun slide down Diamond Head, and breathed in the night.

The house sealed itself at nightfall, all doors locked, all windows latched against the low, shifting wind that carried both ocean salt and the rumor of rain. Inside, the air was dense with the buzz of cicadas and the mechanical rasp of the ancient box fan that had seen three generations through the endless Honolulu summers. The blue glow of the city below crept in around the edges, but the house itself was a blind, protected shell.

Leilani sat on the guest bed. The room now repurposed as a catch-all for holiday decorations, outgrown school uniforms, and the odd, lumpy box of family photos. She folded laundry with the absentminded grace of someone whose hands had memorized the task before her brain ever engaged. Each towel and t-shirt landed in its proper pile, neat and soft and scented with the same green detergent her mother had always used.

The walls were thin enough to let in the muffled soundtrack of the TV, punctuated by the sleepy giggles of Kai in the next room over, where he should be reading but was almost certainly building another secret pillow fort.

On the bed beside her, the spiral notebook lay open to a page crowded with names and arrows and cryptic notes. Sonny Alana—developers? / Union $$ = old grudges / Red hoodie—link to Bluejay? / "They wear suits now." The handwriting slanted more urgently with each new connection, as if urgency alone could force the clues into order.

She was circling the phrase old families for the fifth time when her phone vibrated on the nightstand, a single, insistent buzz, not the triple-pulse she'd set for the precinct. The screen flashed an unknown local number, the kind that always preceded a robocall, a wrong number or something worse.

She let it buzz once more. No call, but a text.

She opened the app, thumb moving with the practiced caution of a person who'd been burned by digital threats before.

*DROP THE CASE*

The words were in block capitals, nothing else. Not even a period at the end.

For a heartbeat, nothing happened. Her pulse quickened, and every hair on her arm stood up as if she'd touched a live wire.

She checked the timestamp. 21:13. She scanned the directory for the number. Not in her contacts, but the prefix was from Kaimuki. She checked for attachments, for links, for signs of malware, but it was the three words. Simple, brutal, final.

She fixed her eyes on the message, focusing on the dark rectangle of the window across the room, where the plumeria outside scraped against the glass. She let her mind race through the possibilities. Who knew her number? Who would risk a direct threat? Who might sit in a car outside? What Now, watching for her response.

She dropped the laundry onto the floor and saved a picture of the text, placing it in a secure folder. She forwarded the message to her work account with the subject line, Threat, Active Investigation, and blind-copied herself at an encrypted personal address, in case the department servers malfunctioned again.

She stood and swept the perimeter of the room. Window closed, check the lock. Closet clear, under the bed clear. She crossed the hall, paused at Kai's room, and listened for the slow, syrupy rhythm of his breath. He was out cold, a book still open on his chest, the quilt drawn up to his chin. She watched, counting the seconds between each inhale and exhale. When she was sure, she closed the door gently and returned to her own room.

She pulled the old .38 from her overnight bag, a department relic, but more reliable than the new polymer stuff, and set it down, within easy reach. She held her phone to her ear and called the station, but the night desk was probably eating noodles and watching the game, because it went straight to voicemail.

She hung up without leaving a message. She didn't want this to live in the system until she'd had a chance to run it down herself.

She sat back on the bed, phone in one hand and gun in the other, and let her mind circle the drain of suspicion.

Who would send a message like that, knowing it would make her more determined? Who knew her personal number, her habits, her exact assignment on the case? The roster was shorter than she'd hoped.

She considered calling her mother. Could

already picture the way Naalei would take the news, half practical and half superstitious, sure that some old curse had come home for them all. But she held back. Not yet. Not until she could tell the whole story, or at least more of it than she had now.

Instead, she opened her notebook and wrote in block capitals, matching the threat.

THEY'RE WATCHING. WHO ARE THEY?

She underlined it twice.

In the quiet that followed, the cicadas swelled, the city hummed, and the wind shifted the plumeria branches, so they knocked a soft rhythm against the siding. She reviewed the message one more time, looking for anything she'd missed. Nothing changed.

She set her phone down, slid the gun under her pillow, and lay back, staring at the stippled shadows the fan threw onto the ceiling. She let her eyes close when she heard, through the thin wall, the steady pulse of her son's sleep.

She would not drop the case.

But she would not sleep easily again, either.

# CHAPTER SIX

## *Another Body Falls*

A blue ribbon of irrigation canal ran between two ridges, hidden from the main road by thickets of ironwood and spider lilies gone feral. In the hour before dawn, the air was heavy with moisture. Leilani turned the Explorer's headlights off a quarter mile from the site and coasted under the cover of gray. Her tires bounced through puddles, frogs silenced as she passed, resuming their call in ragged harmony behind her.

Yellow tape stretched from a rusty irrigation pump to a battered sign warning TRESPASSERS WILL BE PROSECUTED. The scene, already claimed by two uniforms and two out-of-shape crime techs, was alive with the frantic energy of people who hadn't expected to earn overtime today. Beyond the tape, a dozen onlookers clustered with arms folded or hands shoved in pockets—most wore the hoodie of the 'Āina Defenders or the patched vest of a local paddling club. They glared with the flat, impersonal resentment of people who'd shown up too late to change anything.

Leilani parked at the berm, checked her phone for updates (none, except a stale all-caps "DROP THE CASE" still topmost in her inbox), and shouldered the evidence kit. At the tape, a uniformed officer tried to block her path, realized who she was, and pivoted with a nervous laugh. "Detective." The boot print in the mud where he'd tried to plant his stance would be immortalized in the morning's photo log.

She ducked under the tape, ignoring the gaze of the crowd, and squatted near the water's edge. The body, male, medium build, face pressed into the mud below the surface, had drifted to the cattails during the night. It wore an old surf brand T-shirt and nylon board shorts, calves pocked with mosquito bites, soles crusted with the same iron red as the shore. In the pale light, the hands seemed unnaturally bright; the knuckles bleached by water. The only sounds were the drone of insects and, farther up the ridge, the mechanical wheeze of someone's ancient weed-whacker.

The scene reeked of pond scum and decay, but underneath, old oil, burned plastic, and something sharper, like the inside of a dental office. Leilani catalogued the details in the same order she always had, clothes, visible injuries, jewelry (none), the context, the proximity to the tape, the angle of the limbs, the curious path the body had taken to rest here, as if guided by a hand that had been uncertain until the end.

The coroner's tech, a small, tense man named Kimo, arrived with a clipboard, tucking the snap-off scalpel into his vest like a gunslinger. He greeted Leilani with a minimal nod, more focused on the corpse than the detective. "You ready for this?" he asked, already donning fresh gloves.

She snapped on a pair of nitrile gloves, gave a single nod, and settled into a crouch beside him. "What's the read?"

Kimo peeled back the sodden shirt, exposing the back, and ribs mottled with postmortem bruising. He whistled low, pointing with the capped end of a pen. "Livor mortis on the backside, so he floated belly up after death. But see the wrists?" He rolled one arm gently, a bracelet of purple-black bruises, half-mooned by smaller cuts. "Either someone grabbed him hard, or he fought for his life. Maybe both."

Leilani grunted, pulled out her phone, snapping close shots from three angles. The flesh around the fingers was torn, as if the victim had clawed at something, rope, fabric, or perhaps the face of his killer. She thumbed the digital recorder to a fresh file. "Victim exhibits restraint type bruising on both wrists, abrasion under left thumbnail consistent with recent struggle."

Kimo turned the body, careful not to spill more of the muck onto his own shoes. "Check this out," he said, motioning to the mouth. "Sand and leaves, but not enough to suggest he drowned here. Probably choked elsewhere. This could be a dumpsite."

"Water in the lungs?" Leilani asked, rolling the corpse a few degrees to check the nose and jaw for obvious trauma.

"That's the thing," Kimo said. "It's pond water, but not this pond. The mineral content is different. I can smell it. I bet we'll find high chlorine and possibly fertilizer residue?"

Leilani said nothing. She pivoted to the nearest patch of flattened reeds, catalogued the sequence. Drag marks in the mud, interrupted by a single clean footprint, Converse or similar, large size. Male, or a woman with big feet and something to prove. A smaller barefoot print overlapped it, toes splayed, the kind left by someone running for balance. She flagged both with a marker and used a collapsible ruler for the scale.

A few yards downstream, a wad of what looked like torn notebook paper floated, the edge caught in a snarl of algae. She fished it out with tweezers, shaking off the excess water, and pressed it flat inside an evidence bag. On the lined surface, the ink had run, but some words were still legible. Meet tonight, old pump, and, in the margin, a doodle of a whale breaching above what looked like a police badge.

"Victim ID?" she asked Kimo.

He held up an evidence bag. "Found a wallet in the pocket. Mako Pahoa, twenty-two, local address, no known warrants. Student at UH, marine bio major." He passed over the plastic bag with the wallet inside, the cards fanned out for viewing.

Leilani inspected the ID and checked for credit cards before turning her attention to a small waterproof backpack half buried at the water's edge. Inside were two crushed cans of energy drink, a half-eaten bag of shrimp chips, and a battered flash drive taped to the inside lining. The USB casing was cracked, but the tape had shielded it from the worst of the water. She slid the backpack into an evidence bag and made a note to run the drive at the earliest opportunity.

Across the pond, the first true sun of the morning crested the ridge, drawing sharp shadows on the far bank. Leilani squinted into the glare, feeling the heat congeal on her back, the humidity thickening by the minute.

Kimo stood, careful to avoid the evidence markers. "You want me to take him in, or you need another look?"

She waved him on. "You know the drill. Tag and bag, call me if anything pops on the tox screen."

He signaled to the waiting team at the tape. Two uniforms moved with the awkwardness of men who'd never handled a corpse outside of the training mannequin. The body was rolled onto a plastic sled, secured, and covered with a dark blanket that did nothing to disguise the angles and bulk beneath.

With the body gone, Leilani stood at the water's edge, scanning for secondary evidence. A shoe print, a torn candy wrapper, the persistent foam on the surface where Mako's body had lain. She photographed everything as she moved to the far bank, picking her way along the wet berm where the reeds grew tallest.

It was there, near the foot of the old irrigation pump, that she found the second message. It was written on a scrap of cardboard, lashed to the pump handle with zip ties. The letters were uneven, printed in marker.

NO MORE LIES. NO MORE BLOOD. THIS IS FOR SONNY.

The last three words were underlined, the marker bleeding into the cardboard like a fresh wound.

Leilani bagged the note, stood back and took a slow panorama of the site, the yellow tape colored gold by the rising sun. At the perimeter, two environmental activists, their faces painted with black streaks under their eyes, watched her with silent accusation. She ignored them, but logged their presence, their faces and the connection to the protest groups that had escalated after the Sonny Alana murder.

She logged the time, snapped the final sequence of photos, and radioed the precinct. "Kealoha to dispatch. Crime scene secure, body en route to the medical examiner. Suspected homicide, evidence logged." She hesitated, adding, "Media already present at the perimeter. Request Public Affairs on site in twenty."

After clipping the radio back to her vest, she looked one last time at the pond. Already, dragonflies had resumed their circuits above the water, their wings slicing the air.

She headed up the berm to the waiting Explorer, where a new message glowed on her phone.

*CALL ME IMMEDIATELY, LT. UYEDA.*

She let it wait while she thumbed through her case notes, piecing together the preliminary narrative.

Victim: Mako Pahoa. Age 22.

Evidence: Wrist bruising, possible restraint; water in lungs inconsistent with scene; message at pump handle; note and flash drive; strong suggestion of targeted killing, likely tied to the Sonny Alana case.

Perp: Unknown, but footprint suggests male, large, possibly known to victim.

She rolled the window down, letting the thick morning air wash over her, and drew a breath. The patterns were emerging, escalation, copycat, or coordinated strike, maybe all three. The threat from last night rang in her mind, a pulse she couldn't shake.

She watched as the evidence techs loaded the body bag into the van; the activists craned their necks for a glimpse, and typed a note into her phone.

"Check flash drive. Review activist manifestos. Call Kimo, autopsy priority."

She started the car and was about to drive away when the officer at the tape waved her over. She stopped the car, slid out and walked towards him. He was standing next to a medium height, trim, bleach blond with a dark tan. The woman was crying uncontrollably.

"Detective, this is Ailani Hale. She says her boyfriend is missing, and she drove up here when she heard about the dead body. Her boyfriend's name is Mako Pahoa."

Leilani took the woman aside. "We have tentatively identified the body as that of Mako Pahoa," said Leilani.

The woman's knees gave out, and Leilani and the officer grabbed her arms to hold her up. Leilani pointed towards her Explorer, and they half carried, half led her to the vehicle and placed her in the front passenger seat. Her body shook with sobs, and tears flowed like rainwater. Leilani gave her a few minutes to calm down.

The inside of the department SUV still smelled faintly of last week's spilled POG and, beneath that, the industrial foam that lined every city vehicle since the state's lawsuit. Leilani kept the engine running to hold off the heat. The AC humming loud enough to muffle the noise outside. She had parked at the old access road, facing away from the pond, using the hood as a physical and psychic buffer between herself and the swarm of uniforms, med techs and curious onlookers still gathering near the tape.

Ailani slid into the passenger seat, hands tucked between her knees. She wore cut-off jeans, a stretched-out tee, and the blank, starved look of someone who'd already spent all of her tears before the interview started. Her hair, streaked with sun-bleach, hung in limp ropes against her cheeks. She kept her eyes down, but every few seconds she flicked a glance at the rearview, as if something might sneak up from behind.

Leilani pulled a legal pad from the dash compartment, clicking the pen twice for the rhythm. She laid it flat on her knee. "We're recording, but this is for my notes, okay? Nothing formal yet. I need to get your sense of what happened."

Ailani nodded, but it was more a reflex than consent.

"Start wherever," Leilani prompted, voice as level as she could make it. "What did you and Mako do yesterday?"

Ailani worked her jaw. "He should have been in class, but he came home early." Her voice gave out. She started again. "He said people were watching him. Not only the cops, like everyone. The neighbors, the guys at the bodega, people in the park."

Leilani wrote escalation, paranoia, and check security cam coverage near victim's house in her phone's notepad.

"Did he say why? Was there a group or a person he thought was after him?"

Ailani hesitated, stared out the window, her voice low. "He wouldn't tell me. He said if I didn't know, I'd be safer. He used to laugh at people who got like this, you know? Who saw feds in the bushes. But after Sonny Alana died, he started acting differently."

Leilani's pen stalled. "Did he know Sonny?"

Ailani's face twisted. "Everyone knew him. He was at every rally, every water rights thing. But after the murder, people started looking at each other sideways, like there was a traitor in the group."

Leilani circled "rally" and "traitor" on her pad.

"Did Mako say he was being threatened?"

"No," Ailani whispered. "But he got two calls last week, one from a blocked number, one from somewhere on the mainland. After that, he started locking his laptop with a different password every day, and he kept all his notes on paper. He burned them when he was done. I thought it was a joke, but he was scared."

Leilani flipped to a new page. "Did he have enemies in the movement? Anyone mad enough to hurt him?"

Ailani's hands made little fists under her thighs. "They all have disagreements, but it's verbal. The worst they do is kick you out of the group. But Mako wasn't talking to most of them anymore. He said it was bigger than the protests. He said there were people on both sides who'd kill to keep things quiet."

The words sat heavy in the car, the AC suddenly too loud. Ailani glanced at the clock on her phone, as if time itself might close the distance to some rescue.

"Did he meet anyone yesterday?" Leilani asked. "Or go anywhere unusual?"

Ailani's voice trembled. "Last night, he left around midnight. He said he was going to the store, but he took the old backpack, not the one he uses for class. He left his phone at home. I asked if I should wait up, but he said to keep the door locked and not let anyone in if he didn't come back by morning."

"Did he say why?"

Ailani shook her head hard. "He never did. He told me he loved me and not to open the door unless it's me or the cops."

Leilani felt the echo of the threat from her own phone, the sick certainty that these things traveled in circles, always coming home.

"Was he carrying anything else? USB drives, documents, cash?"

Ailani nodded. "He kept a blue flash drive in the bathroom vent. He showed me where, in case something happened. He said it was encrypted, but if I ever needed to, there were instructions on how to open it."

Leilani sat forward, urgency blooming. "Is it still there?"

Ailani's eyes were wide and rimmed with red.

"No. When I got the call this morning about the body, I checked. The vent cover was off. The drive was gone."

Leilani made the note, all caps, MISSING DRIVE. Her pulse spiked, and she tried to slow it with a breath. "Did you tell anyone else about it?"

"No," Ailani said, almost childlike. "Only you."

Leilani ran her thumb along the badge. "Thank you, Ailani. You did the right thing." She passed over a card. "If you remember anything, or if anyone tries to contact you about Mako, call this number right away. Day or night."

Ailani nodded, turning the card in her hands until it bent.

They sat in silence, everything unsaid growing heavier. Outside, the activist crowd at the tape had grown, a chant starting up, low and rhythmic, meant for the cameras that would surely arrive soon.

"Are they going to say Mako was a terrorist?" Ailani asked, voice cracking. "He wasn't. He wanted to help the fish. He loved this stupid island."

Leilani's thoughts drifted, remembering the boys she'd grown up with who'd ended up dead or missing or disappeared into the long shadow of the law. "We're going to find out what happened," she said, hoping the promise wasn't a lie.

Ailani bowed her head, silent tears tracking down her cheeks, but she made no sound. Leilani offered a tissue from the center console. She waited until Ailani was calm enough to exit the Explorer and offered her a ride home, but Ailani refused.

She watched as Ailani made her way down the road, shoulders hunched, arms wrapped tight across her middle. The activist crowd surged toward her, a few reaching out in comfort or solidarity, the rest watching to see if she would break.

Leilani stayed in the SUV, letting the AC blast, and opened a fresh file on her tablet. She began typing the notes. Every fact and suspicion lined up in a neat black font. But as the sun crept higher, and the shadows receded from the pond, the pattern that emerged was far from neat.

She wrote:

Victim: Mako Pahoa, marine bio, deepening paranoia after Sonny Alana's murder. Secret meetings. Evidence: missing encrypted drive. Girlfriend observed the vent tampered with after death.

Threat assessment: escalation. Possible mole in activist group. Possible connection to the development lobby or law enforcement. Urgent: check blue flash drive.

She set the tablet aside and imagined what she would tell her own mother if this were Kai. The anger, the helplessness, the certainty that the people who promised to protect you were the same ones who had already written your story.

She opened her eyes and steadied her hands. They had a lot of work to do and very little time to get it done.

Leilani finished her notes and stepped back onto the access road. The crowd beyond the yellow tape had doubled in size and intensity. What had started as a silent watch line had swollen into a mass of bodies and banners, the latter spray painted on old bed sheets or cardboard. PROTECT OUR 'ĀINA, read one. JUSTICE FOR MAKO, another, the letters uneven and bleeding. At the front, a makeshift altar, ti leaves, bundles of dried ginger, and a cracked conch shell filling with flies.

A TV truck was pulling up, disgorging a cameraman in khaki shorts and a reporter already dabbing powder onto her cheeks. The buzz of the lens and the shifting of tripods sent ripples through the crowd, like a school of fish reacting to a shark.

Leilani moved along the tape, ignoring the questions that got tossed her way ("Is it true the cops did this?" "Are you gonna arrest his girlfriend?" "Why won't you let us see the body?") and focused on threading the space between the uniforms and the civilians. Her badge, visible on her hip, acted less like a shield and more as a beacon for the angriest eyes in the mob.

She stopped to check her phone for any missed messages, and that's when she saw her. Malia, her mother's cousin's daughter, standing in the crowd. She wore a black hoodie, the same one from a Kahoʻolawe occupation years before. The activist group's logo was faded out at the breast. Her arms were crossed, but her hands weren't hiding the tattoo on her wrist. Three kalo leaves in a triangle, the old family mark, unmistakable to anyone who knew what to look for.

Their eyes met. Malia froze, a rabbit in the headlights, her breath hitching, visible from this distance. For a split second, Leilani saw the girl she used to babysit, before the years had turned her hard and angular and fluent in the language of protest. Malia spun on her heel, ducking her head, and began pushing through the tangle of bodies with desperate speed.

Leilani moved to follow, but the crowd surged as the reporter began her stand-up, blocking her path with a wall of phones and voices. She tried to angle around, but the protesters bunched together, backs rigid, shoulders locked as if to say, you don't get to take another one.

"Malia!" she called, but it was swallowed by the chant that erupted: "A'OLE KANAWAI PALAA —IWI, LAND, NOT FOR SALE." The words hit in waves, thumping against her chest with every syllable.

She ducked under a banner, but the gap was already closed. Malia was gone, her dark hoodie swallowed by the tide of humanity.

Leilani stopped by the crowd and braced against a eucalyptus trunk, sweat running cold under the band of her watch. She scanned for another glimpse; nothing but the swirl of banners, the murmur of plotting, and the buzz of the cameras. She wanted to scream, but years of training turned the impulse into a sharp, inward breath.

A patrolman tried to get her attention. "Detective, command wants you on a call with Lieutenant Uyeda. Like now."

She nodded and shouldered past the line. Every step away from the crowd seemed like a failure. Every echo of the chant, a reminder of the rift.

When she reached the Explorer, she leaned against the door, eyes on the blacktop, and slowed her pulse. Malia was in the middle now; a witness, or a suspect, or another casualty in a war that wouldn't end. The old shame and anger rose in her, along with the understanding that her choices, everyone's, no matter how well-intended, only ever widened the gap.

She started the Explorer but didn't drive. She sat in the suffocating silence, phone pressed to her ear, waiting for the line to connect. The sun was all the way up now, burning the dew off the pond and striping the dashboard with yellow.

She looked up, saw the crowd still chanting, still holding, and she hated them all for being so certain, so pure, so ready to see her as the enemy.

She saw Ailani again, standing at the road's shoulder, arms around herself, eyes on the spot where Mako had gone into the bag.

Her phone chimed with an incoming text from her boss.

*NEEDED AT HEADQUARTERS, NOW.*

She pulled away and promised herself she would not run. Not from this, not from the island, not from the blood she carried in her own veins.

But as she crested the hill, and the crowd fell away behind her, Leilani knew that the case had changed. It wasn't work anymore. It was family, and history, and the last shot at fixing something before it all drowned.

She drove toward headquarters; the chant echoing in her ears long after the road went quiet.

# CHAPTER SEVEN

## *Unexpected Allies*

The records room kept its own climate: fluorescent, unrepentant, and twenty degrees colder than the rest of the station. At 2 a.m. it was a bunker for the desperate or the damned. Detective Kealoha counted herself in both categories. The whine of the light fixtures set her teeth on edge, and the air tasted like stale toner, cardboard, and the dying ember of her last caffeine hit. She'd set up camp at the central desk, evidence files rising in battlements around her: old case folders, digital forensics printouts and a scatter of sticky notes so thick you could track the drift in her handwriting from hope to resignation.

She'd been combing the city's financial records for five straight hours. Ever since her three-hour meeting with her boss, Lieutenant Uyeda, and the mayor. They wanted answers to questions she herself hadn't answered yet. The mayor was concerned the city might erupt at any minute, and he wanted the murders solved right away. He didn't care that she had little to go on. He was more concerned with appearances, and he wanted to look like he was doing everything to lead the investigation. Of course, elections were coming up in a few months, and he needed a feather in his cap to boost his campaign.

She was focused on the developer's latest project to open, hoping to find answers related to their current developments. The resort's paper trail was less a line and more a delta, branching through shell companies and PO boxes with predatory intelligence. Each time she got close to the center, the money forked and vanished into Delaware, Hong Kong, or a triple-fronted LLC in the Caymans. Somewhere there was the motive for two murders and a city's worth of unrest. The answer neared pattern recognition yet remained elusive. She rubbed her eyes, blinking the spreadsheet haze into focus, and took another bitter swig of coffee, lukewarm and tasty as ditch water.

The door's security bar clanked, and she tensed, hand sliding by reflex toward her pistol. Visitors at this hour were never good. The new arrival paused, letting his shadow stretch across the floor before stepping in. He wore the haircut and posture of a man who'd never once been late in his life, dark suit, pressed shirt, zero jewelry except for a battered watch and the sharp glint of his shield at the lapel.

"Detective Kealoha?" the man said, voice warm, touch of SoCal behind the vowels. "Sorry to break your flow. I'm Special Agent Isaac Torres. FBI."

He had a smile that came on easily, and a handshake that said he wasn't here for formality but wasn't above using it for effect. She didn't offer her hand, but he took the rebuff in stride, lowering himself into the visitor's chair with practiced nonchalance. He set a folder, much thinner than hers, on the desk between them, followed by a biodegradable cup that steamed like it was freshly made.

Leilani braced herself. "Didn't realize this was a joint op."

He gestured at her pile of paperwork. "Looks like you don't need one. But they asked me to assist, and here I am. Hope you don't mind."

She did mind, obviously, and let it show. "I work better alone."

He grinned, refusing to flinch. "That's what I told my Quantico instructor. Still, two sets of eyes see more than one. Or so I'm told."

She side eyed the fresh coffee, not trusting the gesture, not trusting the man. His suit fit too well for a mainlander in humidity, and his smile had the built-in patience typical of somebody who'd done homework on her. She scanned for the flaw, the chip in the armor, but all she got was a trace of aftershave, citrus, not too sharp, and the faintest hint of fatigue at the corners of his eyes.

She returned to her monitor, typing with more force than necessary. "You here to chase eco-terrorists, or to supervise the locals?"

His smile took a hit, replaced by something like genuine interest. "I'm here because your Commissioner Lau asked for help on the Alana case. Apparently, you have a thing for pissing off the right people."

She snorted. "That's my best skill set."

He let the silence sprawl as he leaned in enough to suggest confidence rather than a threat. "What's your read on the money? I know you've been at it for a while."

She knew he'd been briefed. The question was a test. Was she going to treat him as a partner, or as another bureaucrat sent to slow her down? Her arms crossed without thinking.

"It's not the usual dirty money. No direct bribes, no obvious skimming. The project is bankrolled by a syndicate that changes names every quarter. I keep tracing it, but the owner-of-record is always two companies away from anyone you can indict."

He nodded, sipping his own coffee. "That's why they keep us up at night."

The flicker in his expression was almost imperceptible, but she caught it. A mixture of empathy and exhaustion, like he'd run this same play before.

He set his cup down, took a breath. "I looked at your arrest history. You're not afraid to make waves. Most local detectives let this stuff slide, but you keep following leads, no matter what it costs you."

It wasn't a compliment. It was an admission. He knew her rep, probably her whole file. She fought the urge to bristle, but it was hard wired in her now.

Her tone was flat. "Is that why you're here? To see if I'll play nice with outsiders?"

"I'm here because you've made more progress in three weeks than the last team did in a year. I'm here because someone thought you'd appreciate a little backup."

He let that land, his smile tight. "Besides, I make a mean cappuccino. This place is a graveyard for good coffee. You might as well have someone who's suffered through worse."

She almost laughed but stifled it. He clocked the slip, filed it away, but didn't exploit it.

She turned the monitor so he could see,

pointed at the spreadsheet. "You see that? That's a forty-thousand-dollar payment to a lobbying group. The group doesn't exist. The address is a PO box registered to a shell in Nevada."

He leaned closer, his gaze sharp. "And the shell's been open six months."

She nodded. "Someone's moving cash to buy public opinion, or to disappear it entirely. I've got subpoenas out, but so far, the records come back blank or redacted."

He whistled, appreciation real this time. "You're good."

"I'm thorough," she corrected, not smiling.

He let the word hang, easing back and stretching his shoulders against the stiff plastic chair. "So, how do you want to play it?"

She paused, recalibrating. Torres was relentless but not aggressive, warm without the patronizing she expected from mainland help. He was competent, and worse, he was polite about it. She couldn't decide if that made him less trustworthy or more.

She met his eyes. "We're going to need warrants for the developer's in-house servers. The DA drags his feet if he thinks we're going after campaign donors, so if you've got federal strings, use them. Otherwise, follow my lead and stay out of the protest PR disaster."

He nodded, making a show of jotting notes but giving her space. "You got it. I'll run point on the legal. You want me to cover the next-of-kin interviews, or are you attached to those, too?"

She weighed it. The old version of herself would have said yes, absolutely, I do everything. But she hadn't slept over three hours in as many nights, and the feeling in her gut said she was missing something crucial by chasing her own tail. Torres saw her hesitation and didn't press.

"I'll do the interviews," she decided. "But if you can pull the old case files or cross check social ties, have at it."

He smiled almost triumphantly but dialed it back to professional. "Deal."

He rose, careful to keep his distance from her side of the desk, and reached for the door. As he left, he said, "I'm an early riser, Detective. I'll have the FISA paperwork started before you finish your first round of emails."

She waited until he was gone before pulling the new coffee closer. She eyed it like it might be poisoned. She took a careful sip. It was better than anything she'd had since the investigation started. She scowled, annoyed at the concession, but drank anyway.

The records room settled back into its peculiar climate. But now, when she returned to the spreadsheets, she found the patterns easier to see, the threads less tangled, the trail less opaque. She'd never admit it out loud, but Torres might be right. Two sets of eyes saw more than one.

She cracked her knuckles, squared her shoulders, and dove back in, ready for whatever came next.

The clock on the conference room wall stuttered past midnight, the minute hand trembling between numbers like it wanted to quit. The glass table was a landfill: takeout cartons bleeding soy sauce, half-empty water bottles, the plastic shrapnel of energy bars. Printouts formed a second layer, crime scene reports, campaign donations, the annotated transcripts of angry, desperate people. Leilani and Torres sat across from each other, posture melting into exhaustion, still scraping at the last marrow of the day.

Torres had shed his tie completely, looped it over the chair. His shirt sleeves were rolled high, and Leilani noticed the tattoo. An old-school compass rose on the left forearm. The lines faded at the edges, as if he'd worn it through more than sunlight.

She sipped her cooling coffee, following the lines of ink down to his watch. "You always bring work home with you?" she asked, half-teasing.

He saw the tattoo and smiled. "You could

say that. Family tradition, apparently. My uncle was a detective in San Diego before it got too expensive for anyone with a conscience."

She raised her eyebrows, waiting for the punchline.

He delivered it with a shrug. "He told me, you get lost, you need something to bring you back. Otherwise, the job floats you out to sea. I didn't listen for years, but." His fingers drummed the table, soft and restless. "I guess you reach a point where the thing that feels like home is the work."

She understood the undertow. In this job, obsession was both lifeline and liability. "I was going to be a marine biologist," she said, surprising herself. "Chasing monk seals, not criminals."

He grinned. "Still ended up in deep water, though."

She laughed. It was strange, like an old scar stretching.

They ate in silence, picking at the dregs of a limp Caesar salad. Overhead, the fluorescent lighting rendered their skin the color of boiled chicken, every flaw, and fatigue line unmercifully exposed. The AC rattled somewhere in the ductwork, too faint to make a difference.

Torres broke the silence. "You've got family

here, Detective?"

She hesitated, automatic defense clicking into place. "My son. Kai. Ten years old, stubborn as a goat. He hates that I'm never around, but he builds a volcano for school and names it after me." The confession was like stripping off armor, but she let it hang.

Torres's expression softened, a crease forming at the corner of his eye. "Do you see him much?"

"Not enough," she admitted. "His teacher probably thinks I'm a myth. All my signatures are digital."

He sipped his coffee, turning the cup in slow circles, matching the motion she'd been doing for the last hour. "My nephew's the same. He's seven. I missed his birthday again last week." He raked a hand through his hair, suddenly years older. "It's the third one I've missed. Not my proudest stat."

They sat together, both leaning forward now, arms folded, the space between them filled with nothing but shared absence.

"I used to think the sacrifice was noble," Leilani said. "That it'd count for something. But every year, the case numbers stay the same, and the thing that changes is how much you owe to the people waiting at home."

He nodded, looking at her not as an adversary,

not as a colleague, but as a fellow traveler through the same wasteland. "You ever think about quitting?"

She thought of it every day, but she smiled instead. "I think about it every week, but someone would cut me off in traffic, and I'd be right in the thick of it."

He laughed deeply. "That's what my mother says. She tells me you'll always be a cop, even if they take the badge."

"Maybe that's the problem," Leilani said, but without bitterness.

The hour was thick with fatigue, but neither of them made a move to leave. It was easier, here in the artificial night, to be honest with a stranger than with anyone who'd ever changed your diapers or memorized your favorite color.

She watched him, the way he sat, the way he watched her right back. There was no game, no flirtation, only mutual recognition. Two people who'd given everything to the job and now shared the same hunger. Maybe not for each other, not yet, or never, but for understanding, for connection, for someone who knew what it was like to be haunted by the echo of every mistake.

Leilani cleared a patch of table between them, dragging a napkin aside. She hesitated before offering the details she told no one outside her blood. "Kai's father disappeared before he was born. Surfed out past the reef and never came back. They said it was sharks, but more likely he kept going. My mom always said he belonged to the ocean more than to us."

Torres took it in, no judgment. "He never tried to reach out? Send a postcard?"

"Not once. I always said it didn't matter, but." She didn't finish. She didn't need to.

He nodded, a line of empathy joining them. "People will say anything to get themselves off the hook. But it doesn't mean you can't rewrite the story for the kid. It means you've got to be the one to finish it."

She smiled, a small, private thing. "You're not what I expected, Torres."

He shrugged, grinning. "Neither are you, Detective."

They let the silence ride, the only sound being the tick of the clock and the susurrus of paperwork being pushed aside. Torres rolled up a fresh set of evidence printouts, handed half across the table. Their fingers touched, the contact light but deliberate.

"You ready to crack this?" he asked.

She nodded, energy surging back. "Let's finish it."

Together, they leaned over the evidence,

the problem no longer impossible but merely difficult. Their movements were synced, efficient and fluid. They worked as a team, no longer fighting for control, but combining strengths: her doggedness, his creative leaps.

She allowed herself to imagine what it would be like to trust someone with the load.

As they chased the new lead, cross-referencing names and dates, the noise of the station faded to a low, steady background. It was the two of them and the case, and at that moment, the world could wait.

At four-thirty, the bullpen was empty, the blue monitor glow sharpening every tired angle and flaw in the building's geometry. The HPD's second floor space was less a workplace than a holding tank for insomniacs: half-emptied by budget cuts, the rest partitioned into cubicles that preserved sound about as well as a paper napkin.

Now, side by side, they parsed the digital sea. Two ships on a collision course, each radiating its own brand of suppressed energy. Torres worked his laptop, the muscles in his forearm tensing as he typed. Leilani worked faster, fingers staccato on the keys, her posture rigid but less defensive than before. Their silence was companionable in a way she hadn't expected. Their shoulders grazed when they reached for the same scrap of evidence, an accidental but not unwelcome static.

Ambient noise was a third colleague, radio chatter spooling out of a beat cop's radio two cubicles down, the night janitor's vacuum chewing up a lunchroom full of crumbs, and the HVAC grinding out subarctic air in four-minute cycles. The station was never truly asleep, merely recalibrating between bursts of noise.

Between them, the main screen flickered with forensic accounting. Leilani's corner, spreadsheets and subpoena logs, flagged by color and date. Torres's, news clippings, FEC filings, and a gnarly set of encrypted PDFs he'd borrowed from the mainland office. They didn't waste time narrating every thought; both understood the value of uninterrupted focus. Still, she noticed the way Torres muttered under his breath when he cracked a password or hit a dead end. He was the rare breed who didn't take failure personally, but absorbed it, used it as momentum for the next attempt.

For two hours, they worked in close orbit. The spoken words were requests for printouts ("Shift-P," "already did it") and terse observations ("That's not a real charity," "Run the year-over-year, you'll see it"). Leilani marked time by the number of refilled mugs and the slow accumulation of Post-it notes creeping up the bezel of her screen.

Near five, the pattern sharpened. Torres was first to break the silence, sitting back and propping his ankle on a file box, eyes on the ceiling as if searching for a signal.

"They always said follow the money, but this is more like playing chicken with a GPS blindfolded."

She snorted, not disagreeing. "You ever think we're not supposed to find it? Like, the whole point is to make it so fucking tedious that the IRS gives up?"

He smiled. "That's how you know you're close. People get nervous, they overcompensate. They create enough breadcrumbs to be plausible, but not enough for a conviction."

She nodded, tracing a line with her mouse. "Yeah, and you hit a double-entry, and boom, you're back at square one. I've got three aliases all pulling funds from the same corporate trust, but every withdrawal lands in a different offshore account."

Torres leaned in, tapping on a highlighted entry. "See this? Sequence number. It's off by two. If someone were doing payroll, the numbers would be sequential. This is money laundering 101?"

She examined it. He was right. "The shell's not a front. It's a pass-through for another layer."

"Exactly," he said, and their eyes met, a brief spark of mutual appreciation. "You ever hear of Royal Palm Holdings?"

She frowned. "In the environmental hearings. They're the clean face for the new resort. Community liaisons, all that bullshit."

"Yeah, well, they don't exist. Not as a shell company. The entire board of directors is synthetic. The names are generated from an old census."

She arched an eyebrow, impressed despite herself. "How'd you find that?"

He tapped his temple. "Machine learning, baby. They gave me a cloud cluster when I signed on. I let the algorithm run wild."

She almost smiled. "Good thing you're not evil, Torres."

He grinned, showing teeth. "Not my style."

She was about to make another joke when her screen dinged, a new lead, a cross-reference on a wire transfer she'd flagged in last night's comb-through. She drilled in, tracing the payment from a developer's fund through four intermediaries before it landed, neatly, unambiguously, in a trust set up for the re-election campaign of a councilwoman whose name had come up twice in the protest group's complaint letters.

"There," she said, pointing.

At the same moment, Torres, on his own screen, said, "There," his finger hovering over a ledger entry that showed the transfer from a different angle.

They froze, both digits touching the same data point, two vantage points on a single bullet.

An unsteady laugh rising in her throat. He beat her to it, voice low and satisfied. "We've got a live one."

Their shoulders touched, lingering a beat longer than protocol allowed, and the contact registered in her as something like relief.

He spun the monitor so they could both see. He leaned over, crowding the keyboard as he compiled the relevant emails and filings. The synergy was electric. In ten minutes, they had mapped a triangle of influence, developer to shell, shell to lobbyist, lobbyist to campaign. Each point was substantiated by evidence, each thread taut and ready for a prosecutor to pluck.

Torres exhaled, reaching for the marker, uncapping it with his teeth. "Whiteboard?" he asked, already knowing the answer.

They moved to the wall-sized board, erasing someone's weeks-old homicide timeline to make space. Together, they built the web. Red string for money, blue for political leverage, yellow for legal threats. The result was ugly, an impossible tangle, but at its heart, a single knot of criminal intent.

As they pinned the last index card, Leilani stepped back, hands on hips. She sensed the adrenaline dump of having gotten somewhere, the rare satisfaction of the pattern emerging from chaos.

Torres regarded the finished product before looking at her with something approaching respect. "Hell of a thing," he said.

She nodded, letting her guard down for the smallest fraction. "You did good, Torres. Don't let it go to your head."

He tapped the board with the marker. "Mutual effort, Detective. Not bad for two stubborn assholes working overtime."

She met his gaze, this time not backing down. "Don't expect me to carry your coffee every night."

He grinned wide and unforced. "Deal. Next rounds on me."

The janitor's vacuum passed in the hallway, a ghostly whine receding into silence. The only sound was the low thrum of the server room.

The tension in her shoulders loosened, and she caught herself standing a little closer than necessary. She didn't step away.

They surveyed the whiteboard together, like wolves who'd managed not to eat each other. It was almost dawn, but she was awake.

The case had broken open. And so had the walls between her and her new, well, not partner. Not yet.

But it was something.

# CHAPTER EIGHT

## *Sacred Sites and Secret Meetings*

The sun was barely a rumor above the Koʻolau ridge, but already the construction site radiated a heat that smelled of asphalt, diesel and ambition. Leilani stepped out of the Explorer and into the crunch of black cinder underfoot, eyes watering in the glare bouncing off the white trailers lined up like coffins at the proposed resort. Overnight, someone had staked a new line of orange mesh fencing across the ancient dune, and the breeze carried a fine mist of ground coral that scoured the inside of her nose.

Torres parked behind her and killed the engine, letting the mechanical tick of the block settle in the silence. He wore his suit jacket despite the weather, a thumb hooked into his belt, scanning the perimeter with the calm detachment of someone who'd spent years casing crime scenes that had less blood, but more money.

"Nice place," he muttered. "If you're a Komodo dragon."

She grunted. "You should see the sales brochures."

Beyond the mesh fence, a yellow backhoe stood at parade rest, its steel bucket jutting up like a fist. Closer to the beach, a crew of local laborers in blue polos waited around a generator, flicking glances at the two cops and making no pretense of working. One man in a reflective vest took a slow, defiant pull from a can of energy drink, crushed it, and lined it up beside six others at his feet.

Leilani knew every eye was on her, every unspoken calculus about sides and allegiances. She walked the property line, Torres at her shoulder, and watched the path of the mesh fence as it bisected the old kiawe grove. It jogged sharply inland to avoid a group of collapsed stone walls. The land had been bulldozed in wide, hungry strips, the native grasses peeled back like scalp. Here and there, the gouged earth exposed thin slivers of bone, coral and glass— refuse from a thousand years, now leveled in a month.

The on-site liaison found them as they reached the first trailer. He was sixty, short and thick, with a slab face like an Easter Island moai and forearms the color and grain of Koa wood. His badge read, KEKOA MAHOE, CULTURAL CONSULTANT. He wore a navy aloha shirt, a battered straw hat, and had a look that said he'd once been a brawler but now fought wars with paperwork and patience.

"You the detectives?" he asked, skipping the niceties.

Leilani nodded. "Kealoha. Torres. You're Mahoe?"

He held her gaze, unblinking. "Kekoa, if you choose to keep it civil." He gestured with his chin at the gutted landscape. "You here for the morning's entertainment, or the real show?"

"Depends," Torres said. "What's playing?"

Mahoe snorted, a little impressed. "Only the slow-motion murder of everything that ever mattered, but I guess that's not your department." He beckoned them around the side of the trailer. "Walk with me."

They followed him along a path where the coral had been tamped flat by tires and boots. Where a stand of naupaka clung to the last foot of the bluff, and a wooden sawhorse blocked access to a shallow pit. Inside, the shadows curled around a scatter of black stones, ringed with white shells and burned ti leaves.

Mahoe stopped, swept his hat off, and gestured

down. "You know what that is, Detective?"

Leilani studied the shape, an oval, four feet long, lined with smooth water-worn rocks. "Looks like a burial."

"Half right," Mahoe said. "Used to be a burial. Now it's a legal time bomb. They found it last night, stripped the top layer before the survey team could get here. See that?" He pointed at the rim, where a chunk of femur poked out from the blackened roots.

Torres kneeled, careful not to contaminate the scene, and snapped a photo with his phone. "Whose survey team?"

"County. Hired by the developer, so you can guess how well that goes. They subcontracted me to watch their steps, but nobody wants to slow down the build. So, they work nights, push the line every chance."

Leilani crouched by the pit, feeling the old dread of desecration, a mix of anger and shame. The remains were recent, in archaeological terms, but no one had bothered to cordon off the pit. Ants had already claimed the site, making highways between the fragments.

"Anything else?" she asked, brushing the dirt from her hands.

Mahoe shrugged. "Depends how much you care about the law. Or about what comes next."

He led them past the pit to a section of untouched land Twenty square yards of dense grass and flowering shrubs. The air here was cooler, the light more golden, as if the world itself hesitated to intrude. Mahoe kneeled at a low mound, running his palm over the soil. He pointed to a sliver of gray poking through.

"This is what they want to hide," he said. "Come see."

Leilani bent low, tracing the outline with her fingers. The object was a stone blade, an adze, perfectly chipped, haft still lashed with cord that had calcified over centuries. Next to it, a shallow bowl of black lava crusted with white salt. Farther down, there was what looked like a chain of bone beads, each carved into a different animal form, turtle, owl, and dog.

She caught her breath. "This isn't a burial. It's a shrine."

Mahoe nodded, mouth tight. "One of the old ones. Probably predates Cook. They were supposed to do ground-penetrating radar before digging, but the developer's lawyer got them a waiver. Called it low cultural sensitivity." He spat the phrase like poison.

Torres looked at Leilani, eyebrows up. "What's the significance?"

Mahoe's voice dropped, as if they might be overheard. "These artifacts trigger an automatic injunction. No digging, no building, not a fence until the site is cataloged. But the developers got a pipeline to the city council, so they're betting no one will report it. They want to finish grading before the legal can catch up."

Leilani stood, dusting off her pants. "You think this connects to the deaths?"

He gave her a look that could crack granite. "You know how many times I've tried to stop one of these projects? All it takes is one accident, and the problem solves itself. The last guy who tried to halt a build on sacred land, his brakes failed on the Pali Highway. Everyone called it a tragedy. But nobody ever checked for tampering."

Torres took more photos, careful to get the site from every angle. "What about threats? Anything recently?"

Mahoe shrugged, but his hand worked the brim of his hat until it bent. "Always threats. Usually just talk. But last week, someone left a dead bird on my truck. Head twisted off. That's a message."

They lingered at the mound, the three of them ringed by the silence of the site. Leilani sensed the old pressure, the duty to protect, the fear of overstepping, the knowledge that any action she took would make enemies on both sides.

She glanced at the mesh fence. "Who's paying for the security?"

"Developer. Outsourced, mostly mainland guys. But they hired some local heavies to keep the protesters out. A few of them got records, but the owner likes guys who don't ask questions."

Torres gestured towards the workers near the generator. "You think one of them did it?"

Mahoe shook his head. "Those guys are muscle, not brains. If someone's sending a message, it's coming from higher up. The lawyer or the money men. Or someone who wants to remind us where we stand."

Leilani sensed it, the thousand small humiliations, the slow loss of land and memory. She wanted to scream, to grab the backhoe and drive it off the bluff, but all she could do was catalog the evidence and hope the system would still work.

She took another look at the mound. "Should we report this as a crime scene?"

He met her gaze, hard as obsidian. "I want you to report it as a murder, Detective. Of a person, of a culture, of the last thing left that isn't for sale." His voice caught. "I want someone to care."

She nodded, feeling the knot in her chest tighten. "We'll file it. Properly."

They walked to the Explorer in silence, Mahoe leading, Torres behind. At the gate, Mahoe paused, squinting into the rising sun.

"You ever wonder," he said, "why this island eats its own? Why can't we let the dead rest?"

Leilani looked past him, at the bulldozed scar running down to the ocean. "Maybe we're afraid they'll come back."

He laughed, soft and bitter. "They always come back."

He turned and walked away, shoulders hunched against the morning.

Torres unlocked his car, climbed in, and started the engine. "You all right?"

She stood, closing her eyes against the burn. "Fine."

He let the silence stretch. "He's right, you know. About the cover-up," he said.

She nodded. "It's never the muscle. It's always the suits."

He handed her a bottle of water, and she drank half of it in a single pull. Salt and dust lingered on her tongue, a reminder that no matter how many badges or degrees she wore, she'd never stop being from this place.

She flipped through the photos on his phone. Bones, stones, beads and the shadow of her own hand against the dirt. Proof, if anyone still believed in proof.

"Let's get this to the DA," she said, already

knowing what the answer would be.

She walked to her Explorer, slid in and drove away from the construction site. Torres put his car in gear and followed her, the evidence sealed and waiting for a verdict that would never come.

The text came through as they entered police headquarters; the sky was purple and orange thanks to the early dusk. The phone buzzed once, a new number, all digits scrambled. Leilani checked it without thinking, thumb unlocking the screen on muscle memory.

*COORDINATES: 21.2997, -157.8637. TONIGHT. 11 PM. COME ALONE IF YOU WANT TO SEE WHO'S REALLY PULLING THE STRINGS.*

She gazed at the message, the chill it sent through her stomach at odds with the sticky heat of the early evening. No signature, no context, only a raw challenge.

Torres noticed. "Problem?"

She angled the phone so he could see. "Looks like someone wants to have a chat. Alone."

He read it, his jaw flexing. He plugged the coordinates into his navigation app. "That's Sand Island. Old industrial zone. Could be a trap."

"Could be a lead," she said.

He snorted, but the edge in his voice was respectful. "Let me guess, you're not bringing backup."

"Not if we want them to show. Whoever this is, they're watching us already."

Torres thumbed his phone. "Let me at least run the number. It's probably a burner, but sometimes you get lucky."

She watched him work, the quick, economical taps on the virtual keyboard, the way his eyes flicked to the screen and back. He was a creature of systems, always looking for the next node in the network, while she preferred to move through the world sideways, like a crab, trusting intuition over protocol.

"Burner," he confirmed. "Untraceable SIM, probably purchased off a kid at a convenience store. But the coordinates are real." He handed her the phone, where a satellite map showed a dead zone of warehouses, access roads and a narrow strip of shoreline lined with old shipping containers. "Are we going to play it their way?"

The answer bubbled up before he finished. "Yeah. But I want to see what we're walking into."

Torres gave her a sidelong look. "You ever wear a wire?"

"Only to family reunions," she deadpanned.

He almost smiled. "We'll go in separate cars. I'll hang back; you make the meet. But we keep eyes on each other. Deal?"

She nodded, surprised at how natural it

seemed to work alongside him. "Deal."

They spent the next hour in the secure lot behind the station, preparing for the stakeout with the obsessive care of people who understood how quickly plans could go sideways. Torres packed a surveillance kit into a battered duffel: night-vision goggles, a pair of low-light body cams, and a handheld scanner for intercepting police bands. He moved methodically, checking and rechecking, the discipline of someone who had buried more than one friend because of a bad battery or a loose strap.

Leilani loaded her Glock, tucked a backup piece into the ankle holster that had shredded two pairs of her slacks. She considered the taser, decided against it, and instead palmed a canister of pepper gel from the glove box. She always preferred options to escalation.

Torres noticed. "You planning to mace the bad guy?"

"Only if he's allergic to bullets," she said.

He zipped the duffel and handed her an earpiece. "These are encrypted. You press twice to mute, hold for SOS. I'll be on the ridge above the warehouse, but if things get ugly, I'm coming in."

She accepted the earpiece, holding his gaze. "Don't play the hero. I can handle myself."

He shrugged. "Not my style, detective."

They left the station in tandem, Torres peeling off at the Nimitz overpass, Leilani doubling back along the frontage road to loop around from the water side. She rolled down the window, letting the wind whip her hair. She thought about the anonymous sender, the casual threat of the message, and the way the city seemed to vibrate with secrets below the threshold of sound.

She arrived early, parking under a dead streetlight two blocks from the target. The warehouse was a relic from the seventies, all cinderblock and sheet metal, the paint on the side a sun-bleached ad for a trucking company that had vanished before she was born. Piles of broken pallets and shredded tarps littered the lot, and weeds grew high enough to hide a body, or several.

She did a slow circuit on foot, keeping to the shadows, marking the exits and sightlines. The place was a natural kill box, with long windows on the south side, but no easy egress except the main roll-up door. She spotted Torres' car parked on the embankment, camouflaged under a dusting of beach sand and a sun faded hula girl on the dash.

She keyed the earpiece. "In position."

His voice came back, tight and clear. "Copy. You see any movement?"

"Negative. But I smell old cigarettes and poor decisions."

He chuckled. "Ten minutes to go. You ready?"

She watched the moon climb behind the storm clouds and exhaled. "Always."

As the hour crept closer, she could feel her nerves wake up. First the fingers, followed by the soles of her feet, and last, the old tick behind her left eye that signaled adrenaline was staging a coup. She looked at her watch.

At 10:56 p.m., headlights swept the street. A black SUV, windows tinted past legal, idled at the curb, nosing forward until it blocked the warehouse loading dock. Two silhouettes inside, driver and passenger, the latter bigger, bulkier, but nothing else visible. They sat until the driver cut the engine. The parking lot grew still.

A long two minutes later, the roll-up door groaned open, and a third figure slipped out, short, wearing a hoodie, face obscured. The figure stood in the doorway, hands in pockets, shifting from foot to foot like someone waiting for a date or a dealer.

She keyed the mic. "Three on site. One in the door, two in the vehicle."

Torres: "Copy. I see them. Go when ready."

Leilani slid her badge onto her belt, zipped her jacket halfway, and crossed the lot with the loose stride of someone who belonged. At twenty feet, the figure in the doorway raised a hand, half wave, half warning.

"You alone?" the voice said, masculine, but nervous.

Leilani stopped outside of arm's reach. "You asked for me. I'm here."

The hooded figure flicked eyes left, right, and jerked his chin toward the open warehouse. "Inside. Fewer eyes."

She followed, letting him take the lead. The air inside was hot and wet, thick with mold and the smell of spilled solvents. The main bay had been gutted, but a folding table near the back held a battered laptop, a pile of manila folders, and a box of white latex gloves.

He motioned for her to sit. She didn't.

"You have something for me?" she asked.

The man hesitated before sliding a file across the table. "Are you curious who's behind the land deals? It's not who you think. The council, the cops, the protesters, they're all meat shields. The money's coming from offshore. Japan, Australia, and mainland hedge funds. All hidden behind shell companies with local faces."

She thumbed through the folder, skimming the names, the payment schedules, the scanned invoices. It was damning, if you could prove any of it. "Why are you giving me this?"

"Because people are dying," the man hissed. "And I don't want to be next."

"Who's targeting them?"

"You wouldn't believe me. It's not the unions. It's not the families. There's someone new in town, and they don't care about tradition or keeping things quiet. They want to own the entire island."

A beat. "And if I talk to you, I might get to leave. Or at least go out on my own terms."

"Why me? Why not the Feds, or a reporter?"

The man glanced at her badge. "Because you're the only one who's not bought and paid for. And you're local. That still counts for something."

She picked up the file. "Thank you. But if you're lying to me."

The man held up both hands. "I'm not. Be back here at two-thirty and you can see for yourself. Don't try to find me after tonight. Do what you can, Detective."

She turned to go but paused. "What should I call you?"

He smiled, sad and scared. "Call me a ghost."

She stepped back into the night, the air sharp and clean after the warehouse stench. She saw the black SUV already turning onto the main road, taillights vanishing into the dark.

Torres waited, his arms folded, eyes on the door.

"You, okay?" he said.

She nodded, handing over the folder. "I've been waiting my whole life for a break like this. I hope it's real."

He scanned the contents, lips tight. "It's real enough for now. You did good. But let's see who shows later."

She shrugged, fighting the shiver that ran through her. "Let's get the file folder to the office before someone decides they want it back. We'll regroup, come back and see who our late night visitors are."

He walked her to her Explorer, silent, watchful, and she didn't mind the company.

Sand Island was a knife of rock and landfill shoved between the harbor and the dark slab of the reef. From the ridge above the warehouse, the city was a necklace of lights strung tight, and the only sound was the clatter of unseen trucks and the far-off roll of surf. Torres parked a quarter mile up the access road and hiked the last leg in silence, boots muffled in the hardpan. Leilani followed, every nerve alive to the night's static.

They set up on the old spillway, Torres unpacking his gear with surgeon's hands while

Leilani glassed the target with a battered pair of night-vision binoculars. The warehouse lay below, painted silver by the sodium vapor lamps at the periphery; the lot itself was a black pool. Ten yards from the main entrance, a new Mercedes idled with the engine ticking, two men inside sharing the quiet calculation of men who'd already weighed every outcome.

Torres fit the parabolic dish onto the tripod and thumbed the receiver, one hand to his earpiece. "We're up," he whispered, voice close in the darkness. He handed Leilani the video camera. "What do you see?"

She scanned the lot. "Two in the car, not the usual bouncers."

Torres checked the channel. "Encrypted comms, but I'm pulling the local band. Try channel six." He handed her a second earpiece, and the sounds of the night flooded in. The rush of wind, the chirr of insects, and underneath it, the low-frequency murmur of human conversation.

At two-thirty, the show began.

A black Lexus pulled into the lot, followed by a pearl-white Land Cruiser. The Lexus belonged to a city councilman. Leilani recognized the plates from a past DUI that had gone away after a single phone call from the mayor's office. The Land Cruiser was developer stock, driven by a woman who wore her hair in a bun so tight it looked like it might snap her skull. She exited with a briefcase and a tablet under one arm, eyes sharp, gait steady as a sniper's aim.

More cars arrived in sequence: a silver Tesla, another Mercedes, a Ford Explorer with the county seal still faint on the door. At two-thirty-five, the black SUV rolled in, slow and deliberate, parking nose to nose with the Lexus. The driver emerged first, tall, in a tailored suit, face turned away. But the passenger was the one who mattered, a figure in a hooded jacket, gloves on in this heat, posture like someone built from anger and wire.

Leilani's stomach dropped. "Got our ringleader," she muttered.

She zeroed in with the camera lens focused tight. "You want video or audio?"

"Both," he said. "No one believes what they can't see."

From their vantage point, they watched the attendees file into the warehouse. No handshakes, no names, only curt nods and a sense of urgency. The private security at the door frisked them perfunctorily and scanned the lot for stragglers. Leilani ducked lower, counting bodies. Nine, including the hooded figure.

Inside, the meeting started fast. The parabolic mic caught fragments. "Timeline is nonnegotiable." "Protesters will be neutralized." "Council votes already in the bag." A man's voice, slick and persuasive, suggested "optics management" for the next week, and laid out a plan to "frame the eco group for arson" using pre-planted accelerants. Laughter, low and practiced, echoed in the tin-roofed space.

The hooded figure spoke. The voice was unplaceable, masked, but every word was deliberate, clipped, and cold as dry ice.

"You are not here to debate. We are here to execute. The media will get their evidence, the activists will implode, and the land will be ours by the end of the quarter. You have your assignments. Don't fail, or the cleanup will be permanent."

The room was still. Leilani felt the temperature drop.

She keyed the earpiece. "You getting this?"

Torres, voice tight: "Every word."

The meeting adjourned with a single command. The attendees filed out in reverse order, each pausing at the door to check for shadows or flashes. The hooded figure waited until the last. He walked to the SUV with a liquid confidence that bordered on the supernatural. Leilani tried to capture a photo, but the night-vision washed out the face.

The SUV reversed, paused, and for one heart-stopping moment, Leilani thought it was about to gun straight up the ridge. But it turned hard, fishtailed in the gravel, and vanished toward the city. One by one, the other vehicles slipped away, until all that remained were the sodium lights and the empty lot.

They waited ten minutes to be certain; afterward, Torres packed the gear, his hands less steady than before. "You recognize that voice?" he asked, low.

Leilani shook her head, but the chill at the base of her spine told her it would come to her, eventually, in a dream or a memory. She remembered her uncle's warning, the fear in his eyes. She thought of all the bones in the earth, the thousand small betrayals that built the city one lie at a time.

She stood, stretching out the cramp in her legs. "That's the one my uncle told me about," she said. "The real boss. No name, no record, just a voice in the dark."

Torres sealed the camera in its pouch. "We've made ourselves the next targets."

She smiled, thin and savage. "If they wanted us dead, they'd have done it already. This is a warning. They want to see what we'll do."

They hiked to the car in silence, the city humming like a bad conscience. At the car,

Torres paused. "You trust me, Kealoha?" he asked

She thought about it. "Yeah. For now."

He smiled. "Good. Because whatever comes next, we're in it together."

They got in, locked the doors, and watched the ridge behind them for taillights. None followed.

As they drove away, the camera bag on her lap seemed heavier than it had going in.

# CHAPTER NINE

## *Family in the Crosshairs*

The little coffee shop sat wedged between a defunct laundromat and a tattoo parlor, its sign barely lit, the O in COFFEE flickering at odd intervals as if refusing to be fully awake at this hour. The place was empty but for a kid in a delivery apron nodding off over a tablet and a barista with the spiked lashes of a woman who'd worked the night shift since high school. Leilani scoped the perimeter by habit. She spotted Malia at a two-top by the window, facing the door, hands wrapped tight around a chipped mug. The black hoodie was unmistakable, the same one from the scene, the old protest patch faded on the sleeve.

Leilani climbed into the seat across from her cousin, peeled off her own jacket, her badge neatly tucked out of sight but close enough to heat her ribs.

Malia looked up, the twitch in her cheek a tell from childhood. She never could hide guilt, or fear, or the pulse of anger she carried like a charge. Her eyes darted around the room, logging the exits, the cameras, the regulars. She was ready to run.

"Hey, Lei," she said, voice pitched low. "You want something? I can order."

"I'm good." She allowed the silence to fill the gap, let the morning traffic outside form a muffled buffer. She studied Malia's face, which seemed to have thinned since the last reunion, jaw sharpened, shadows beneath the eyes smudged permanently.

"You look like hell," Leilani said, keeping it light.

Malia snorted. "You should see the other guy."

They let that hang as Malia leaned in, her voice barely audible. "You following me now? Or is this a social call?"

Leilani gave a little shrug, performed for both of them. "You missed the last two family dinners. Auntie is convinced you joined a cult."

"Isn't that what she says about everyone who won't go to church?" Malia's smile was a crack, nothing more. She fidgeted with her mug, rotating it three times before pointing the handle at the door.

Leilani watched, hands steady. "Malia. We need to talk."

"Thought we were."

"No, we're doing the dance. I need the real."

Malia's eyes narrowed. Leilani thought she might bolt, but she rolled her shoulders and folded in, chin down, eyes on her hands.

"You're investigating the Alana thing, right?" she said, not quite a question.

"That's part of it."

"So, what, you think I had something to do with it?"

Leilani didn't answer right away. Her face remained neutral, the way she had at every suspect interview and more than a few Christmas Eves. "You were at the pond," she said. "Not as a bystander."

The lie came instantly: "No, I."

"Save it. I saw you. I have you in four different witness photos, and at least one has you close enough to touch the tape."

Malia flinched but recovered. "It's my right. I live here too."

Leilani suppressed a sigh. "You know what happened to Mako, right? You know how he died?"

Malia looked away, face hollow. "Everyone knows."

"Not the way I do." Leilani leaned forward.

"Look, I'm not here to screw you over. I'm not here as a cop. But I need you to be straight with me. Are you still running with the Defenders?"

Malia hesitated. Her left foot jiggled under the table, a rapid fire Morse Code. "They're not what people say. It's not some eco-terrorist thing. We try to protect land, yeah, but."

Leilani cut her off gently. "You're on a list now. That's not going away. And neither is the threat."

The coffee kid got up, dumped his mug, and shuffled out the side door. Now they were alone except for the barista, who was busy filling a pastry case with frozen malasadas. Malia dropped her voice further, hands now wringing the fabric of her hoodie.

"Are you curious if I know who killed Mako?" she said, her voice flat.

"Yeah."

Malia watched a bus crawl past. Her voice cracked. "He was my friend, Lei. I wouldn't hurt him. I swear, we don't believe in that shit, violence, I mean. The worst anyone ever did was tag a sign or block a bulldozer. They got scared after what happened to Sonny."

She looked up, desperation leaking through the anger. "We want to keep something for ourselves, you know? Before they pave everything over."

Leilani's jaw got tight. She wanted to reach across the table and grab Malia's hand the way she used to when they were kids, but the memory of the badge burned too close.

"You ever hear of a group inside the Defenders, or offshoot, who might do more than protest?"

Malia stood there, her eyes wide. "No. Nobody talks like that. There are always rumors, but mostly it's paranoia. The last six months, it's been worse. Feds, locals, everyone thinks they're being tailed." Her hands made small fists. "Half the meetings now are spent arguing about who might be a snitch."

"You trust everyone in your circle?"

A humorless laugh. "I don't trust anyone, Lei. But I trust you. And I trust that whoever's doing this is trying to make it look like us. So, the next time there's a protest, it won't be rubber bullets. It'll be real."

Leilani studied her cousin's face. Sweat glistened on Malia's upper lip. The air in the café seemed to have thickened, muggy with fear and the sharp edge of regret.

She tried to let it go but couldn't. "The night Mako died, where were you?"

Malia's mouth worked and went slack. "At home. Ask my mom."

"I did. She said you were at band practice."

A grimace. "She means the meeting. Look, I was at the fundraiser at the rec center. After that, I was home. Maybe two, 3 a.m.. I don't know. I was sick the next day."

"You see him that night?"

"No." Malia's voice dropped to a whisper. "He'd been hiding out. Said someone was following him."

Leilani's pulse quickened. "Did he say who?"

"He called it the gray suit. Said if anything happened to him, we should check the university records. That's all."

Leilani made a mental note but kept her features calm. She drew a long breath and let it out. "Okay. I believe you."

Malia relaxed a fraction. "But?"

"You need to be careful. I don't want to see you on a slab, Malia."

A tiny, sad smile. "That's not your call anymore, Detective."

She looked at her. "Maybe not. But if I find out you're lying to me, I will come for you first. You get that?"

Malia snorted. "Now you sound like Auntie."

At that instance, they were two girls again, trading barbs over popsicles, not the cop and the radical, not the loyal and the lost.

The barista called out "last call" with a forced cheer. Leilani stood but didn't reach for her cousin. Malia rose as well, still wringing her hands, eyes fixed on some point above Leilani's shoulder.

Leilani relented, stepped in, and wrapped her cousin in a quick, hard hug, the kind that hurt more coming from a grownup. Malia clung back, subsequently releasing her grip.

"Take care of yourself," Leilani said, voice rough.

"You too," Malia said. "And Lei, don't trust anyone from the city. Especially not your own."

Leilani nodded and walked out, the bell above the door ringing sharply. She didn't look back, didn't allow herself to feel the weight on her shoulders. Not yet.

Outside, the world was growing dark; the air filling with the sharp resin of new asphalt and the faint, omnipresent tang of salt. She walked to her car, sat for a minute with the engine off, and let her hands shake in her lap.

When it passed, she fired up the Explorer, tossed the file on the seat, and merged into the current. She had a university to visit. She had a cousin to protect.

She had no idea how to do either.

The drive home took Leilani past the chain

of battered storefronts, the last rays of daylight reflecting off the greasy windows of lunch spots and vacant lots. She stopped at the corner for a gallon of skim milk, per her pediatrician's strict instructions, before continuing the five blocks to her residence outside of Palolo. The house sat in a row of identical houses, each with bikes and flip-flops on the stoop. From the curb, her house looked indistinguishable from the others, a tiny fortress of normalcy in a city where nothing stayed normal for long.

She climbed the front steps, noting the scuff marks from Kai's skateboard wheels, the faint, sticky footprints from his last barefoot dash through the puddles. The door was unlocked. She tested the knob out of habit and found the bolt thrown, but the latch disengaged.

Inside the scene was a familiar wreckage. Kai's backpack lay exploded open by the door. Science worksheets, paper clipped and abandoned, and a pair of sneakers aimed at the baseboard like two sinking boats. The kitchen was perfumed with a faint funk of forgotten banana peel; the sink filled with the bowls and chopsticks of this morning's cereal binge. On the table, Kai had left a menagerie of clay Pokémon, each lovingly painted with an old brush and a near-lethal dose of model glue.

After putting the milk away, she inspected the house. Locks on the slider, check. Back bedroom window, check. She relaxed a fraction.

"Kai!" she called.

A moment of silence, followed by the thump and skitter of him bounding out from his room. He wore swim trunks and a purple rashguard, face shiny with sweat, and had engineered a rubber band ball the size of a fist.

"Hey Mom! Did you get milk? Mrs. Kila says my bones will turn to dust if I don't drink at least one glass a day, and she showed us x-rays in class, and it was so gross, but also, hey! Can I show you something?"

She nodded, setting her purse on the counter, and braced as he launched into a rapid fire demonstration of his latest contraption, a catapult made from popsicle sticks and duct tape. She watched as he attempted to hurl a jellybean across the room, succeeding only in hitting the ceiling fan and bouncing the projectile directly into her coffee mug.

"Nice trajectory," she said, ruffling his hair.

Kai grinned, all teeth and pride, and began dissecting the device to see if it could be weaponized further. She let him be, turned on the rice cooker, and started assembling dinner from the Tupperware units of last night's leftovers; half a laulau, some soggy shumai, and two scoops of mac salad. She set the table with mismatched chopsticks and bent forks and called him in.

"Five minutes to dinner," she warned.

He appeared in three, hands scrubbed and hair damp from an overenthusiastic rinse at the sink. They ate together, the rhythm unspoken. She'd scoop the rice; he'd attack the protein. Afterward, they'd trade halfway through. For five minutes, she forgot the day's tension, the way her cousin's arms had seemed fragile and insubstantial that morning.

"Did you get the video I sent you?" Kai asked, mouth full of rice.

"Not yet. I haven't checked my phone since lunch."

He arched an eyebrow, skeptical. "I bet it's full of cop calls."

"Some," she admitted. "But I always make time for you."

He glowed at that, and the house was what she'd always hoped for, a safe place, a clean slate, a home that wasn't shadowed by anyone else's history.

After dinner, Kai retreated to his room, leaving the door open a crack. A little kid's version of privacy, a silent invitation for company. Leilani let him go, cleared the dishes, loaded the dishwasher, and ran a hand along the side of the sink, grounding herself. The night outside pressed against the windows, thick and black, and she flicked on every light in the kitchen before pulling out her case folder.

She worked at the table, the clicking of Kai's LEGOs in the other room forming a white noise. She thumbed through the interviews from the day, the forensics on Mako's body, the transcripts from her time with Torres. The clues lined up like dominoes, but the sense of imminent collapse was still out of reach.

At nine, she peeked in on Kai, found him curled in his comforter, the glow of his tablet painting his face ghost-blue. She grabbed the device, set it on his desk, and tucked him in, making a show of tucking the blanket around his feet so tight he squealed.

"Will you check for monsters?" he asked, the old joke.

She kneeled, looked under the bed, and made a big show of examining the shadows. "None today. Maybe tomorrow."

He smiled, drowsy now, eyes already fluttering. "Love you, Mom."

"Love you too, bug," she said, kissing his forehead.

She lingered at the doorway, watching the rise and fall of his breath, the flutter of his eyelids as he drifted away. She closed the door softly.

She poured herself a glass of water and sat at the table, case files spread out like a roadmap to hell. She scribbled notes in the margin, circled *gray suit* and *university records* and *Malia, still hiding something*. She underlined "Kai" and drew an arrow to the margin, where she wrote, "He's all that matters."

The clock crept past ten, then eleven. Outside, the night was silent except for the distant yowl of a feral cat. She was halfway through reading the toxicology report when the sound came; a sharp, percussive crash from the living room, as if someone had hurled a cinder block through the glass.

She was on her feet before she realized, her hand moving by reflex to the gun in the side table drawer. She thumbed the safety, heart pounding, and crept toward the source.

The window above the couch was a jagged, star-shaped wound, glass teeth glittering on the carpet. The wind, heavy with salt, pressed into the room, bringing with it a chill that made the hair stand on end. The TV was toppled, and the remotes scattered. A large landscape rock was in the middle of the mess.

She covered the room, her gun raised, adrenaline scorching her nerves. No movement, no sound, only the relentless noise of her own pulse. She swept the kitchen and the hallway.

The back door was still locked. She examined the window. It had been shattered from the outside.

She dialed 911 on her phone, thumb shaking on the touchscreen, but stopped herself before hitting send. Instead, she called the precinct direct, got patched through to the night sergeant.

"Kealoha, what's going on?" the voice croaked.

"Attempted break-in at my place. Palolo, you have the address. They smashed the window, didn't see anyone in the yard, but could use a sweep. My son's here."

"Copy. Patrol ETA ten minutes. You need medical?"

"No. We're good."

She hung up, scanning the floor, searching for anything that didn't belong. That was when she saw the envelope, white and thick, taped to the rock with painter's tape. She pried it loose, hands steady now, and opened it.

Inside was a single sheet of printer paper. The words in block letters, black ink bled through.

BACK OFF OR YOUR SON IS NEXT.

The letters slanted up, angry, the handwriting aggressive and unfamiliar. She read it twice, and a third time, until the words blurred at the edges.

She stood there; the gun hanging limp at her side; the letter trembling in her grip. Her thoughts turned to Kai, the trust in his voice when he said love you, Mom. The thought made her chest tighten so hard she thought her ribs would snap.

She bolted down the hall, flung open his door. Kai was still asleep, sprawled under the crocodile-print comforter, mouth open, limbs splayed like a cartoon starfish. She placed her hand on his forehead, and back, to be sure.

He didn't stir.

She watched him; the terror receding enough to let the anger flood in. She holstered the gun, returned to the room, sweeping the mess into piles, gloving up to collect the glass and evidence for the patrol team.

As she waited for the black-and-whites, she read the note, letting every letter burn itself into her memory.

It was no longer about her job, or the case, or justice. They'd made it personal now. They'd made it about blood.

She sat in the ruined living room; the lights blazing in every window, and planned how she'd burn them down to the last man.

The squad cars arrived, and the house was lit up like a Christmas parade. Leilani met them on the stoop, badge on, sidearm holstered, and walked them through the evidence, the glass, the note, the exact spot where the rock had left a print in the soft patch of the rug. Her voice stayed even, detailed, unflinching, cop mode, a shell so thick the responding officers looked sideways, like they were waiting for her to break.

The cops found an old piece of plywood from the last hurricane and in a few minutes had it screwed to the front window frame, covering up the shattered glass.

While the techs dusted and the uniforms canvassed the block, she slipped into Kai's room, shut the door behind her, and braced herself against the weight of the moment.

She sat on the bed, watching his chest rise and fall, counting each breath the way she'd done when he was a newborn, jaundiced and sweating through his first fever. She let herself be a mother. She snapped off the night light and got to work.

She moved through the house with surgical precision: zipped two changes of clothes into his daypack, threw in his battered Kindle, a box of granola bars, and a flashlight. She added the inhaler, the emergency contact list, the charger cord wound tight as a noose. She packed her own overnight clothes in the black gym bag, loaded the Glock and two spare mags, and slipped her badge into the side pocket. She inspected the windows, the doors and the car alarm. Every motion was exact and practiced, but her fingers kept trembling, missing zippers, fumbling keys. The muscle memory of fear.

She woke Kai with a hand on his shoulder, gentle but insistent.

"Hey, bug. Time to get up."

He rolled toward her, groggy and annoyed. "Is it morning?"

"No. It's an adventure. We're going to Tutu's house for a sleepover."

He perked up at that, confusion evaporating in a second. "Now? It's dark."

She ruffled his hair, smoothed it down, and let herself look at him longer than necessary. "Yeah, now. I need your help to be brave, okay?"

He nodded, dead serious. "Okay, Mom."

She dressed him in the hallway, slipped his bare feet into Crocs, zipped up his hoodie. He didn't ask why. He clung to her hand and shouldered the bag, a pint-sized soldier on a forced march. She checked the porch for the patrol officer, after which she hurried him to the car, the Explorer still radiating warmth.

Only when he was belted in did she call her mother. The phone rang twice. Naalei answered, voice instantly awake and vibrating with the promise of trouble.

"Lei? What is it?"

Her voice faltered slightly. "Can you open the gate for us? We're coming over. Now."

"Is it Kai?"

"Yes," she said, the word thick. "Someone threatened him, Mom. I can't." The rest choked in her throat, but Naalei didn't need more.

"I'll wait on the steps. Don't stop for anything."

She ended the call, put the car in drive, and pulled away from the curb. The police still milled on the sidewalk, blue and white lights washing the houses in a toxic strobe. She gave them a nod, and floored it down the block, not slowing until the last cruiser was a memory in the rearview.

Kai watched the houses slide past, silent at first. As they hit the turn up St. Louis Heights, he asked, "Did someone try to rob us?"

She hesitated. "Something like that. But I'm here. I'll keep you safe."

He nodded, pulling the hoodie over his head, shrinking into the seat. She glanced at him again. The angle of his jaw was so much like his father it made her chest ache.

Halfway up the ridge, she realized she'd forgotten his night buddy—the grimy, mint-green chameleon he'd slept with since he was three. She nearly turned the car around, but spotted the comfort animal jammed under his arm, half hidden by the folds of the sweatshirt.

She almost wept with relief, but kept her eyes dry and forward.

At Naalei's, the gate was open, and the porch light blazed. Her mother waited in a housecoat, bare feet on the cool stone. She opened the car door before it fully stopped, pulling Kai into her arms and ushering him inside. No fuss, no questions, only action.

Leilani stayed at the door, breathing in the night, willing her hands to steady. She had to be strong now; her mother returned, eyes hard, face set. "You find out who did this, Lei."

She nodded. "I will."

Naalei pressed a Tupperware into her hands. "Eat something before you go."

She let herself be hugged.

She walked to the car alone, the bag heavier than it had been. She slid into the driver's seat, gripping the wheel until her knuckles turned pale. She picked up her phone, saw the unread messages stacking up, the case file icon pulsing like a threat.

She put the food in the cupholder, started the engine, and checked the mirror one last time.

Through the window, she saw her son, small and safe, curled on her mother's couch, chameleon clutched tight. The image burned into her mind. A shield against whatever waited outside.

She put the Explorer in gear and drove into the night, determined to end it on her own terms.

# CHAPTER TEN

## *Unearthed Connections*

The digital forensics lab was at police headquarters. At 4 a.m., every corridor above it throbbed with motion, cops shuffling reports, detainees lobbing obscenities, dispatchers rehearsing the next disaster. In here, the world reduced itself to an endless fluorescent hush, humming racks of servers, fans spinning perpetual wind, and rows of monitors flickering in shades of pale blue that painted everything in the colors of drowning.

Leilani walked in, trailing ocean damp from the street, an evidence bag tucked under one arm. She signed the chain-of-custody clipboard, the tech on duty watching her from behind the acrylic sneeze shield with the bored intensity of a TSA agent. The badge clipped to his lab coat read T. Lee. His hair was a fresh buzz and his face was so cleanly shaven it looked like a baby's heel.

"Need access to the cage, Detective?" he said, not quite making it a question.

Leilani nodded, offered her badge, and waited while he typed her in. The security door gave a sad pneumatic sigh before unlocking, admitting her into the core of the lab. It was colder here; the AC worked triple time to offset the body heat of the machines.

She took a moment to center herself at the evidence table, white laminate, nothing on top but a bar coded tray and a set of nitrile gloves folded into a neat blue square. After gloving up, she unzipped the evidence pouch. Mako Pahoa's laptop slid out with a sound like a deck of cards being cut, slim, silver, caked at the corners with grime from a thousand dorm room desks. The screen wore a patchwork of cracked resin and missing key caps. There was a faded sticker across the palm rest, an old campaign slogan that had been half peeled off and written over in Sharpie.

SAVE THE STREAMS, DON'T DROWN THE FUTURE.

She lined the laptop up with the evidence tag, snapped a digital photo for the log, and signed the case number on a fresh chain-of-custody strip. The ritual steadied her. The gloves reduced her sense of touch; however; she perceived the pulse in her fingertips, a nervous expectation that something here was more important than it seemed.

She started her work at the perimeter, cataloguing every external feature. The manufacturer's name had been abraded off, but the serial number was intact, so she recorded it. She flipped the device over to examine the battery compartment. A thin line of adhesive marked the edge, but it looked factory - made, nothing added. She levered the latch with a microspudger, feeling the satisfying click as the battery slid free.

There, a seam, subtle and wrong, running the length of the housing. She angled the light; a portion of the plastic was melted, re-glued, and camouflaged with marker to match the original matte finish. She snapped more photos, took a dental pick to the seam, and teased it open with careful, patient pressure.

Inside, buried in the void where the battery's cells should have been, was a small flash drive wrapped in electrical tape. She paused, letting the magnitude settle in. Mako had built a hollow in his own hardware, and after that stashed something inside. For what? Blackmail? Insurance? Desperation?

A rush of admiration warred with dread. If you were twenty-two and knew someone was hunting you, this was what you did. Hide your secrets and challenge the world to discover them.

She extracted the drive, careful not to touch any surface that might carry prints. Set it next to the laptop. The tech, Lee, had wandered over, curiosity overcoming his boredom.

"Nice catch," he said, hands hovering over the table, but not daring to touch.

"Took half my life to find it," Leilani replied, but she said it under her breath. She filled out the supplementary log, documenting every detail. When she looked up, Lee was still there, shifting his weight from foot to foot.

"Uh, Agent Torres called. Said he's on his way in. Wants to help run the image if you get stuck. He said you'd know what that meant."

Leilani tried not to sigh, but the air escaped her, anyway. "I can handle it," she said.

Lee grinned. "I mean, sure, but the encryption on these is no joke. And Torres, he's kind of a freak about this stuff. Scares some of the techs."

Leilani's expression pinched tight, but she offered a shrug. "I'll let him know when I need him."

"Suit yourself," Lee said. He wandered back to his station, which was a command post for managing email tickets and the fantasy basketball league.

She settled at the nearest forensic imaging bay. The monitor was retina-burn white; the peripherals arrayed in perfect rows, SATA adapters, USB analyzers, every variety of cable known to man. She booted the write-blocked workstation and plugged the flash drive in, waiting for the standard new device chime. The drive spun up, but the partition was unreadable. She launched the forensic suite, set it to mirror the raw data, and started a header analysis to check for buried partitions or shadow files.

It was an hour of labor, most of it spent watching slow progress bars and hex dumps scroll like green rain. The longer she stared, the more her mind wandered. Not to the crime, not to the victim, but to Mako's hands. The exacting patience it took to carve open a battery shell and hide your last will and testament inside. She imagined him in some crowded dorm, sweating over the plastic with a soldering iron, his phone propped up to stream a how-to video. Every minute, aware that someone could come through the door and end the experiment forever.

She'd seen the pattern before. In the kids she used to chase out of the skate park when she was on patrol. Paranoia as self-defense. You only needed to be right once.

The screen beeped. Hidden volume found. She tunneled in, following the signature bytes to a nested directory named Koa. She clicked through, finding three encrypted containers, each the size of the drive itself. A name floated in the directory index, set as the administrator, Mahoe.

A pulse of electricity ran up her arms. Mahoe, the name from the old cases, the community brawler who'd turned up at every protest in the last decade. She typed the name, hit return. No luck. Password protected and set to lock after three failed tries.

She made two attempts, both standard, both rejected with a passive aggressive chirp. She hesitated, thumb hovering over the enter key, when she heard footsteps approaching from the hallway. Heavy, measured, but with the light tread of someone who didn't want to alert security.

Isaac arrived before the sun. He came through the precinct's sally port with two paper cups balanced in his hand, his collared shirt untucked, and his face etched with the map of a night spent awake and moving. The tech at the evidence cage buzzed him through with the knowing nod reserved for the people who lived in the building when they weren't on shift.

He found Leilani in the far corner of the digital lab, huddled over the ghost image she'd spent all night building. The blue glow limned her cheekbones and threw hard shadows under her eyes, but the way she clicked through file trees and cycled passwords spoke of caffeinated resolve. She didn't look up when he set the coffee next to her elbow.

"Do you ever sleep?" he asked.

She grunted. "Last week." She took the coffee anyway, sipped it, letting the warmth rush over her.

He sat in the chair beside her, eyes on the mirrored data. "You found it."

"Barely," she said. She told him about the battery compartment, the layers of tape, the Mahoe name.

He scanned the error log. "You get three more tries before it fries itself. They always build in a kill switch."

Isaac pulled up a rolling stool, setting his bag beside hers. He glanced at the mirrored drive and whistled. "Nice work. That's a lot of data for a dead kid."

"He wasn't a kid," Leilani said, but the defensiveness was more for herself than for the room. "He outsmarted half the adults on the island."

"Guess you needed the right motivation." He powered up a forensic suite on a second terminal, syncing it to the network. For a while, they typed in tandem: her hands dancing over the UI, his digging through system logs and user profiles, pursuing different threads through the same labyrinth.

The first hour flew by quickly. They brute-forced known passwords, ran strings against the drive, cross-referenced names from protest logs and university directories. Leilani grew increasingly tight, knuckles whitening on the mouse every time another attempt came up 401 Unauthorized.

Isaac, meanwhile, maintained a running commentary. "He salted the hash. Smart. But the salt itself is too short for true random. It's probably a phrase or a date. Maybe a local one, holidays, or family."

Leilani barked a laugh. "No one here remembers their own birthday, let alone anyone else's."

He liked the way she bantered, deflection layered over worry. She'd been burned enough times by friendly fire that an alliance seemed like an audition.

She tried another password set. Classic protest dates, the year of statehood, the city's founding. All failed.

Isaac reached across her, keying up the error logs. The screens were so close, their shoulders touched, and neither moved. He smelled of dark roast and sweat and something metallic, like dried blood. It made her want to recoil, and to lean in further, so she did neither.

"Look, the lockout time changes with each attempt, but never by more than three seconds. That's a deliberate buffer, not to keep us out, but to slow down someone impatient," he said.

"Which is everyone in this building," Leilani said, but she saw what he meant. Whoever built the encryption wanted it to be broken, but only by the right hands.

"Did you ever meet Mahoe?" Isaac asked, eyes on the screen.

"I read his file. Guy was a rock star in the day. Now he's a ghost."

Isaac's hands slowed as he scanned the process log. "You know, when I was a new agent, my mentor told me, if you want to know how a man thinks, look at how he eats breakfast."

She made a face. "You profiling my granola bars now?"

He smiled. "I'm saying some people hide in plain sight. And some people want you to chase your tail before you find them."

Over the next hour, they cycled through password variations, local sports teams, street names, and family genealogies. The system batted them away, each time stacking up the error message with a gentle condescension.

Isaac rested his chin on his hand and watched

her work. "You ever think it's not about the victim?"

She scowled. "What do you mean me?"

"I mean it could be about someone watching you. About getting your attention."

She rolled her eyes, but the thought lingered. "You sound like my mother."

He grinned. "She sounds like a smart lady."

They huddled closer, elbows bumping as they typed. The lab's humming settled into the white noise background of their focus. She could feel his pulse through his wrist when he reached over her to switch tabs, a steady rhythm that was at odds with her own, which had gone fast and staccato.

Leilani took a breath, thinking. "What would you use as the password?"

Torres smirked. "If it's Mahoe, probably something ceremonial. Kumu always used dates for the first crack, founder's birthday, last day of protest, stuff like that."

She tried the date of the last legal injunction against the development. It Failed.

Torres tapped the desk. "Try the opposite. The date the project broke ground. Pain points."

Isaac typed another command into the terminal. This time, the system paused a full four seconds and returned a new prompt.

Leilani frowned. "That's different."

"Maybe it wants you to try something else." He glanced at her. "What about your badge number? Or your father's?"

She flinched, hand hovering above the keyboard. The mention of her father made her skin crawl, an old wound barely crusted over.

"I haven't used that number since I was a rookie. Why would Mahoe know it?"

Isaac shrugged, face softening. "People leave fingerprints on each other. Maybe it's a message, detective."

She hated the idea, but she tried anyway, typing her father's badge number into the prompt. Nothing. She tried the reverse, the number backwards. Still nothing.

On impulse, she added the year he was sworn in and the year he died. She hit enter.

The screen turned green. The new folder labeled Pu'uhonua opened. The screen flickered. The file opened in read-only mode.

Inside, PDFs, spreadsheets and an org chart so dense it looked like the wiring diagram for an entire government. Leilani scrolled, scanning the file names. Near the bottom, an audio file labeled, in case. She double clicked, and a voice, Makos, tremulous and urgent, filled the lab.

"If you're hearing this, I'm already gone. Don't trust anyone from the developer's side. The families are involved, and at least one council member. Find Mahoe. He's the one who can explain the numbers. And if you can, tell my mom I'm sorry. She was right all along."

The words hovered, unerasable. The harsh glare from the screens accentuated the shadows on Leilani's face, making her look both older and more tired.

Torres was silent. "That's your case breaker."

She nodded, teeth clenched. "We need to find Mahoe. And we need to do it before they realize we've cracked this."

They watched the files as the system parsed them: spreadsheets, emails, voice memos, photos. Pages and pages of account ledgers, payment schedules and bribe agreements disguised as consulting fees. There were lists of council members, names circled in red. Some files were dated days ago; others stretched back over two decades.

Leilani's mouth went dry. "He kept everything. All of it."

Isaac nodded, expression gone flat. "The bastard built a failsafe. If anything happened to him, or anyone, this would be the grenade." The glare from the screens highlighted the contours of Leilani's face, giving her an ageless appearance.

Torres closed his eyes, rubbed at his temple, and smiled. A slow, predatory thing. "I'll run interference. You finish the data pull."

She didn't thank him. She didn't need to. She powered through the next steps, fingers working faster than her mind could keep up. The war was now in the open, and the only thing left was to finish it.

Leilani leaned back, breathing hard. She could feel the energy radiating off Isaac—his pride, and his fear, and something else.

She didn't want to meet his eyes, but she did anyway. "You did good," she said.

He reached out, almost instinctively, and touched her hand. "So did you."

For a moment, they sat with the glow of the screen between them, a wall and a bridge at the same time. The secrets on the drive were bigger than the both of them. But together they were large enough to face it down.

She downloaded the files to the precinct's secure server and made a copy for the DA. Outside, dawn had clawed its way up the skyline, bruised purple and yellow. She'd been in the lab for so long that her sense of time had burned out; she knew that the next move would define everything that came after.

When she logged off, the glow from the screens had faded to gray. She peeled off the gloves, tossed them into the evidence bin, and felt the ache in her bones as a signal. There was no going back. Not now.

Isaac stood and stretched, rolling the tension out of his neck. "How about some breakfast?"

She thought about saying no, but remembered the last time she ate alone, staring at the phone and waiting for a name that would never come. She packed up the evidence, zipped her bag, and looked at him. "I could eat."

"Good," he said, smiling. "You drive."

She led the way out of the office, the pressure of the unlocked secrets thudding against her chest with every step. For now, it was enough.

Much to his chagrin, they ate breakfast out of vending machine wrappers. Granola bars for her, black coffee and a Red Bull for Isaac. The precinct cafeteria didn't open for another hour, and besides, no one wanted to face the sun yet. Instead, they sat at the battered steel desk in her cubicle, ringed by evidence bags and the hum of machines digesting data. The flash drive was a gold vein now, every folder opening into new rooms of information, some half-lit, some roaring with revelation.

Leilani started with the spreadsheets. Each one was a temple to organized crime.

Line after line of transfer numbers, shell corporations in four countries, wire instructions coded as community grants, and impact study reimbursements. At first, the numbers were numbers, long and impersonal, like a flood gauge. But as she worked, the patterns became inescapable. Every payment coincided with a permit approval, a council vote or a suppression order against the 'Āina Defenders. Every transaction told a story, and every story led to someone with a badge, a suit, or a last name that meant something on this island.

Next came the ledgers, slick with secrecy. They exposed the arteries of money that ran from the mainland to the developers, from the developers to the fixers, from the fixers to the handful of trusted advisors who could make things happen or make things vanish. Some names on the payroll stung. A judge Leilani had once respected a councilwoman who'd shaken her hand at a fundraiser, the son of her mother's oldest friend. She scrolled faster, each click a new wound.

Isaac hovered behind her, his energy different now. At first, he'd offered a running commentary. "Look at that transfer." "That's a big chunk for a cleanup crew." "How many aliases does a guy need?" As the file tree grew, his words dwindled and grew silent. Once, he placed a hand on her shoulder, light as a moth landing; she didn't shake him off, but she didn't lean back, either. The contact grounded her, kept her from tumbling into the blue-lit abyss of numbers and names.

The emails were last. They read like a hit list masquerading as a CC thread. Developers threatening to speed up projects unless certain obstacles were removed; city officials responding with promises of cooperation and optics management. There were attached scans of falsified environmental reports, doctored impact assessments, and in one case, a photo of a protest leader's car with a rifle scope centered on the hood.

Leilani scrolled, jaw set. This was what they'd killed for. Not oil, not gold, a little more dirt, a little more beach. A tiny slice of paradise turned to concrete. She kept clicking, absorbing every detail, feeling both vindicated and nauseated. She wanted to print out the whole directory and shove it under the nose of every cop, every council member, every ancestor who ever told her to keep the faith.

She saw her own last name.

At first it was a line in a memo, a reference buried in a mass of double talk. But the more she read, the clearer it became. A decade old payment, small, not five figures, wired to her father's old credit union account. The note attached: For services rendered, expedited review per phone call.

She stopped breathing. The office was freezing, and the noise of the machines was too loud. Her hand hovered over the trackpad, fingers rigid.

She read the line again, and again, and again. Every time, it said the same thing.

Her father had taken money. Maybe for a favor, or for something more. The records were unambiguous. The deposit was real; the timing damning. She remembered the story from her childhood, the one she'd always believed, how her father died on the job because he'd refused to look the other way, refused to let corruption through the door. She'd built her life on that story, made it her own personal constitution. And now, here it was, rewritten in black and white.

She sat, staring, unable to move. A single tear broke loose, running down her cheek, and she wiped it away with her hand, like she used to scrape sand from her eyes at the beach. She gripped the desk so hard the wood creaked.

Behind her, Isaac said nothing. She could feel him watching, but his gaze was gentle, unintrusive. After a moment, he squeezed her shoulder.

Leilani closed the file. She stood up, her legs unsteady, and walked out of the bullpen without a word.

She drifted down the empty hallway, the overhead lights strobing in a slow, nauseating rhythm. She found the bathroom, locked herself in a stall, and sat on the lid. She pushed her fists against her thighs and forced herself to breathe.

She had always believed in evidence, in the clean logic of facts. She had never expected to become evidence herself, to see her own name in the same toxic ledger as the men she hunted. She closed her eyes and there he was, not as a memory but as a presence. Her father, standing in a taro field, hands streaked with dirt, explaining to her why the stream mattered more than the shopping mall it might one day water. The way he'd thrown her on his shoulders at marches, his voice booming louder than the megaphone as he taught her the old chants. How he always cleaned up after the protests, how he took her with him to meet with the other families when someone got arrested, how he'd given her that first battered pair of handcuffs with a smile and a warning. "Never use these to hold yourself back, only to catch the bad guys."

She remembered him coming home after his shifts, the tired way he'd set his service piece on top of the fridge, the way he'd wink at her and say, "It's a job, baby. The real fight is what you do after you take off the badge." She remembered the funeral, the speeches about honor, the promises that he'd never be forgotten.

And she remembered the day she found out the case had been closed because of insufficient evidence and that her father's killer had never been named.

Now she knew why. And it made her want to tear down the wall in front of her, to prove that something could still be unbroken.

She stayed there, listening to her heart, to the distant, irregular tick of the precinct's pipes. That was when she realized she'd lost all sense of how long she'd been sitting there that she finally stood, splashed water on her face, and stared into the mirror.

She looked older or simply hollowed out. But she noticed her father in her reflection, the line of her jaw, the set of her brow. She was tempted to smash the mirror, but she didn't.

Instead, she left the bathroom, composed and silent. She walked into the bullpen, to the evidence, and to the work that would not let her go.

Isaac was still there. He met her eyes, offered no platitudes, no apology. An unspoken contract. We finish this together.

She nodded, sat down, and scrolled to the next name. Isaac stood behind her.

"Do you need to talk?" he said, not pushing it.

She shook her head, but he didn't move, so she spoke anyway. "He was one of the good ones. Not perfect, but better than the rest. I grew up thinking he was..." She exhaled, long and shaky. "I built everything on that. Every time I arrested some shitbag, every time I had to lie to a mom about why her kid wasn't coming home, I did it because I believed he did the right thing. Even when it cost him."

She folded her arms, hugging her own elbows. "What if it was all a lie?"

Isaac leaned against the opposite wall. "You ever hear the one about the cop who spent his whole life chasing ghosts?"

She rolled her eyes but didn't tell him to stop.

"He caught a few and let a few go. But every time he closed a case, he was a little emptier. One day, he found out that the first ghost he ever chased, his own dad, wasn't a ghost at all, but a man who made a bad choice and paid for it."

Leilani looked up and met his eyes. "I don't need comfort, Torres."

He smiled. "I know. But maybe you need permission to be pissed off at him. Or to forgive him. Or both."

They stood in silence, the electric ballast humming above their heads.

"I don't know what to do with this. How do

you keep going when you realize you're no better than the people you're trying to catch?"

Isaac's hand hovered, settling gently on her arm. "You don't have to be better, Lei. You have to not give up."

She laughed. "You sound like my mother. She'd like you."

"Everyone likes me," he said. "Especially you."

She snorted, but she didn't pull away. She let the comfort land. She straightened, jaw set.

"We finish the case," she said. "We burn it all down."

He nodded, accepting her resolve. "Together."

"Together," she echoed.

Her hands moved across the keyboard. The screensaver had kicked in, a slow ripple of the HPD logo. Torres stood behind her, one hand resting on the chair, an anchor more than an intrusion.

She opened a fresh window and drafted the report, names, dates, connections, every ugly truth she'd spent a lifetime refusing to believe. When she finished, she sent the entire case file to the DA, cc'd her supervisor, and blind-copied herself at every email she could think of. She added a single line at the top.

**All evidence attached. Pursue all leads**

**regardless of origin. L. Kealoha.**

She hit send.

The room was silent for a while. Isaac reached down, squeezed her hand, and let her go.

She smiled at him, at the blue glow painting the creases around his mouth and eyes. "Let's get breakfast," she said, and this time it wasn't a joke.

He grinned. "Always."

They left the precinct together, stepping out into the world with nothing left to lose and everything to prove. The dawn was ugly, sharp-edged, full of trash trucks and squawking Mynas, but it was honest. It was theirs.

And for the first time in a long time, she was almost free.

# CHAPTER ELEVEN

## *The Mastermind's Shadow*

A text message woke Leilani from her dream. No preface, merely a string of numbers and a promise.

*ANSWERS YOU SEEK. COME ALONE.*

No callback, no signature, the sender ID a scrambled burn code that made the hairs rise on Leilani's arms. After reading it three times, she opened the GPS. The coordinates placed it on the west side, out past the recycling plant and the last strip of big box retail, deep in the old industrial grid where the vagrants gave the warehouses a wide berth.

She thought about deleting it, thought about copying Torres, thought about rolling over and finishing the two hours of sleep her body craved. But the word alone, throbbed in her skull, a dare, and a command, and in the raw, ragged state she now lived in, that was enough. She pulled on a fresh tee, clipped her badge and gun to her belt, and holstered her backup piece at her ankle before locking the door behind her. She checked to make sure Kai was still asleep, kissed him on the forehead, and walked out of his room. Kai's chameleon peeked out from the mountain of comforters on the couch, one lazy eye tracking her as she crept past. She gave it a nod. "Protect the home front bug," she said, and stepped into the humid dark.

The drive was mercifully quick. The city's neon and sodium vapor bled together in the mirrors, watching for any tail but seeing only the anonymous drift of delivery vans and lifted Tacomas, nobody out there by accident after midnight. The rental lot gave way to a wasteland of chain link and corrugated metal. The ocean's stink layered with burned plastic and the smell of old machinery. She killed the headlights a block early, rolling the last hundred yards in silence, senses primed by every cop story she'd ever been told about ambushes and set-ups and the sick genius of a criminal with too much time.

The building squatted at the end of a gravel spur, two stories of rust and rot, windows blacked out with cardboard or webbed with spider cracks. The roof sagged at the center, and the paint had once been blue but was now a mottled scab, salt-licked and ready to flake off at a whisper. She coasted to a stop behind a stack of busted shipping crates, the engine ticking as the heat bled off. She waited, counting heartbeats, watching for movement at the loading dock, the roofline, the shadowed alley behind the dumpsters. Nothing. Not a stray cat.

She palmed her phone, double checked the address, and scanned the street for cameras, found two, both aimed at the gates of the next property over, probably set up to catch employee theft and illegal dumping. Not for her. Still, she wore her hat low and her stride casual, every sense stretched thin as a fishing line. At the main entrance, she found the padlock had been snapped off; the shank left hanging. She drew her weapon slowly, pushed the door inward and stepped into the dark.

The interior was colder than outside; the air thick with dust and old oil. It took a few seconds for her eyes to adjust. At first, all she saw was the expected entropy, sagging shelves of mildewed boxes, a toppled drum of something sticky pooling around its base, a workbench littered with shattered glass and mouse droppings. Her boots crunched on a grit of rust flakes and glass, echoing sharply in the silence. She held her breath, waited for the shuffle or scrape that meant a watcher, a camera, a trap. Nothing.

Near the wall, dead center in a spill of light from one of the lot lights, someone had constructed a tableau. A six by ten section of drywall, propped on sawhorses and painted matte white, was plastered edge to edge with photos, maps, printouts, sticky notes and strings in the classic paranoid style. Red yarn mapped connections between faces, sites, money trails, and here and there, the familiar outline of the HPD badge or a snippet from the case files Leilani herself had filed.

She circled the display with her weapon up, but after a few passes, she lowered it. Whoever built this wanted her alive, at least until the next act.

She stepped closer, cataloguing each element with the speed and precision of a lifetime spent in evidence rooms. The faces up top were the major players. Politicians with practiced smiles, resort developers in polo shirts, and the current and former chiefs of police. Clustered below were the activists. Some she recognized; others she'd seen in mugshots or protest livestreams. Photos traced their arcs from rallies to arrests to funerals, a visual timeline of the movement's rise and attrition.

To the left, a spiderweb of news clippings and city council minutes. Financial disclosures and property deeds, each annotated in a looping, aggressive hand. Here, a transfer from an offshore account. There, a subpoenaed memo with three lines redacted, but restored in pen at the margin. She saw names she'd circled in her own notes, and others she'd never thought to connect. Union reps, mid-tier lobbyists, a priest from her childhood parish. Every page bore a code in the corner, as if someone was building their own master index, the kind you make when you already know what the outcome will be.

The right panel held maps. Aerial photos of the island, overlays marking out sacred sites, water rights, old burial grounds. On one, someone had drawn a thick red line around the latest development, and X'd out each point of resistance. First the protest camp, next the city's environmental review office, and the home address of Kekoa Mahoe, his name circled three times in black ink.

At the very center, anchoring the chaos, was a single white card. It bore a silhouette, a blank, stylized face, and beneath it the caption. THE MASTERMIND. No other info. Every string on the board, every arrow and underlined word, led to this blank. It wasn't only a suspect. It was a signature.

Leilani's skin prickled, a slow crawl of recognition and anger and something that might have been admiration. She swept the room with her phone, snapping photos from every angle, making sure not to touch or disturb the arrangement. Each flash caught new details. A stray fingerprint on a document, a torn envelope from a university lab, a watermarked memo she'd never seen in the DA's discovery.

She scanned for traps. Not the physical kind, but the kind that lived in information. The wall was a weapon, and she could see the outlines of her own case, mirrored and distorted, laid bare by a mind as obsessive as her own. She sensed the pulse of a challenge, the way predators circled before a kill. The word, alone, echoed in her head, this time as a taunt.

Low on the wall, almost hidden behind a stapled row of protest photos, was a trio of old newsprint stories. They were all about her father.

She went cold. The first article was a yellowed scan from the Advertizer, headlined LOCAL WHISTLEBLOWER FACES THREATS. Below it, a blurry photo of her father at a podium, flanked by lawyers, eyes wild but proud. The next was an op-ed, two weeks later, decrying the cost of police corruption investigations and implying her father had made enemies on both sides of the line. The third was a brief, an obituary, if you read between the lines, though he'd lived another five years after they fired him for cause. Someone had marked it up with a red highlighter.

She read them all, jaw locked. Every string from those stories fed to the central silhouette. The message was clear. Everything old was new again, and no one, not even a cop's kid, got to change the script.

She stepped back, centering herself. The room

seemed smaller now, the walls closer. There was a tremor in her hands. Not fear, but a sharp, almost chemical excitement. She'd been summoned here for a reason, and now she had the invitation in hand.

She was not alone in this story. Not anymore.

She swept the warehouse, clearing corners and cubbies, half expecting a camera, a watcher, a trigger. Nothing. Only the hum of the highway and the crackle of salt air through a broken pane.

Before leaving, she circled the evidence board one last time, letting her gaze linger on the gaps, the spaces where a critical truth still waited. She realized, with a start, that half the files pinned here were things the HPD had missed. The Mastermind wasn't following the case; they were driving it, one step ahead, planting clues for the cop most likely to chase them down.

Her phone vibrated, a silent notification. She checked it. A new message from the same unknown number.

*YOU SEE IT NOW. NEXT MOVE IS YOURS. DON'T BE LATE.*

No coordinates this time. Only the dare.

She had finished photographing the last quadrant of the evidence wall, her phone's memory maxed, the battery crawling toward zero, when the warehouse changed. Not a sound at first, but a feeling. The way silence can deform, can develop a texture you taste at the back of your teeth. Something was different in the air.

Leilani moved her left hand, checked the sightlines over her shoulder, and caught the shift of a shadow along the wall by the old loading ramp. She thought, cat, but, no, that's two feet. As soon as her mind issued the order to draw, the new presence was already moving.

She pivoted to the right, using her own body as a shield for the phone. The assailant came in low, A classic tackle, and took her at the hip, above the joint. The shock knocked the air from her lungs, but years of rolling with waves and wrestling idiot cousins at the tide pools kicked in. She dropped her center of gravity, planted her left knee, and rolled with the force, letting them both hit the concrete instead of being bowled clean over.

The phone skittered across the floor, a glint of pink plastic flashing as it tumbled under the sawhorses. For half a second, she saw her attacker in full. Average height, trim, arms corded with muscle under a black fleece jacket, hands gloved in leather. The face was covered, a balaclava over the lower half and mirrored sunglasses above, ridiculous in the warehouse gloom, but somehow more menacing.

The stranger's hands were on her throat.

Not crushing, more a test, a sizing up. She snapped her arms upward, breaking the hold, and brought her head up fast enough to crack the bridge of the mask with her forehead. There was a grunt and a retaliatory elbow that smashed into her shoulder. She pivoted, dropped them both sideways, and used her legs to entangle, jiu-jitsu style, but the attacker was already angling for leverage.

They rolled, knees and elbows, legs scissoring, dust and blood thick in Leilani's mouth. She got her right hand free, jammed it between the mask and the attacker's jaw, and touched for a split second the slick, clean-shaven skin of someone who didn't expect to be touched. She grabbed for the mask to rip it away, but the assailant clamped a hand around her wrist and squeezed. The bones ground together, sharp enough to make her vision fuzz out in black and white stars.

The fight condensed into seconds, every move automatic and desperate. Leilani drove her heel into the attacker's thigh, deadening the muscle, and rolled on top. The move would have ended most street fights, but this was no amateur. The attacker twisted at the waist, snapped an arm around her throat, and levered her backward, dragging her into a chokehold. She let her body go slack, feigned fainting, and clawed backward with her nails, aiming for eyes or anything exposed. Her fingers caught skin. She wasn't sure where, possibly the neck, and dug in, earning a hiss and the wet, coppery smell of blood.

The attacker let go long enough for her to break free, but before she could turn and get up, the assailant slammed a fist into her ribs. She folded, breath howling out, but kept her elbows tucked and rolled away, scooping up a length of metal pipe that had clattered free during the struggle. She brought it up in a two-handed grip, ready for the follow-up.

Instead, the attacker backed off, standing loose and casual, as if nothing had happened. He or she couldn't be sure, but the build suggested male, flexed his left hand, where her nails had torn open a fresh line of blood, drawing a thumb across his throat in a slow, deliberate arc.

"Next time," he said, the voice disguised by a mechanical rasp, almost cartoonish. But the threat in it was primal, unfiltered.

Leilani's chest heaved, sweat stinging her eyes, but she raised the pipe, determined not to give an inch. The stranger faded into the gloom of the warehouse. His retreating boots muffled on the thick layer of old sawdust and detritus.

She stood still, counting seconds, listening for the double back, the sucker punch, but nothing came. After a minute, her own pulse slowed enough that she could assess the damage. Her lip was split, her ribs ached with the promise of a bruise, and her right wrist throbbed. She'd lost her phone, but not her weapon; she'd lost the element of surprise, but not the will to fight.

She paced the perimeter, checking for any sign of ambush. She found the blood droplets where she'd gouged the attacker. They led in a staggered line to the back exit, where the lock was twisted and the door left open an inch. She poked her head through, saw nothing, and closed and bolted the door behind her.

Back at the evidence wall, she retrieved her phone and checked the photos. All intact. She took a quick selfie; her face already blooming with a new bruise, hair wild, eyes black with adrenaline, and attached it to the last photo, sending the sequence to Torres with the subject line. Shit's getting real. She scrolled through the new messages, searching for any clue she'd missed.

Her breath came in short, raw gasps. She spit blood onto the concrete, wiped her face on her sleeve, and worked to steady her hands. Humiliation filled her mouth, but there was something else: excitement. The case wasn't a puzzle anymore. It was a war.

She glared at the blank silhouette on the wall, the red string vibrating with the memory of her fight, and she was sure. The Mastermind knew her, knew her methods, knew her family. And if he wanted her scared, he'd have to do better than that.

She should have left. Every cop sense in her body shrieked it, every case study screamed don't chase the unknown alone, but pride and the wound on her face made her reckless. Her own blood had a way of clarifying the world. She paced the main floor of the warehouse, the length of rusted pipe gripped tight in one hand, gun still holstered but ready, eyes pinging off every beam and puddle of shadow. Each breath hurt. Somewhere, water dripped in the guts of the place; every few seconds a muffled clang echoed from the rafters, the afterimage of a footstep, or the metal cooling in the night. She moved around the space, methodically, letting her vision adjust, letting her heart slow. Her mind drew a map of the place, blind alleys, likely choke points, the doorways, and crawl spaces where a grown person could hide or double back. She listened for the twin beats of pursuit, hers and her enemy.

The attacker was gone. No sign, no sound. A single black thread snagged on a splintered support post, and a wet line of blood across the floor.

Leilani's hands shook as the adrenaline faded. She dropped the pipe with a clang that echoed through the warehouse, flexed her bruised wrist, and wiped her mouth with the inside of her elbow. The pain was clean, manageable, but the anger underneath it was messy. She hated being outplayed.

She doubled back, every nerve tuned to the possibility of an ambush. This time, she checked the ground for anything left behind: cigarette butts, a dropped glove, a receipt, anything. Nothing, except.

Her foot caught something under the sawhorses, where she'd first seen the evidence wall. She crouched and picked it up. It was a folded square of cheap printer paper, weighed down with a single rusty washer. The handwriting was blocky, each letter knifed into the sheet as if the pen were angry.

Your father couldn't stop it. Neither will you.

She held it between thumb and forefinger, avoiding any prints. The line chilled her, but not for the reason it was meant to. If anything, it made her laugh, one sharp, bitter bark that startled her. She had lived her whole life in the shadow of her father's failure. She'd built a career on the idea that any fight could be won if you refused to let go. The fact this was supposed to break her made her dig in harder.

She photographed the note with her phone and bagged it in an evidence pouch from her pocket. She turned her attention to the wall, looking at it with fresh eyes. The organization was military, obsessive. Every pin and string had been placed to communicate and to document. It was more than a web. It was a challenge, a demonstration of superiority. The face in the middle, THE MASTERMIND, was not a blank; it was a mirror, reflecting whoever came to hunt it.

She spent ten minutes cataloguing the wall, cross-referencing every clue. She peeled off a few documents that looked original, handwritten ledgers, a polaroid photo of Mahoe at a protest, a child's drawing with a date and a coded message on the back. She saw the layering, the way the topmost clues always led back to her or to people she'd trusted. There was a photo of her at the last protest she'd broken up, off duty, face half in shadow, unguarded and raw. Underneath, a newspaper clipping of her father's badge number, the one she'd used to open the encrypted files at the lab.

She backed away, breathing through the sting in her lungs, trying to imagine who would do all this. Not the skill, but the patience, the gall. Someone who had watched her for months, maybe years. Someone who knew the city's arteries better than she did.

She typed a quick note to Torres.

Possible suspect, confirmed surveillance on both of us, will call after secure. Watch your six.

As she left the warehouse, she paused on the

threshold, letting her eyes adjust to the lights from the parking lot. She listened for a car, a watcher, anything, but the street was still. The city was waking up, out of sight, its machinery already grinding toward another day of secrets.

She walked to her car, unlocked it, and climbed into the driver's seat for a full minute before starting the engine. Her knuckles left bloody crescents on the wheel. The evidence bag with the note sat on the passenger seat, humming with potential energy.

She drove home, making sure she wasn't tailed. The world outside was a blur of blue and orange. She ran through the fight in her mind a dozen times, plotting every move, every mistake, every advantage she'd learned for next time. She thought of her father, the old stories, the way every generation made the same war with different enemies.

Once she pulled into her driveway, the pain was a dull memory, and the anger was a warm, steady coal.

She'd been marked. Not as a cop, but as a target. The game had always been personal. Now at least, she had a name for it.

She stepped inside, locked the door, and started planning her next move.

# CHAPTER TWELVE

## *Fractured Trust*

The drive to her uncle's house seemed like trespassing. The houses grew taller and shinier, palaces climbing the slope above the old king's beaches, glass cubes with infinity pools aimed at the sunset. Leilani's battered Explorer rolled past the security gate on a borrowed code, suspension groaning as it crested the rise and spat her out in front of Edward's house, a showpiece that the TV tour guides called "legacy construction." There was no security guard, only a neat plaque with the surname in staid block letters and a winding stone path to the door, wide enough for a bride and her train.

She killed the engine, got out, and checked her reflection in the window. The bruise on her lip was swollen, a thumbprint of rage in full bloom. She considered raising her collar, leaving it as a message instead. She'd worn her badge on a lanyard but tucked it under her jacket. This was still family, no matter how official today was. She pushed open the door.

She walked across the marble expanse of the foyer, into a living room that faced the ocean through a triple-arched wall of glass. It could have doubled as a museum, bronze kahili on the mantle, carved driftwood tables, prints of extinct birds. The air smelled of lemon and money.

He was waiting in the study, mid-60s, fit, with hair like the bleached top of a sugarcane field and skin tanned to a high-polish antique. The resemblance was there, in the set of the jaw and the spread of the eyebrows, but everything else was an act. The linen shirt, the antique watch, the lazy sprawl behind the koa wood desk.

He didn't stand. "Leilani, twice in one week. To what do I owe the pleasure?"

She closed the door behind her, sensed the snap of cold AC on her neck. "We need to talk."

The study was a shrine to heritage. Old medals, the warped paddle from a childhood canoe, framed deeds from Kamehameha's time, and the family tree filled the wall. Every branch had its photo, going back to daguerreotypes, but the line that included her was conspicuously thin. Her own father was a childhood face, skipped in the later generations. She gritted her teeth. She hated the wall every time she saw it.

She sat in the visitor's chair, set the folder on his desk, and opened it without invitation. The papers inside were Xeroxed copies, with most bearing the evidence seals of the HPD. She set three sheets into a fan. A wire transfer slip, a set of emails, and the second page of a notarized land transfer.

His gaze shot upward, quicker than a car alarm. "You've been busy."

She waited. If you let them fill the air, they always said more than they meant to.

He reached for the papers with a surgeon's delicacy, spreading them across the desk as if afraid they'd combust. "You realize these aren't admissible. Chain-of-custody and all."

"It's not about court, Uncle." The word came out like broken coral. "It's about why a community fund meant for stream clean up routed seventy grand into a shell company registered in Delaware, which transferred it to you as consulting fees."

He pinched the bridge of his nose, closing his eyes for a full second. "You wouldn't understand."

She snorted. "Try me."

"Every election cycle, the rules change. The only way to keep any leverage is to." He paused, eyes narrowing. "It's not illegal, Leilani. Not the way you think."

"So, explain it to me," she said, voice flat. "Tell me why the same shell company is on the donors' list for the councilwoman trying to fast-track the Haumea development."

A muscle in his jaw ticked. "That land is dead, Lei. You think you're saving it, but it's already bought and sold. The best I could do was make sure our family got something before it's turned into another golf course for tourists who never learn to say mahalo."

She shoved the second set of papers across the desk. This time, the motion knocked a glass paperweight to the floor, where it spun and wobbled like a tiny planet about to end. "You think Sonny Alana died for your leverage?" she asked. "You think the threats and the payoffs are victimless?"

He didn't answer. His fingers drummed on the desk, a tempo that betrayed the nerves beneath the tan.

She leaned in, voice low. "Who's the Mastermind? The one pulling the strings on all this. I know you're the messenger. So, who?"

He inhaled slowly, and when he spoke, it was almost gentle. "There are bigger players, Leilani. People who wouldn't think twice about making you or your mother or." He stopped and flicked his eyes at the family wall. "You want to survive this? You stop asking questions. You bury it."

Her laugh was ugly. "You don't get to tell me what to bury."

He stood, all six-feet-two of old-school gravitas. The burden of a lifetime of expectation pointed at her like a loaded gun. His hands clenched, relaxed, palms open on the desk as if he were about to make a blessing. "I can protect you. I can't save everyone, but I can protect you, Lei."

She marshaled every old memory of him as her father's older brother, the one who used to buy her rainbow shave ice and let her drive the boat on the slow afternoons. "You've been lying to me from the start."

His eyes were sharp, flat as river rocks. "You still don't get it. Your father never did either. Some secrets are kept buried for a reason."

"Like what?"

He looked down at the desk, as if reading his own future in the grain of the Koa. "Like the fact that every cop who ever tried to fix this island wound up dead or in exile. You want that for yourself, or for your son?"

She could feel her pulse. "You think threatening me changes anything?"

"It's not a threat. It's a warning. You keep digging, you'll find the bottom, and you'll wish you hadn't."

The phone buzzed on her hip, her work cell, the tone coded for "active" not "urgent." She picked it up, thumbed the answer button, and kept her eyes on her uncle.

The voice was clipped, cop-cold, and carried the badge of a fellow officer. "Detective. I need you at 87-002 Hakimo. Right now. It's your cousin. She's not answering the door, and there's blood on the threshold."

She was numb. Her uncle's face, reflected in the polished desk, showed features crumpling before settling into a blank expression. The phone beeped in her hand; the officer waited.

"I'll be there in fifteen," she said. She stood, swept the papers back into the folder, and fixed her uncle with a look that was all teeth.

He started to speak but thought better of it.

She left him in the study, a man surrounded by the prizes of a life spent winning, now alone in his own echo chamber. As she walked out, she passed the family tree again, paused, and noted the missing leaves. She touched her father's photo with a fingertip and walked out, the sound of her own footfalls the only answer he'd get.

She hit the street with the phone already out, her finger flicking through contacts, her other hand trembling so hard she had to clutch the wheel to keep it from showing. The voice on the other end, a sergeant from the intelligence unit, answered on the first ring. She spat orders in clipped bursts.

"I need you to set up surveillance on my uncle Edward, now, not later; no marked cars, no uniforms, nothing that would tip him to the net closing in. Use the utility vans and rotate shifts every four; cover the driveway, the oceanfront, the private service access that ran under the lawn." She listed his routines, the runs before sunrise, the standing tennis match, the Tuesday trips to the club, and told the sergeant to assume her uncle would bolt the instant he saw something he didn't like.

The voice took it all in, repeated it back. "Copy. Full assets, twenty-four hours. What about your mother's place?"

Leilani thought of her mother's cottage, the battered minivan parked in the carport, the way Naalei never locked her doors before midnight. "One officer, plainclothes, nothing visible. If he's got leverage, he'll use her."

"Understood. And you?"

She ended the call. The inside of the Explorer stank of stress, sweat, and last week's takeout. She parked behind the patrol unit by Malia's ground floor apartment, slid out, and pulled the lanyard out from under her shirt. She walked up to the officer standing by the door.

"Did you check the patio door?" she asked.

He nodded. "Place is locked up tight. No sounds from inside."

"Why are you here?" she asked.

"Precinct got a call asking us to do a welfare check," said the officer. "Your cousin didn't show up for work for her last two shifts. When they couldn't reach her, they called us."

He pointed to the bloody handprint on the doorjamb, by the lockset. "Looks like someone got their fingers crushed in the door."

Leilani looked up and down the street. "Her car is missing. Go ahead and get back on patrol. I'll deal with this," she said. "Thanks for the call."

The officer nodded and slid into his cruiser. Leilani slid into her Explorer. She pressed her forehead to the steering wheel and let herself feel it. Fear, yes, but also the galloping pulse of hatred. Not only for Edward. For herself, for dragging Malia into this. For letting any of it touch the only person in the city who still looked at her without a record of disappointment.

She ground the gear into reverse, clipped the side mirror backing down the drive, and pointed the car toward town. She parked and headed into the building. She passed through the security desk with a scowl, taking the back stairwell two at a time to the third floor. Torres's voice carried over the cubicle walls, louder than usual, probably fueling up on caffeine and adrenaline.

She found him hunched over an evidence table, a mess of printouts spread before him, with a dry-erase board at his back filling with lines and circles. He looked up as she entered, and he stayed silent. No joke, no greeting. A direct look at the bruise on her cheek. "You, okay?"

She ignored it, pulled out the office chair opposite, and dumped her folder into the mess. "I want you to cross check these with the last three months of council fund dispersals," she said, already booting up the terminal. "And the fake companies, find out which are actually on the islands and which are tax holes."

He scanned the top document and raised his eyebrows. "You got this from Edward?"

"In person. He didn't flinch when I showed him the wire transfer."

"Did he confirm?"

"He tried to spin it. Said he was protecting family, taking the best deal before someone else fucked us all."

Torres frowned, jaw tight. "You believe him?"

She gazed at the screen, jaw clenched. "Doesn't matter. I want him caged. But I need to find Malia first."

He nodded and flicked through the next two sheets. He typed with one hand while his other reached for the dry-erase marker. "You think she ran, or got taken?"

"She missed two shifts at the bar, didn't respond to texts, and stopped posting at 3 a.m. yesterday. Her landlady saw a strange car outside the unit, said the guy at the door was an insurance salesman but never left a card."

Torres swore under his breath, scrawled a string of numbers on the board, and said, "Are you looking to do a digital dragnet, or go physical?"

"Both," she said. "Start with every property the developer has touched, especially the old resorts they shuttered for environmental study. I'll pull the traffic cam footage. She's in a white Nissan, plates NXR 310."

She pulled up traffic cameras around Malia's apartment. There were no close cameras, and she was getting frustrated. She spotted the car heading west on the H1 but lost it at the next camera. The car must have exited the highway and was on surface streets. Camera coverage was light. Torres pulled up a map of the area.

Leilani scrubbed her hands over her face. "Let's get creative. If she's alive, they'll keep her close, but not too close to anything with cameras or civilians. Abandoned properties, commercial."

"There's a warehouse out past Lagoon that got re-zoned two weeks ago," he said. "It's listed as a holding site for construction equipment, but the utilities never turned on. No cameras, no guards. Nothing eles in that area."

"Get me the address."

He pulled it up, tapped the screen, and spun the monitor. "What's your plan?"

"I'm going to find her."

Torres's hand hovered near hers on the desk, an offer of contact. She took it, squeezing once, hard.

"We'll find her," he said.

The room contracted around their resolve. He dug into the digital records, layering city grid maps with recent traffic, while she called the nearest patrol units to prep for a low-profile sweep. She could feel herself running out of adrenaline, the emotional void threatening to crack, but every time she caught herself slipping, she gripped the desk until her knuckles hurt.

Her phone buzzed, a blocked number. She answered on speaker, expecting nothing, but the voice on the other end was inhuman, a slurry of audio filters and low bandwidth.

"Detective Kealoha. If you want your cousin alive, you stop all investigations. Drop the case, drop the files, and do not contact the press."

Her blood iced. "Where is she?"

A pause. "You have twenty-four hours."

The call cut off. The timestamp on the log showed it came from a number in Dubai, bounced across six proxies. Torres sat back, eyes wide.

"Did you record?" he asked.

She nodded. "Already sent to the audio lab. I want forensics on the background noise."

"Can do." He drummed his fingers on the keyboard. "You're not going to stop, are you?"

She laughed, but it was a brittle, splintered thing. "Not until she's home."

The next hour was triage. She took the file from the surveillance team, tracked Edward's every move since her visit, checked with her mother (still asleep, unbothered, but she'd left a voicemail anyway), and called in every favor she had left in the department. She sent a text to Kai, told him to stay at his grandma's until further notice, and to not open the door for anyone.

At seven sharp, a package arrived at the main desk, hand-delivered by a courier with no return address. It was the kind of box you put a cake in, or a bomb. She opened it in the evidence bay, Torres at her side.

Inside was a flash drive, labeled simply FOR YOU. She took it to her desk.

She plugged it in with shaking fingers. The

screen filled with a video, grainy, fixed angle, the kind used by ransomers and murderers in movies. Malia was in the frame, tied to a chair, a gag biting into her mouth. Her eyes were red, and mascara ran in streaks down her cheeks.

A voice played over the video, modulated, but slow and distinct. "You have until 6 a.m. tomorrow. If you continue your investigation, she dies. This is the only warning."

Malia's head jerked up at the sound, her gaze stabbing the camera. She mouthed something, but the tape was too tight. The video cut out before Leilani could read the message in her cousin's eyes.

Torres's hand was on her shoulder, steadying her, but the room was a centrifuge, spinning out and away from itself. She watched the blank screen, replayed the last frame in her mind until it stung.

"We'll get her back," Torres whispered. "We will."

She nodded, but her vision blurred. The pain was bright, undiluted. There was nothing left but the hunt.

She picked up her phone and started again.

# CHAPTER THIRTEEN

## *Race Against Time*

The precinct after midnight was a mausoleum for lost causes, every corridor echoing with half-spoken threats and the dying breath of overhead fluorescents. Someone had turned the thermostat down to sixty and the air shimmered with a clinical chill, sour with disinfectant and the ghost of a hundred cigarette breaks. In the open bullpen, the light throbbed and flickered, painting every tired face with the jaundiced pallor of a coroner's report.

Leilani hunched over a desk cluttered with the detritus of the long siege. Coffee cups were stacked into wobbly towers, case files bled open and devoured, half a box of malaise-glazed donuts, a child's crayon drawing (Goku and Pikachu fighting a dinosaur), and an evidence bag with the edges already chewed by worry. Her phone buzzed, rattling across the faux-wood veneer, only to be silenced by a reflexive slap of her palm. Another update, another dead end. She scrolled, her eyes narrow and red-rimmed, as the room ticked with the nervous energy of people held together by caffeine, rage and duct tape.

Isaac Torres sat across from her, his shirtsleeves rolled, a gauze bandage taped above his left wrist from some injury she'd missed in the day's storm. He ran on imported espresso and the wired vigilance of a man who'd forgotten how to sleep. Every few minutes, he fired off a call, sometimes to a contact at the bureau, sometimes to someone deeper in the alphabet. His voice was low, urgent, the same pitch he'd used when first talking her down from the ledge of her own rage.

"Got a ping on the Nissan," he said, not bothering to look up from his battered laptop. "Last camera was near the Kapalama Canal, right before 3 a.m.. The next sighting was half an hour later, on the airport access road."

Leilani grunted and flipped a page on the printout. It was a satellite photo of Oahu's industrial fringe, annotated with the spidery handwriting of someone who took paranoia as gospel. "Anything on the plates after that?"

"Nothing," he said. "Either switched them, or it's deep in a warehouse."

She jabbed a pen at the line of entry points between Nimitz and Sand Island. "They won't risk surface streets this close to the cordon. They go below, or by water."

Torres splayed the new map on top of the old, aligning the grid with an engineer's precision. "These buildings," he circled three rectangles with a coffee-stained thumb, "are all owned by shell corps with Delaware registration. Some are offshore trusts. They overlap with every major resort deal from the last two years."

"Family's got deep roots," Leilani said, her jaw set so hard it clicked. "And money to dig in."

He slid her a bunch of manifests, the top one marked CONFIDENTIAL in red. "These shipping logs don't match the declared cargo. That's how they did it: laundered bodies in shipping containers. You'd never spot it unless you cross check against the port logs."

She read the first page. Four containers scheduled for off-load, but only three signed out. The paperwork was tight, but not perfect. The dates slanted, the sequence numbers reversed, like someone counting time backwards. She caught the error instantly.

"Look at this," she said, stabbing the manifest with her pen. "Second shipment, declared as agricultural equipment, but the weight class is double the listed items. And here," she thumbed to the next page, "the timestamp's off by a full day. If they're moving Malia, it's in that window."

Torres nodded, half a smile bleeding through his stubble. "You ever consider joining the bureau?"

She barked a laugh. "Too many secrets. I like to see my enemies' faces."

He dialed another number, this time pulling a favor from someone who owed him from the mainland. While the call connected, Leilani let her eyes drift to her desk. There, wedged between a tangle of wires and the mug with the world's worst pun ("FBI: Female Body Inspector"), was a photo of her son, Kai, shirtless, hair wild, squinting in the white light of an afternoon at Magic Island. She stared at it until her eyes blurred, the guilt swelling up from her gut like bile. He was safe, tucked in the next zip code with her mother and enough cartoon DVDs to keep him from noticing how empty the house had become. She should have been relieved. Instead, the distance stung worse than the bruises along her ribs.

Checking her phone, she thumbed through the open apps, and saw two missed texts from Naalei.

*9:42 PM: KAI ASKED IF YOU'RE CHASING BAD GUYS AGAIN. SHOULD I TELL HIM BEDTIME OR LET HIM WAIT UP?*

*10:11 PM: HE'S SLEEPING WITH HIS BACKPACK IN CASE YOU NEED TO LEAVE FAST.*

*NO WORRIES, I'LL MAKE SURE HE GETS TO SCHOOL.*

She read them twice, after which she pocketed the phone, unsure if she could bear to reply.

Torres leaned in, his voice pitched so only she could hear. "We'll find her. I promise you, Lei."

She ignored the promise and focused on the map. "They've got Malia, so they need leverage. They won't kill her until they know they've bled us dry."

He arched a brow. "Meaning?"

"They want me to shut down the investigation." Her lips peeled back from her teeth. "But they know me. If they wanted to cut me out, they'd have dumped the body by now."

Torres nodded, understanding. "So, we smoke them out."

"Yeah," she said. "But first, we find the lockup."

Over the next hour, they battered the evidence into shape. Every time she faltered, Torres would nudge the conversation forward, keeping her mind on the hunt and off the abyss. They built timelines, cross-indexed cell pings, and ran facial recognition on every rent-a-cop in the port district. As the night progressed, the light remained harsh, and the coffee grew colder, turned bitter, and was eventually gone.

At some point, the captain drifted by, saw the

spread, and grunted. "You two going to crack it before morning?"

Torres didn't miss a beat. "If we do, you get the press conference."

The captain nodded and shuffled away, his own ghosts making his gait uneven.

As the clock slid past 2 a.m., Leilani found the detail she needed. A service request, filed under a fake ID, for a loading crew at Pier 36, scheduled for sunrise. No return address, only a contact number that stopped working after one ring. But the access log was there, showing a badge scan registered to a temp with no history in the union.

She pushed it across the desk to Torres. "Here. This is where they'll make the handoff."

He studied it, smiling for real this time. "You ever think you're too smart for your own good?"

She smiled. "Too stubborn."

They sat in the monitor's glow, the world outside reduced to the low drone of street traffic and the nervous clatter of keyboards. For a few seconds, they said nothing.

Torres broke the spell. "We'll need backup. No uniforms, but people we can trust."

"I'll call in the night sergeant," Leilani said. "We keep it small. And I want to be in the first car."

He mock-saluted. "Wouldn't have it any other way."

She stood, shook the tension from her arms, and began pulling together the essentials: her piece, two spare mags, a box of disposable gloves, and a packet of sour Skittles for the blood sugar crash that always hit in the last hour before dawn. Torres rolled up the map, stuck it in his back pocket, and slung his jacket over one shoulder.

Before leaving, Leilani glanced once more at the photo of her son, before turning it face down. She had to believe she'd be there to turn it back up.

They left the bullpen side by side, two insomniacs against the tide, neither admitting how much of themselves they'd already mortgaged to the fight. As the elevator doors closed, the last flicker of light caught her badge, and she looked the way her father always had in her memory, tired, battered, and more alive than anyone else in the room.

Honolulu Harbor never slept. The shipping lanes cut the city in two, cargo moving day and night between the blue and the gray, the air a permanent stew of diesel and seawater and overheated metal. The docks themselves were a low-slung skyline. Cranes, stacks of containers, prefab warehouses faded by twenty years of salt and sun, and a tangle of chain link and razor wire. On a Saturday, in the early morning hours, there were always men at work, most of them pretending not to see the things their bosses paid them to ignore.

Leilani drove the unmarked Ford along the perimeter road, eyes flicking from the line of idling semis to the guard shacks posted every quarter mile. She wore a thrift store aloha shirt over her tactical vest, her hair in a messy knot, and the badge on a lanyard around her neck. Isaac rode shotgun, a battered Thermos in hand, scanning the slip numbers and jotting quick notes in the margin of the map book balanced on his knee.

"Pier 36 is ahead," he said, voice tight. "Don't pull in, not unless we want to be on camera."

She grunted, gliding the Ford past a side lot and into the shadow of a massive cinderblock warehouse. The pavement here was cracked, the weeds tall enough to tangle an ankle. Isaac checked the rearview, pointing at a cluster of workers smoking by the old vending machine. "Third from the left. Blue hard hat, orange vest."

"Copy that. Eyes on."

They waited for the dockworker to finish his cigarette. When he peeled off from the group, they stepped out of the car, making themselves obvious but not cop-obvious, just two more idiots from admin lost in the maze. The man's name was Keoni, local, fifty if a day, skin like sandpaper and hands so cracked they looked sculpted. He took one look at Isaac and Leilani and walked the other way, but Isaac was on him fast, using the bored, patient voice that worked on both witnesses and street kids.

"Keoni, right? You, the guy with the forklift cert?"

Keoni turned, his eyes wide, before narrowing with suspicion. "Maybe. Who's asking?"

"Looking for a delivery. Lost in the shuffle. You work this shift?"

Keoni looked past them like he was counting on someone else to intervene. No one did. He dropped his voice to a mutter. "Depends who wants to know."

Leilani cut to the chase. "We're looking for a white Nissan. Came through last night after hours. Belongs to a friend."

The man's posture sagged. "You cops?"

She didn't answer, meeting his eyes. It was enough.

Having scratched his scalp, he nodded towards the end of the pier. "Saw it. Came in with a black van, no markings. I wasn't working, but the foreman called me for overtime. Said I could take cash if I didn't sign the punch sheet."

Isaac pulled a folded twenty from his pocket and pressed it into Keoni's palm. "That's for your next lunch. Anything else weird?"

Keoni tucked the bill away. He leaned in. "Warehouse over there, number twenty-seven. They only use it at night. Doors reinforced, guys with guns, not local security."

"What about cameras?" Leilani asked.

"Maybe on the inside, not outside. The foreman doesn't want anyone recordings."

Leilani made a mental note. "You see anyone go in with the van?"

"Couple haoles. One looked like army, crew cut, big neck. Other one watched. They wheeled something in. Couldn't see what, but it was heavy. Took four guys to get it off the dolly."

"Thanks, Keoni," Isaac said, voice soft. "You did good."

The dockworker jerked a nod and retreated into the nearest gap between containers, vanishing as if he'd never been there. Leilani watched the space for a beat. She turned to Isaac.

"You believe him?"

He shrugged. "He's got no reason to lie. And if he's dirty, that was the world's shittiest shake."

They walked to the car, every sense open to the possibility of being watched. There were eyes everywhere on the waterfront, union guys, security, the occasional drifter, or tweaker looking for a loose load to fence. Leilani's palms were sweaty, the old, sour taste of adrenaline in her throat. She hadn't slept for over two hours, but every nerve in her body was awake.

In the safety of the car, Isaac opened his laptop, fired up the bureau's satellite overlay, and pointed at the rectangle of blue painted warehouses. "Look here," he said, zooming in on the roof. "Last month, they did a build-out. Air handlers, plus a bunch of comms gear. Power draw spiked after hours, dropped at shift change."

Leilani chewed her lip. "They're running servers in there, or a dark office. Not just a stash."

He nodded. "If I were holding someone, I'd want cameras and a cell jammer, too. But it makes them less likely to run until they have to."

Leilani scanned the lot with binoculars. There were three cars in the employee section, a Civic with a rusted hood, a gold Tacoma with the bumper held on by zip ties, and, parked tight against the fence, a silver Nissan Sentra. The plate was streaked with dust, but the numbers matched.

She tapped Isaac on the shoulder. "There. That's Malia's."

He drew a quick diagram on his notepad,

labeling possible points of entry and egress. "So, we watch and wait, or we go in loud?"

"Neither," she said. "We get backup, but keep it tight. If they're holding her, they'll panic fast if they see lights."

He agreed. "I'll call the Feds, see if they can get a drone up for thermal."

She keyed the radio, patched through to the precinct. "Dispatch, this is Kealoha. I need a discreet assist at Pier 36, warehouse twenty-seven. Approach from makai side, park at the strip mall lot and walk in. Plainclothes only."

The dispatcher confirmed the request.

Leilani hung up. "How fast you think they can get here?"

He checked his watch. "Fifteen, twenty minutes. There's little traffic this early."

"We don't have that long," she muttered. "If they get spooked, they'll move her."

They spent the next five minutes watching the warehouse. Nothing moved at first, but a side door opened and a man in a green work shirt walked out. He scanned the yard, checked the sky, and walked the perimeter. His arms were roped with muscles, and his head was shaved slick as a cue ball. Military, Leilani thought. Maybe ex-military, but not out long enough to go soft.

He checked the Nissan, circled it once, keyed his radio, and walked back inside.

"They're expecting company," Isaac said.

"Yeah," she answered, jaw clenching so hard she noticed the pop of old scar tissue. "Us."

Her eyes were glued to the scene. She ran through scenarios. Hostage inside, maybe restrained, at least one guard on her. They'd have routes planned, escape baked in. But the guard was nervous, which was clear in the stiffness of his movements.

The precinct team arrived just before four, two unmarked cars, four plainclothes officers, all local and all hand-picked for loyalty. They parked as instructed and walked in pairs, like they were just casing the neighborhood for a lost dog. Leilani briefed them, her voice clipped but calm. "Primary objective is extraction, secondary is evidence preservation. No heroics. We go in at the signal."

The officers nodded, the look in their eyes the same one she saw in the mirror every morning.

Isaac checked his weapon. The click of the magazine sharp in the quiet. "You ready?"

She nodded, rolling her shoulders to loosen the knot of tension that had built overnight. "Let's finish this."

She watched the warehouse, the darkness

behind the top windows. Somewhere in there, her cousin was alive, and counting on her. The thought made her hands steady, her voice sure.

She switched to the precinct frequency, gave the signal to move, and believed, for one breathless moment, that this time the story would end with someone coming home.

The sun had set behind the Ko'olau, and the night sucked up every color but the sodium vapor orange that bathed the empty lot two blocks from the target. The tactical team circled around the trunk of an unmarked Crown Vic, loading mags and assembling rifles, everything done in mime so as not to wake the neighborhood's regular ghosts. The air was sharp with the scent of engine coolant and the warm plastic off-gassing from the newly unwrapped body armor.

Leilani stood at the hood, hair pulled back with a battered scrunchie that had survived three prior stakeouts and one attempted arson. She drew her plan on the portable whiteboard, just a rectangle with three points of entry, two marked decoy, the third, a thinner line denoted with a star. "That's the access. Service door, east side. Fewer cameras, fewer eyes."

Isaac watched her from the side, working a ballpoint in quick nervous stabs as he updated the sketch for last-minute changes. He pointed at the rear of the warehouse, where the containers made a little fortress of steel. "If you were inside, you'd expect the front breach. You'd guard the catwalk and post up a guy near the loading bay."

She nodded. "So, we bait the front, sneak in through the side. Priority is live extraction. If you get eyes on Malia, don't wait for backup. You pull her out."

The four officers she'd hand-picked, Kaipo, Flores, Matsumoto and Old Man Iosefa, checked their gear with the resigned discipline of men who'd seen every plan fall apart by the second room. Kaipo had already duct-taped his boots to mute the scuff, and Flores cinched his gloves until the knuckles turned white. They were nervous, but no one asked questions. They trusted her, and she hated that responsibility.

She gave the last instructions in a whisper. "We go in quiet, find her, get out. No one dies unless it's us or her. Clear?"

They nodded.

Matsumoto patted her on the shoulder, a dry old gesture from their rookie days. "You lead the wedge, Lei?"

"I'll take point. Isaac, you're with me. Kaipo and Flores sweep the office. Iosefa stays by the exit for evac."

She turned and found Isaac's eyes waiting.

The same look from the bullpen, but now it carried weight, an anchor to reality. She touched his wrist, long enough for the memory of it to register. "You ready?"

He studied the warehouse, a jagged blue shape against the stars. "Yeah. Ready."

After jogging the blocks in silence, they moved between parked trailers and shipping crates, each step calculated to avoid gravel or stray rebar. The lot behind the warehouse was empty except for a single dead forklift, a rat's nest of extension cords, and the glow of a cracked security lamp that painted everything in the sickly yellow of a two-day bruise.

Kaipo and Flores peeled off at the front, sweeping their periphery and settling in behind an old vending machine. Leilani and Isaac moved low along the fence, breath visible in the cooling night. They found the service door as described. The lock was a new model, but Iosefa's kit made fast work of it. One slim Jim, a gentle pressure and the click was soft as a heartbeat. She waited for Isaac to slip in and followed.

Inside, the darkness was near-total. She thumbed the low light on her TacLight, holding the beam chest-high so it wouldn't silhouette her face. The warehouse was a warren of stacked crates, most of them marked with codes she recognized from the shipping manifests.

She whispered. "This way." Isaac nodded and followed close.

They crept the perimeter, avoiding the pool of light in the main bay. Twice, a shadow passed overhead, probably a guard, pacing the catwalk. Leilani counted the steps, the hesitation, the rhythm of a man killing time. She led Isaac to a narrow corridor; the walls lined with pallets and an old Pepsi fridge buzzing like an insect hive. At the end was a door, marked OFFICE, a slice of light beneath.

She pressed her ear to the steel, heard nothing but the soft whine of electronics and the distant thump of bass from a radio, somewhere on the other side.

"Now," she mouthed.

She twisted the handle, soft and slow, and eased the door open enough to see inside. The office was empty but for two chairs and a folding table. There was a cheap laptop, a pile of old phones, and a half-drained bottle of water. She scanned for signs of a struggle but found nothing. No Malia, no blood. But there was a smell, sharp and human, fear or someone trying not to cry.

Isaac signaled for Leilani to clear the room. He ducked in and started flipping through the laptop's contents, his fingers ghosting over the keyboard to avoid triggering any alarms.

Leilani swept the room, opened the supply closet, and found the real prize, a battered duffel bag, zippered halfway open. Inside were bundles of cash, a coil of plastic zip ties, and a cheap burner phone with blood on the case. The sight of it made her skin crawl.

She pocketed the phone, turning to Isaac. "Anything?"

"Locked up. I could force it, but not here."

She nodded. "Move. They'll check this place soon."

They backed out, closed the office door behind them, and signaled the team to regroup at the side exit. Kaipo and Flores joined them, breathing heavy but unhurt.

"All clear up front," Kaipo whispered. "But there's at least two on the catwalk. Didn't see the boss, though."

"Any sign of Malia?" Leilani asked.

Flores shook his head. "They're hiding her. Or moving her now."

She cursed under her breath. She signaled to fan out. "Sweep the loading bay. If she's here, that's where she goes next."

They moved in formation, tight as a single body. At the entrance to the main warehouse, she flicked her flashlight once, cutting the dark in a quick surgical sweep. Shadows moved on the high catwalks, but she focused on the crates at ground level, searching for any hint of human presence.

That's when the red dot appeared, dancing on the floor, up the wall, centering on Isaac's chest.

He froze, eyes wide, and dropped flat as Leilani shouted, "DOWN!"

The world exploded in noise, gunfire, ricochets, the crash of glass as someone above fired blind into the dark. Leilani pushed Isaac behind a row of steel drums, her own heart pounding so loud she barely heard the shouts of her team.

Kaipo's voice cut through: "Sniper, mezzanine! Two more up top!"

She grabbed Isaac's arm, shoved him deeper into cover, and signaled the rest to flank left and right. The scene changed from silent to mayhem in seconds, the air thick with smoke and panic and the cold thrill of being alive only because someone else wasn't aiming straight.

She reloaded, waited for a lull, and crawled forward, inch by inch, hoping to God the next bullet missed.

They were inside now, and there was no way out but through.

Gunfire stripped the air, sharp, staccato, ricocheting off the metal racks with a sound like hail on a tin roof. Another team member returned fire, the muzzle flare pulsing orange in the dark, momentarily painting the warehouse in an x-ray of moving bodies and rising smoke.

"Left flank, now!" she barked, not caring who heard. Flores and Matsumoto peeled off, using the maze of crates as cover. Kaipo was already moving low, sweeping with controlled bursts, each round aimed to pin the shooters up on the mezzanine. The smell of gunpowder grew heavy, a smell that cut through the deeper rot of seawater and warehouse mold.

Leilani poked her head up, drew a bead on the nearest shadow, and squeezed off two shots. The first missed, but the second clipped the catwalk, drawing a startled shout and a curse. She ducked as the return volley chewed the lip of the crate, splintering the plywood. She signaled Isaac with three fingers. Covering fire. She prepared to move.

He nodded, popped up, and let loose a barrage that sent the gunmen scrambling back along the catwalk. She took the chance, sprinting in a crouch toward the next pile of pallets. Behind her, the team's movements were choreographed chaos, each member leapfrogging to the next position, shouting to keep track in the mayhem.

A round zipped past her cheek, hot enough that she felt the sizzle before she heard the crack. She tumbled behind some drums, heart pounding in her ears, checking the field again.

That's when she saw it, a figure up on the catwalk, broad shouldered, in a blue windbreaker. He was dragging something, or someone, behind him. A limp shape, a mess of black hair and the glint of bare skin on an outstretched arm.

Leilani froze. "Malia!" she screamed, voice raw to her own ears.

The figure jerked at the shout, heaved the limp body over his shoulder, and bolted for the exit. Leilani's world shrank into a tunnel. The catwalk, the woman, nothing else.

She moved before she thought, breaking from cover and tearing across the open floor. Bullets chased her, one slamming into a crate at her knee, another whistling through the gap between her ribs and her arm. Isaac roared her name, but she ignored it, skidding behind a pillar, and running up a set of metal stairs that led to the catwalk.

The first shooter met her at the landing, crouched behind a steel support with a submachine gun in his hands. She leveled her Glock and fired. The bullet caught him in the thigh, sending him sprawling; the gun clattered down the stairs. She ran past him, her boots hammering the metal, every step exploding in her bad knee.

At the top, the world was a strobe of light and shadow. The second guard took a shot from fifty feet and missed. She ran after him, the length of the catwalk trembling under their combined weight. The target was still dragging Malia, who was now struggling, weak but alive.

"Stop!" Leilani shouted, firing a round at the man's feet.

He spun, using Malia as a shield, his own pistol digging into her temple. Everything slowed. The breath in her chest, the noise below and the tremor in Malia's eyelids as she recognized Leilani through a haze of blood and sweat.

Leilani leveled her weapon, steady as ever. "Let her go."

The man sneered. "Back off, or she's dead." He moved towards the exit door, dragging Malia along.

Isaac's voice came from the stairs behind: "Lei, move!"

The warning hit a split second before the pain. A round grazed her left arm, slicing through sleeve and skin alike. The heat was intense. She staggered, dropped to a knee, and returned fire blindly, hoping to keep the shooters pinned.

The catwalk trembled with every step, old metal and older bolts, never meant to hold two people running for their lives. Leilani reached the midpoint as Isaac gained on her, both their breath clouds lit by the muzzle flashes from below. She glanced back, saw him gaining, face set and determined, his right arm cradled against his body but his aim still sure.

The next burst of gunfire came from above, the angle all wrong. A hidden shooter perched on the warehouse rafters, smarter than the rest, sent a trio of rounds sizzling through the dark. Leilani dove flat as the world seemed to explode. She hit the grating hard, ribs screaming, and watched in slow-motion horror as the shooter adjusted, zeroing in on the ladder where Isaac was climbing.

He should have ducked. He should have let her take the next shot. But Isaac Torres wasn't built that way. He reached the landing, saw the glint of a barrel in the dark, and lunged forward, shoving Leilani sideways into the solid safety of a support beam.

The bullet caught him high on the shoulder outside his vest, ripping through cloth and flesh with a wet, sick crack. He spun, his back slamming into the guardrail, and collapsed to his knees, blood blooming down his arm in an instant.

Leilani raced to him, all instincts warring: cop, medic, sister-in-arms, friend. She pressed both hands over the wound, feeling the hot slip of blood as it ran through her fingers.

"Goddamn it, Isaac, stay with me."

He looked up, face gone gray already, but his voice was calm. "Go," he said. "You have to go."

She hesitated, adrenaline and dread freezing her in place. Her hands wouldn't stop shaking. "Not leaving you."

He grabbed her wrist with his good hand, grip bruising. "If you don't, they get away with Malia. You know that."

She bit back the tears, and forced herself to breathe. "Hold pressure. Backup's right behind us." She ripped off her jacket, wadded it against the wound, and leaned in close. "If you die, who's gonna bring me good coffee in the morning?"

He smiled.

Below, the shooter took another potshot, but missed, the round pinging off a vertical beam. Leilani keyed her radio with a bloody thumb. "Officer down, catwalk! GSW to the shoulder, bleeding bad but conscious. Need medics, now!"

The comm replied instantly, static overlaying Kaipo's voice. "Copy, moving up!"

Leilani squeezed Isaac's hand once, hard. She propped him in place, jacket jammed tight against the wound. He slumped against the rail, eyes blazing with something beyond pain. "Find her," he said again. "Go."

She went.

The last she saw of Isaac, he was cursing the shooter below, his free hand cradling his own arm, face twisted in fury and pride. She ran the length of the catwalk, boots leaving bloody prints on the mesh, and reached the door.

The interior was worse than the outside, dim, close; the walls streaked with mold and the floor wet from a leak in the ceiling. A streak of blood on the handle showed where the suspect had dragged Malia, using her as both leverage and a shield.

Leilani followed, mind gone to a narrow slit of intention. There were no thoughts, only actions. She breached the next door and found herself in a stairwell; the concrete spiraling up and up to a hatch marked ROOF ACCESS. The sound of rotors was faint but growing, the low, insistent thump of a helicopter spooling up somewhere above.

Her chest ached, lungs raw, but she kept moving, taking the stairs two at a time. At the landing, she saw the suspect, a massive man, one hand locked around Malia's throat, the other holding a pistol outstretched. He was yelling into the radio, words lost in the thrum of the chopper.

Malia was awake, eyes wild with terror but not defeat. She locked eyes with Leilani and in that heartbeat, all the years of family, all the pain and pride, came flooding back.

Leilani squared up, took aim, and shouted, "Let her go!"

The man spun, dragging Malia in front of him. They hung there, no one moving, the air thick with the promise of death.

The man's gun barked twice. The sting of a round tearing through the edge of her vest, followed by the numb cold as blood seeped. She fired two shots, both wide in the chaos, but the noise was enough. The suspect flinched, and his grip on Malia loosened.

Malia twisted, bit his wrist, and yanked herself free. She fell on the landing, gasping for air.

The suspect bellowed in rage, gun swinging back to bear on Leilani. But this time she was ready, and her shot was true, catching him in the thigh. He staggered, cursed, and stumbled up the last stairs and out onto the roof, the chopper's noise now deafening.

Leilani grabbed Malia and hauled her to her feet. "Can you walk?"

Malia nodded as her legs threatened to fold. "Yeah. I got you."

Together, they stumbled up the last few stairs. The roof was a chaos of wind and noise. The suspect, already bleeding, had made it to the chopper, where two more men in black stood ready to haul him inside.

For a split second, Leilani considered going after him. But Malia was here, alive, and the chopper was lifting, rising, the downdraft ripping at her hair and the blood thick in her mouth.

She let them go. She had what mattered.

On the way down the stairs, Malia held tight to her arm. "You, okay?" she whispered, voice trembling.

Leilani laughed, shaky and wet. "Not even close."

From below, the gunfire had ceased, replaced by the chaos of the other officers securing the perimeter and hauling out any remaining resistance. Flores called up, "All clear, boss! Warehouse secure."

Isaac clapped her on the good shoulder, face split with equal parts relief and terror. "You, good?"

She nodded, but the world was going gray at the edges. She held Malia, who was trying to smile through the pain, and knew she'd stay conscious as long as her cousin needed her.

On the ground floor, Kaipo and Flores had already reached Isaac, pressing gauze to his wound and cursing him for not ducking.

He looked up at Leilani; her smile was weak

but present. "You did it."

She nodded, and the pressure of the day settled, heavy and final.

They waited together on the cracked concrete until the medics came, the city's lights flickering in the distant dark, and Leilani allowed herself to believe that the cycle could be broken.

Outside the warehouse, the world was a kaleidoscope of emergency lights, white and blue, strobed the stacks of cargo and the faces of the paramedics as they swarmed the scene. Isaac lay on the stretcher, shirt half-shredded, blood pooled black around his shoulder and arm. He was conscious, but his breath was ragged, teeth bared against the oxygen mask as the EMTs worked to stabilize him.

Leilani hovered, hands still sticky with blood, his and her own, though she could no longer tell the difference. The medics offered her gloves and a blanket, but she shook them off. She had to be raw for this moment, to feel every inch of her own survival.

Malia stood a few feet away, wrapped in a silver emergency blanket, face pale but unbroken. They locked eyes; nothing needed to be said. The family history was there. She could see it in the set of Malia's jaw and the stubborn defiance in her bruised eyes. Leilani let the tension bleed off, turning her attention to the surrounding chaos.

A plainclothes officer, one she barely recognized, jogged up with a Ziploc bag full of evidence; shipping manifests, half a dozen burner phones, and a folder marked with the developer's logo. "We found this in the upstairs office, Detective. There's a list of names, most of them flagged from your last report. Looks like payments, scheduled pickups, and." He checked his notes, brow furrowing. "And references to helicopter flights. There's a helipad marked on a map, north of the quarry, near Ka'ena Point."

Leilani took the evidence, flipping through quickly. The phones were still warm from use, one buzzing with a fresh text as she handled it.

Another officer ran up, the headset dangling, his face bright with bad news. "Chopper got away. They headed west, cut inland, and lost them at the ridge. Airport radar is pulling the transponder log now."

She nodded. "Anyone at the quarry? Any eyes?"

"Not yet. You want us to deploy a team?"

"Do it," she said, voice clear as steel.

She returned to Isaac, who was fighting the straps as the paramedics tried to move him. "I'll see you at Queens," she said. "Don't pull a martyr, okay?"

He managed a grin, the color returning to his lips. "Only if you promise to finish this."

Having squeezed his good hand tight, she watched as the paramedics loaded him into the ambulance.

The door slammed. The siren whooped once, and the ambulance took off, blue lights flickering in the puddles left by the night's rain.

Malia came over, silent at first. She hugged Leilani, holding on with a strength that was more like forgiveness than need. "You're not done, are you?" she whispered.

"Not even close," Leilani answered.

A paramedic led her to an ambulance and sat her on the back step. He helped her unsnap her vest and laid it on the ground. He lifted her shirt and evaluated the wounds, one on her upper arm and one below her armpit. "You're gonna need stitches. They're grazing wounds. not too deep." He cleaned the wounds, sprayed them with an antibiotic film and covered them with butterfly bandages and a clean gauze. He told her to go to the hospital and get stitches and a tetanus shot.

He offered to take her in the ambulance, but she needed her car, so she told him she would drive herself.

She thanked him and stepped away from the ambulance.

A fellow officer hovered, eager to report. "Dispatch says the chopper could land in a dozen places. They've got the FAA watching, and the feds are sending a bird from Pearl."

Leilani nodded. "Send me the grid. Every site, every landing pad. And get me the satellite on standby."

The officer hurried off, dialing as he moved.

She stared at her hands, blood already drying in the lines of her palms. She thought of Kai, at home, safe, probably asleep, unaware of the universe his mother had torn in half.

She touched her sidearm, squared her shoulders, and looked up at the sky.

The night was bright. The stars scattered like buckshot. Somewhere out there, her quarry ran free. But she was alive. And she was hunting.

"Time to go," she said, to no one in particular. And she walked toward the waiting future, unbroken.

# CHAPTER FOURTEEN

## *Sins of the Father*

L eilani pulled the Explorer to the curb, cut the lights, and stared through the windshield at the old cottage. It sat low and stubborn under a jacaranda canopy, porch light flickering, a lopsided string of paper lanterns still faintly glowing from last month's festival. Her mother's van hunched in the carport, the rear window fogged over, and the side panel plastered with faded stickers: My Child Is an Honor Student; E Ala E; Protect The ʻĀina. The digital clock on the dash flashed 12:27. It reset itself to 12:01, a hiccup of old wiring, the thing she never fixed.

She exhaled, rolled her neck to snap the tension, and fished a battered container of ibuprofen from the cupholder. Two pills, dry swallow, bitter on the tongue. Her phone chimed. One text from Kai (half an emoji, the kind he sent when words were too big), and three missed calls from her mother, which she ignored for now. She was running on fumes, stitches in her arm itching beneath the makeshift bandage, her body a patchwork of bruises, some earned, some inherited.

She climbed the porch steps, boots thudding softly on the weathered boards, and knocked twice before letting herself in. The entryway was the same as always, a row of slippers by the mat, a hula skirt drying on a plastic hanger, the sharp scent of ginger and something frying. She slipped off her boots, padded into the kitchen, and stopped.

Her mother was at the stove, sleeves rolled up, singing old words in a voice pitched low to keep from waking Kai. The table was set with a chipped platter of poke, a nest of purple sweet potato, and a bowl of rice steamed to glossy perfection. The clock over the fridge read 1 a.m., always a little fast, and the calendar next to it was three months behind. Leilani wanted nothing more than to step backward into that simpler time, when the worst thing that could happen was a burned casserole or a call from the principal.

"Look at you," Naalei said, not turning, but with a smile in her voice. "Late again. You trying to make me worry myself into the next life?"

"Sorry, Mom. It was a day." She dropped her bag onto the bench and slouched into her usual seat.

"Every day is a day with you. Eat. I made too much, as always."

Leilani let herself be served, let her mother ladle a mound of lomi salmon onto her plate with pickled onion and a fat wedge of mango. The first mouthful hit her like a homecoming, a rush of brine and umami and memory. She chewed in silence, too hungry and too tired for conversation, but Naalei didn't let the quiet win for long.

"You find her?" Naalei asked, eyes fixed on the rolling boil of the pot.

Leilani nodded. "Yeah. Got her out. She'll be okay. The doctors at Queens say she might be out before the weekend." She reached for the soy sauce, splashed it over everything, then added, "Isaac took a bullet. But he'll live. That idiot could get hit by a truck and still walk it off."

Naalei's shoulders eased, her hands slowing their work at the cutting board. "You bring him here when he's ready. I'll make him tea."

"Not sure he drinks tea," Leilani said. "But I'll tell him."

Naalei's eyes landed on the bandage peeking out from under her sleeve. She didn't say anything, and Leilani let it go.

They ate like that for a few minutes, trading

small talk, pretending neither could see the exhaustion that radiated from Leilani's skin or the lines that had deepened around her mother's eyes. The food filled the cracks, warmed her bones, and made it almost possible to believe that the world was still safe on the other side of the door.

But as she ate, Leilani knew her thoughts were turning to what she'd been avoiding: the flash drive, the files, and the old betrayal in her father's name.

When she finished her second helping, she sat back and rubbed the bridge of her nose. "There's something else. About the case."

Naalei wiped her hands on a dish towel and faced her, eyes dark and unblinking. "You found the man behind it all?"

"Not yet. But I found." She paused, hunting for the right words. "I found Dad's name. In the developer's files. From before he died. Payments, meetings. I don't know what to think."

Naalei's face didn't move, but her hands closed around the counter. "What do you mean, payments?"

"Exactly what it sounds like. Wire transfers, consulting fees, land contracts. I don't want to believe it, but." She glared at her mother, and all the old anger was there, mixed with something rawer and less defined. "Did you know? Were you part of it?"

The air in the kitchen was still. Outside, a night bird shrieked. Naalei turned to the stove, lifted the lid and shut off the burner with a click.

"I always wondered when you'd find out," she whispered. "Your father did things I'll never forgive. But not what you think."

Leilani's fists were clenched in her lap. "I need to know everything. No more secrets."

For a few seconds, her mother didn't answer. She poured a cup of tea and set it in front of Leilani. She moved farther into the room where a battered filing cabinet leaned against the wall. From the bottom drawer, she pulled a box, Koa wood, carved with the old symbols, and the finish rubbed smooth at the corners. She carried it to the table and set it between them.

"I hoped this day would never come," she said, voice trembling. She opened the lid and spread the contents across the table. There were letters in careful script, Polaroids from rallies, and newspaper clippings yellowed with age. There was a badge in its cracked leather case, and a photo of her father in his uniform, smiling with his face the way he only ever had for family.

Leilani looked at the evidence, the cop in her cataloguing every detail as the daughter in her wanted to push it all away.

Naalei sat, hands folded, and saw her daughter with an honesty that made Leilani flinch. "You want to know? Fine. But you listen. And you believe me when I say your father tried to stop it. He died because he wouldn't take their money. Not because he did."

Leilani blinked, the ache behind her eyes sharp as glass. "Why are his prints all over their files?"

"That's the proof they wanted you to find, Lei. They paid everyone else. Your father kept the records, took the meetings, made it look like he played along. But he was building a case. He thought if he made them trust him, he could get close enough to bring them all down at once." Naalei's voice broke, and she brushed a stray hair from her face with a hand that shook enough to notice. "He never got the chance."

The kitchen spun, slow and relentless. Leilani pressed her palm flat on the table, grounding herself. "Why didn't you tell me?"

Her mother looked away. "Because I knew what you'd do. You'd chase the truth until it killed you, like it killed him. And I'd rather lose you to a lie than to the same people who." She stopped, and the hurt was a living thing on her face.

Leilani forced her breathing to slow. "It's not going to kill me, Mom."

"You don't know that," Naalei said, almost a

whisper. "But you're going to try anyway, aren't you?"

Leilani nodded. She reached for the badge, tracing the worn edge with her thumb. "I have to. It's the only way this ends."

They sat together in the spill of kitchen light, the silence bigger than any truth spoken between them.

"I'm sorry," Leilani said, and meant it.

"I'm not," her mother replied, voice steady now. "If you're going to finish this, do it with your eyes open."

She rose, gathered the evidence into the box, and placed it in Leilani's lap. "You take it. Whatever you find, you bring it home. Understand?"

Leilani stared at her mother, the resolve in her jaw and the history in her hands, and nodded.

"I will."

Naalei smiled, just a little. "Good. Now eat something sweet before you go back out into that darkness. It's the only armor we get."

Leilani laughed, the tension draining from her shoulders, and let her mother serve her another slice of mango, the sugar sharp on her tongue. The night was not so endless after all.

By the time she finished the mango, the box

had spilled its history onto every surface in the kitchen. But as she handled each artifact, a newspaper clipping, a Polaroid, the edge-creased leaflet from some forgotten rally. Her hands betrayed her: fingertips stained with newsprint, knuckles whitening around a photo, nails digging into the old wood of the box.

Leilani spread the contents in careful rows, evidence first, sentiment later. The earliest documents were prosaic. The water rights surveys, a certificate of employment from a now-defunct realty firm, an architectural rendering of a subdivision with her father's neat signature on the bottom. She perused the letters, searching for code, but found only a young man's optimism. Her father, before the world had made him a cynic. He'd believed in the power of compromise, of making change from the inside out.

The tone darkened. Emails, clipped and urgent, printed on reams of cheap paper, each marked with dates that lined up too well with the rise of the resorts and the demolition of the old neighborhoods. The words urgent, noncompliant, and immediate risk repeated like a refrain, and the recipient list always circled back to the same handful of names. Developers, politicians and lawyers whose grandsons now ran the same offices with different letterheads.

"He thought if he built their trust, he could fix things before they broke," Naalei said, setting a bowl of poi between the piles of history. "He was good at making people believe in him. After he stopped believing in himself."

Leilani ran her thumb over a photograph. Her father standing on the steps of the city building, two protest banners behind him, one arm slung around a younger version of herself. The date on the back was the year before he died. She tried to remember that day, but all she recalled was the sunburn and the itch of too-tight sandals.

"He brought you to every march," Naalei said, reading her mind. "Even when it was dangerous. He said you had to see what the world was like, or you'd believe the stories the newspapers told you."

"Did you ever want him to quit?" Leilani asked, though she already knew.

Her mother smiled, a complicated twist of love and regret. "Of course. But he never could. He used to say, the moment you stop fighting is the moment the ocean takes it all back." She reached for the letters bound in a rubber band after wiping her hands on a dish towel.

"These are the ones I never let you see," she said.

The handwriting was tight, a spiral of energy on every page. The first few were mundane, reminders to pay the cable, notes about picking up groceries. Without warning, the text grew paranoid. Half of them were written after midnight, the pen pressure so hard it cut the page.

"They started threatening him," Naalei said, her voice going flat. "Phone calls. Notes on the car. Sometimes just a man standing in the driveway, watching him leave for work."

Leilani read, eyes skating over the words: "Don't trust anyone. Files at office. If something happens to me, check the lockbox behind the old shed. Tell Lei to finish what I started, only her. Don't let them rewrite the history."

A tightness wound itself around her ribs. "Did you check? The lockbox?"

Naalei nodded. "After the funeral. I burned half of it, for your sake. The rest I sent to the state investigator. They never opened the box."

Of course they didn't. Leilani opened the next letter, dated three days before he died. It was short, as if written in a hurry.

I know who's behind it. We're finished after the meeting tomorrow. If I'm late, don't wait. Take care of Lei. Love you, always.

She read it three times, every word growing heavier. She could almost feel her father's hand on her shoulder, could almost hear the way his voice tightened when he tried not to worry her.

"He knew he was being followed," she said, the

words scraping out. "He must've thought it was worth the risk. Your father believed if you stood your ground long enough, the current would change," she said. "But I watched him drown, little by little, every year."

"He never got to finish it," said Leilani.

Her mother's hands trembled as she poured a glass of water, a bead of condensation tracing down the side. "Maybe it was too big for any one person."

Leilani spread the latest batch of evidence on top of the oldest. The names were familiar, just updated for a new century; the same lawyers, now partners; the same developers, their sons in the company photo; the same dead stream, silted over with promises of green space and community revitalization. Every document was a carbon copy of the last, the cycle unbroken.

"It's the same pattern," she said, the realization slotting into place. "They use the same tricks, the same threats, just with newer technology. The Mastermind didn't start this; he just took the baton."

Naalei smiled. "That's your father in you. Never give up, even when the odds say otherwise."

Every time she thought she understood the case, it cracked open another layer, exposing secrets she wasn't sure she wanted to own. She left the box open on the counter, in case Leilani needed to check it again.

"He wrote you one last letter," Naalei said. "I never mailed it. I didn't know if it would help or hurt."

She handed over a single page, creased and translucent from all the times it had been unfolded and refolded. Leilani read it by the stove light, her heart slowing to match the cadence of her father's words.

Lei,

If you're reading this, you're braver than I ever was. The world will tell you that fighting for what's right is a waste, that the line is already drawn. But you get to choose where you stand. Don't let them change who you are. Whatever they say, whatever you find, remember that the ocean always remembers its own.

With love, always.

The letter fell to the counter, and she rested her head in her hands. The burden of legacy, of old grief and new purpose, pressed down hard.

"Thanks, Mom," she said, voice small.

Naalei squeezed her shoulder. She kissed her on the crown of the head, as she had every first day of school, every scraped knee, and every homecoming from the dark.

"You finish it, Lei," she whispered. "Make it

mean something."

Leilani nodded, wiped her face, and squared the edges of the evidence pile. She was already building the timeline in her head, seeing not just the end but the thread that ran through every chapter.

The Mastermind was next. And this time, she would not be alone.

The hour had gone deep and sideways by the time Leilani was done organizing the documents. The world outside the kitchen window was matte black, broken only by the pulse of the red-blinking comm towers on the ridge and the spatter of porch light on the hibiscus. The only clock she trusted, the one above the rice cooker, read nearly three, the second hand stuttering as if time itself needed to catch its breath.

She paced from counter to sink and back, tracing the same worn stretch of tile her father had favored when he had something on his mind. Naalei watched from the table, making no secret of her worry, hands folded in the manner of a mother who had run out of chores to busy herself.

"I still think you should let it rest," her mother said. "No one's asking you to become a martyr."

"Dad didn't get the choice," Leilani shot back, harsher than she meant. She poured a glass of tap water, drank half in a single gulp, wiping her mouth with her hand. "I know who's at the center now. Or I know what he is. And he knows I'm getting close."

"That doesn't mean you need to walk into his trap."

"I'm not walking in. I'm baiting him." She put the glass down so hard it almost cracked. "That's the difference. He thinks he's got the upper hand. Let him keep thinking it."

Naalei's lips pressed into a line so thin it might have been scar tissue. "I thought I could keep you safe by keeping you ignorant. That was my mistake. But you're not alone anymore, Lei. You have friends, allies. Use them."

Leilani paced, paused, and kneeled next to the memory box. She pulled out her father's badge and held it in her palm. The words on the back, once crisp, had gone almost unreadable with time: Stand firm against the tide. The edges were sharp and cold.

"I am using them," she said. "But the Mastermind doesn't want collateral damage. Not this time. He wants to erase loose ends, make sure there's nothing left that can point back."

She opened the battered notebook where she'd logged every threatening call, every cryptic message. She'd memorized the sequence of numbers, the burner, always with a local prefix, but always routed through a different disposable. But the voicemails all had the same texture, a low hiss under the words, as if each threat was delivered from the inside of a conch shell.

"I'm going to call him," she said, with a finality that made her own skin crawl.

Her mother protested, but Leilani remained stoic, already reaching for the burner phone she'd bought the week prior. "He needs to know that I know," she said. "He needs to believe it's over, that I'm scared, or he'll just keep circling."

Naalei rose and wrapped a cardigan around herself like a blanket. "You're still my little girl," she said, the words soft but fierce. "Even if you don't need me to fight your battles, you can still let me in."

Leilani looked up, and the concern on her mother's face nearly broke her. "I know, Mom. I do."

She dialed the number, thumb steady on the keypad. It rang twice, followed by a hollow click and silence.

She forced her voice to be flat. "I know who you are. I know what you did to my father. If you wish to finish what you started, meet me." She gave the address of the park where her father had taken her for every birthday, every May Day, every time she'd scraped a knee and needed to prove she could get up again.

She ended the call and exhaled, letting the adrenaline soak in before it could twist itself into regret.

For a while, neither of them moved. Without a word, Naalei crossed the kitchen and slid the badge across the table, the metal scraping against the wood. She laid her hand on Leilani's shoulder, her grip equal parts comfort and anchor.

"In the old stories," her mother said, "when someone goes out to fight a monster, they always bring something from home. A rock, a feather, a piece of shell. You take this, you remember who you are."

Leilani tucked the badge into her pocket, its weight both a shield and a debt.

They stood together in the kitchen, silent, the only sound the low tick of the clock and the hum of the refrigerator. Her mother hugged her tight and pressed her lips to Leilani's forehead. She whispered a blessing, old words that meant nothing to outsiders but were like armor to her.

When the embrace ended, Leilani squared her shoulders, grabbed her jacket, and moved to the door.

"Come back," Naalei said, voice steady but trembling at the edges.

"I will," Leilani promised. "And I'll bring the

truth with me."

She opened the door. The night air hit her like a salt slap, sharp and cold, the threat of rain on the wind. She let it clear her mind before stepping into the darkness.

She stood framed in the doorway, the light behind her, the city before her, and her father's badge clutched tight in her hand. She disappeared into the shadows, leaving only the echo of her footsteps and the resolve to finish what had begun a generation ago.

# CHAPTER FIFTEEN

## *Dangerous Gambit*

L aniakea at dawn was an erasure and a promise. The sea, flat as a surgeon's table, spread its slow, shimmering blue toward a horizon the color of old bruises. Low clouds lay heavy on the Koʻolau, suffocating the sun before it could do anything but nudge the world into a half-light, and the famous breakers stood empty, save for a single gull riding thermals over the reef. The sand was untouched, rippled in soft scallops by the night wind, and the only footprints marring the perfection were Leilani's, spaced wide as she picked her way down the slope.

She wore cargo shorts and a gray tee, both thrift shop fare. The mic taped under her bra strap itched with every step. A persistent, low grade reminder of what this morning was supposed to be. She had slept for an hour, fitfully, before waking at three to case the beach and rehearse a thousand variations of how this would go. She'd checked her service weapon twice, checked her backup, deciding to leave the backup in the Explorer; the first rule of these meetings was that if the mark felt threatened, they'd ghost and you'd never get a second chance.

The backup team was already in place, scattered along the shoreline. A fisherman with an empty bucket and a hat too new. A couple pretending to argue over a surfboard lease; and, farther out on the north point, a late night partier in board shorts pretending to nurse a hangover. They had her back, in theory, but she knew from experience how thin the line between theory and fact could get, especially when a man like Alika Kahue was the one you were baiting into the open.

She checked her watch. 5:47. The meeting time was six A.M. on the dot, but the man she was dealing with would arrive early, just to see what happened before the game actually started.

She settled herself near a cluster of lava rocks, half embedded at the wrack line. It gave her a view of both the main beach access and the narrow footpath that snaked in from the jungle behind. She crouched, scooping a palmful of sand and letting it sift through her fingers. It clung to the creases of her skin, stubborn and wet. She wiped her hands on her shorts and tapped the wire under her shirt, a nervous tic that left her fingertips smelling faintly of medical tape and fear.

From here, the world was reduced to a geometry of waiting. The wind was soft, the surf low, but every so often the hush was broken by a far-off shout or the slap of a wave against the outer reef. She played out the likely moves in her head. Alika would circle, would scope the approach, would test the perimeter for tails. He'd show only if he thought he had all the angles, or if the bait, her, and only her, were strong enough to override twenty years of professional paranoia.

A Myna landed near her foot, bold as a thief. It pecked at her laces, flitting off in a spasm of wings, heading for the trash can near the lifeguard stand. Leilani almost envied it; prey could move with confidence if it had no concept of what was hunting it.

She exhaled, eyes darting from the pocked basalt outcrop to the looming green behind her. Her mind catalogued the threats, a snare, a spotter with a scope, an IED if the Mastermind was feeling biblical, but none of them fit the man she'd studied. Alika Kahue was a planner, not a brawler. He'd never left so much as a parking ticket on his record, and if his hands had ever been dirty, they'd been washed with enough money and influence to come up cleaner than God's own soul.

The light shifted. It was 5:53.

She watched the footpath and saw the palms shiver. Movement. Not enough to be a runner, or a dog-walker; but enough to telegraph that someone was testing the water. She pretended not to notice, instead pulling a protein bar from her pocket and unwrapping it with exaggerated care, the bored nothingness that said, I'm here, no drama. She took a bite, chewing slowly, and used the excuse to keep her gaze low. Her peripheral vision turned up to max.

At 5:57, he arrived.

Alika Kahue stepped from the tree line as if stepping onto a stage. Every inch calculated, every gesture pre-scripted. He wore linen slacks and a dark, untucked dress shirt, sleeves rolled to the elbow. No jacket, no tie, but his shoes, narrow, Italian, dusted with a single line of white sand, were the only clue that he was an affectation. His hair, steel-gray and swept back from his face, caught the sunrise and threw it in silver streaks; his goatee was neat, his eyes unreadable behind aviator lenses that reflected the full sweep of the bay.

He paused by the rocks, looking out to sea. The move was deliberate, to make her wait, to show he controlled the clock. As if bored with the view, he turned and made his way toward her, hands empty and easy at his sides. He was trim, early sixties, but moved with a practiced looseness, like a man who had spent his life never worrying about how much space he took up in the world.

"Detective Kealoha," he said, when he was close enough that she could smell the aftershave, cedar, and something citrus, expensive enough to not have a name. "You beat me here."

She shrugged, tossing the wrapper into her backpack. "Early bird, et cetera. Want a seat?" She gestured to the flat shelf of rock beside her.

He glanced at it but remained standing. "You don't trust me," he said, almost amused.

She matched his smile, thin as a knife. "I'd have to know you first to trust you."

He took off his sunglasses, tucking them into his shirt pocket. His eyes were lighter than she'd imagined, pale green, almost yellow in the beach light. They crinkled at the corners, but not from laughter. From years of looking directly at things most men would pay to avoid.

"I know your family," he said, as if it were an opening chess move. "Your mother was a year behind me at Kamehameha. Your father, well. We had our differences."

She remained silent. In an interrogation, the truth always floated up fastest when you let the other person fill the dead air.

"You look like your father," Alika said, his tone

intimate but hollow, as if reading the line off an internal prompter. "He had that same set to his jaw when he was lying through his teeth."

She met his stare, let it hang. "You didn't agree to meet me to reminisce. Say what you came to say."

He smiled. Not the kind that split a face, but the one that meant you'd already lost. "You're efficient. That's good. I never had much patience for nostalgia."

She held her ground, spine as straight as the steel in her badge. The waves behind them were rising, each one closer and more insistent than the last. A crab skittered by her boot, vanished into a mat of limu, and was gone.

He regarded the ocean, turned to her and shrugged. "I suppose you've figured out that all the noise, your cousin, the developer, the dead kids, none of it was random."

"Wasn't hard," Leilani said. "You're known for your theatrics."

He rolled the memory of that on his tongue, tasting it for bitterness. "Theatrics get results. You can quote that to the mayor when you see her."

She clenched her teeth. "You called my father theatrical, too, when you sold him out. Didn't expect him to survive as long as he did, did you?"

Alika's eyes narrowed. The only sign he'd registered the insult was a twitch at the corner of his mouth. "He and I had an understanding before he developed a conscience, or a daughter who made him think he could start over."

Leilani barked a laugh. "Funny, I heard he was working undercover. Said you'd burn anyone who got in your way, including family."

Alika's hands came out of his pockets, palms up. "You want a confession, Detective? Fine. Your father cost me everything I'd built. Twenty years, and he still haunts every deal I make. But this island is constantly changing. It waits for the right storm to sweep the bones clean."

She let the silence stretch, only the ocean and the distant traffic to mark the seconds. "You ran the money through shell companies. Bought politicians, judges. Paid off cops, too, your own people."

He didn't flinch. "Didn't need to pay them all. Only the ones who understood it was a transaction, not a crusade."

"And the ones who didn't?" Leilani stepped forward, voice low. "Like my father?"

He studied her as if calculating risk. "I didn't have your father killed. That's not how it works. He died because he thought the rules did not apply to him, and he was wrong."

"So, all those deaths?" She tried to keep her voice flat, but the words came out scalding. "The protesters, the activists, the kids who thought they could stop you?"

He tilted his head, considering. "I only do what is necessary. Nothing more, nothing less. This island will bury its own, eventually. I just moved the process along."

Something in Leilani's chest constricted, a fist of bile and salt. She'd known, of course. But to hear it out loud, in that dry accountant's voice, made the world shrink to a pinpoint.

She turned her head, scanned the horizon. A fishing boat drifted in the outer bay, its light a faint apology. The sky was closing; the clouds combining to block the rising sun.

"Why now?" she asked. "You had the contracts, the land, the city council. Why drag it out?"

He stared at her. "You wanted to meet. I'm here."

A twitch at the corner of his mouth, something between respect and annoyance. "You're not what I expected," he said. "The reports said you were raw."

"I'm learning," she said, dry as tide-washed coral.

He nodded, as if that confirmed some private

hypothesis. "Did you bring friends?"

She rolled her eyes, cocked her head at the couple up the beach, the fisherman, the hungover plainclothes. "Only the minimum."

He smiled again, this time with a little more teeth. "You're braver than your father. He never enjoyed doing the dirty work himself. He always wanted to solve things from behind a desk."

She bit down the response, let him run the table. "And you prefer the beach at sunrise?"

He looked out to sea, the sun now bleeding through the clouds and lighting the water in strips of fire. He said, "It's a good vantage, you can see what's coming."

She scanned her watch. 6:09.

He followed the gesture, his own hand drifting to the face of his gold-and-black timepiece. "You wanted a confession, Detective. So, ask me."

She sat up straighter, the wire pressing against her chest. "Why did you do it?"

He gave her a look, a slow, indulgent assessment. "Define, it."

She recited, voice flat. "The murders. The threats. The campaign to silence anyone who stood in your way. You ran an operation against this island for two decades and erased anyone who got too close."

He tilted his head, birdlike. "You sound angry."

She looked down and saw her knuckles white against the stone. "I'm curious," she said. "What was worth all that?"

He moved to an outcropping opposite her, settling onto the rock with a grace that betrayed both yoga classes and hours in backroom board meetings. He pulled a shell from the sand, cowry, perfectly formed, and rolled it between thumb and forefinger as he spoke.

"Your father," he said, "didn't just blow the whistle, he burned the whole thing to the ground. I spent twenty years reclaiming what was mine."

She watched the shell, saw it catch the light with each rotation. "You could have left. Started over somewhere else."

He barked a single, humorless laugh. "You think the world lets men like me start over? They want you to disappear, or die."

"So, you made others disappear."

He shrugged. "What's one more corpse on a beach where kings buried their enemies in the sand?"

He laughed, soft and genuine. "You ever spend twenty years being told you can't have what you've already paid for?" His gaze flicked to her face and lingered. "I wanted to savor this. To see what kind of daughter the righteous dead leave behind."

She shifted her weight, thinking how easy it would be to draw on him, to let the gun end it. But she waited, needing him to keep talking. She hadn't gotten the confession she wanted.

Alika's voice softened, almost conspiratorial. "I knew you were coming. From the day you put on that uniform. I read every one of your reports. Saw the pattern. You had the same blind spot he did, believing people are more than their circumstances. But you're not your father. You're better. Colder. More precise."

Leilani smiled, lips drawn tight over her teeth. "You talk a lot for someone who claims to be finished with the past."

He glanced at her. "It's not about the past. It's about the future. My future, and the land your father tried to save. I will build on it. And you'll watch, just like he did, powerless."

She let that hang. The wind was up now, tugging at the fabric of her pants, ruffling his expensive hair. The waves battered the rocks behind them with a sound like distant applause.

Alika watched the water, calculating the shape of her next move. "If you walk away now, you get to keep your mother, your son. I'm not sentimental, but I respect loyalty. I won't threaten them again, not if you let it rest."

She spit, the glob landing between them. "You think I'm afraid of you?"

He shrugged, amused. "No. I think you're afraid of becoming me."

Neither spoke. The only sounds were the waves hitting the rocks and the far-off call of a dog, or a siren. Leilani could feel her pulse in her fingertips.

She drew a breath. "You're going to confess to murder, conspiracy, racketeering. All of it, right here."

He looked past her, out at the horizon. "You won't get it on tape." He reached into his shirt pocket and pulled out a small black box with green and red lights. The light was red. He showed it to her. "I jammed your wire the second you stepped on the beach," he said. "Works on the police band, cellphones, and the old analog recorders. Your backup is down the beach, listening, waiting for a code you'll never send. He's probably wondering why he hasn't heard any conversation. He'll move this way and that would be a shame, because I don't want to see him die on the beach all alone." He grinned, all teeth.

The panic move up her body, but she refused to let him see it. She remained composed.

"You ever wonder why people say it's darkest before the dawn?" he asked.

She stayed silent. Her father used to say the same thing, but in his mouth it sounded like hope. In Alika's, it was a forecast.

He flicked the seashell into the sand, watched as the water covered it. "Because it's true. The worst things always happen right before the sun comes up."

She shifted her stance, readjusted the hang of her badge, kept her hands free and visible. "If you're trying to scare me, you'll have to do better."

He smiled. "That's the thing. I don't need to. You're already scared, or you wouldn't have brought back up."

She made a mental note. "Would you like to finish the story you started? Or would you rather surrender now, before I run out of patience?"

Alika smiled. "You know what I like about you?" he asked. "You see the entire board. You know the moves before anyone else. It's a shame."

He placed the jammer back in his shirt pocket.

Leilani's heart jumped twice. She shifted her weight again, her pistol pressing into her side.

"You won't get away," she said. "You think you're the first to try something like this?"

"I know I'll be the last." He glanced over his shoulder at the sea. He turned back, measuring her. "You ever read Sun Tzu, Detective?"

She didn't dignify that with a response. She was growing tired of all this talk.

He continued anyway. "If you know the enemy and know yourself, you need not fear the result of a hundred battles." He stood and walked towards the water. "I've watched your career. I know every choice you made to get here. And I know how you'll react when I do this."

His left hand moved fast, not for a gun but for a sap, a heavy blackjack, which he swung low. She twisted, catching it on the meat of her thigh, but already her right hand was on the grip of the Glock, safety off, aimed at his heart. She stepped away from the rock. He backed away from her.

He stopped, smiled at the restraint. "Predictable," he said.

Her leg was numb, but her aim was steady. "Try me again."

He shrugged, showed her he was putting the sap into his back pocket, and reached behind his back. When his hand came back around, it contained a small black semi-auto that looked custom and expensive.

"Drop the gun!" she yelled.

He smiled. "I'm not going to shoot you yet. I'm going to give you a chance. You want the shot, so take it," he said, the weapon pointing towards the ground. "But you'll get one or two before I put you down. And you don't want to die on this beach, not after everything you did to get here."

She worked her jaw; the heat radiating from the bruise already rising on her thigh. The ocean was louder now, the wind up, bringing with it the stink of rotting algae and cold brine.

"Are you curious about what happened to your father?" he said, voice almost bored. "He made the same mistake you did. He thought if he played by the rules, he'd win. But the rules mean nothing to men like me. Or to men like him, once he realized he had nothing left to lose."

He backed up, the gun steady, his voice low enough that only she could hear. "Sonny and Mako are dead, yes. But not by my hands. You know why? Because I delegate. Because I know when to trust a professional."

Her breathing got tight; the world narrowing to the circle of his face, the barrel of his gun,

He smiled, and it was the first honest thing he'd shown all night. "I knew your father would send you. That's why I waited this long. I wanted to see if you'd be any different."

"You're stalling," she said, keeping her eyes on the muzzle.

He leaned in, the scent of expensive soap and sweat. "No, Detective. I'm savoring it."

Alika's smile was sad, almost elegiac. "You were always going to lose. But I admire the way you play out every hand."

He turned his back and walked away. She flexed her hand, ready to shoot. "We're not done."

He turned, brushing sand off his cuff. "No, Detective. We're just getting started."

She stood, dusted the sand from her hands, and looked down at him. "You're under arrest," she said quietly. For assaulting a police officer.

He looked up, unafraid. "You think you'll make it to the road?"

The branches on the slope rustled, and she knew he hadn't come alone.

She kept the boulder between them, adrenaline burning off her fatigue. "You're done," she said.

He smiled. "No one's ever done, Detective."

"Shall we discuss family?" he asked, eyes burning now, all pretense gone. "Let's talk about legacy. You ready to die for yours?"

She smiled, just enough. "I don't need to be. You're the one running out of time."

Alika turned his back on her and walked towards the path he came in on. He stopped next to a large piece of driftwood and pivoted. He pulled the trigger, but she was already moving, rolling left, the round creasing the air above her shoulder. He dove behind the driftwood. She fired once; the shot going high as she ducked behind the rocks.

The beach erupted in noise, gunshots, the bellow of waves, the rattle of wind in the chain link fence.

She glanced behind her and saw her backup running down the beach.

Alika fired from behind a driftwood log, his gun trained on her position. Rifle shots filled the air from two locations, hitting the rock and the sand near her. She hunkered down, firing without looking. Hoping to keep their heads down until her team could get there.

"You think this ends with you walking away?" she called.

He barked a laugh. "This ends when you realize you're just like your old man. Stubborn. Alone. Dead. They'll never let you win."

She risked a glance. He was flanking right, using the tide's noise to mask his footsteps. Two men ran out of the bushes firing as they moved. Shots now came from behind them as her back up moved towards the scene. Shots filled the air, and her team dove for cover and returned fire.

She had to neutralize the situation, so she

moved to the side of the rock and fired. Two shots, quick, aimed at one man's legs. One missed; the other hit home, and he went down with a wet grunt.

Alika moved, firing twice, one hitting her vest at an angle and the other skimming past her arm. She felt the sizzle.

She tumbled forward, rolling in the cold sand. She came up on her knees; the pistol aimed square at where Alika had been standing. But he was no longer there. She heard bushes shake to her side and scanned the area. Bullets from the other man glanced off the rock. She dove for the rocks.

Shots came from down the beach and approaching sirens filled the air. There was a grunt from the other shooter and the shooting stopped. She looked over the rocks and saw her backup standing over the shooter. The fisherman ran to her side.

"You okay, Detective? I didn't hear anything until the first shot. What happened?"

"He had a jammer," she said. She looked around. "Where is Alika?"

They looked up and down the beach. Nothing. He had vanished during the commotion.

She walked to the shooter lying near the water. He had a shoulder wound but would live.

The second shooter would have a hard time walking, since his knee had a big hole in it.

Blue and white lights split the early morning light as multiple patrol units pulled into the lot and officers with guns drawn raced down the slope.

"Alika got away. Spread out and search the slope and the parking area. He couldn't have gone far," she yelled. But she knew the search would turn up nothing. She blew her chance.

One officer called the dispatcher and issued a BOLO for Alika and requested two ambulances and paramedics.

Leilani slumped in the wet sand, chest heaving, the cold surf creeping up her calves. She examined her hands, covered in sand, and felt the enormity of what she'd just ended. Or begun.

The shooters were loaded into waiting ambulances and her team and the patrol officers headed for their vehicles. Leilani looked at the fisherman. "Call it a day. I'll wait for the shooting team from the DA's office."

The fisherman nodded and left Leilani alone with her thoughts.

# CHAPTER SIXTEEN

## *Uncle's Betrayal*

When the last of the officers disappeared into the lot, Leilani let her body remember how to breathe.

She sat on the damp sand with her knees drawn up, the blood from her split lip already drying stiff and tacky across her mouth. Her phone was gone, ripped out during the scuffle and swallowed by the tide, for all she knew. Her wire had died in the first moments of the fight, fizzling out with a whine like an angry mosquito. She was alone.

The sun had risen fully, painting the water and the shore in harsh, unflinching light. The north point breakers threw sheets of white across the reef, each wave ending in a low, concussive roar that rolled up the sand and over the scarred basalt. Out here, beyond the lights and the sirens, time stopped moving. She could almost hear her father's voice. "Some days, the only thing that saves you is the ocean's memory.

Everything else gets washed away."

She almost laughed at that. Almost.

A shadow moved along the rocks, slow, careful, too deliberate to be anything but trouble. She wondered if it was the shooting team from the DA's office coming to start their investigation. But she saw the silhouette, tall, the walk loose but predatory, the weight held in the hips like a panther sizing up a wounded deer.

Alika Kahue.

He must have slipped the net during the scrum, doubled back through the reef caves, or he ghosted the periphery until all the uniforms were busy hauling off the grunts. She'd underestimated him, and now here he was, closing in on her like a chess piece after checkmate.

She pushed herself upright, hands leaving two perfect prints in the sand. She considered running, but the futility of that was already a taste in her mouth. She stared at the empty pistol in her hand and the two empty magazines lying at her feet. She swallowed hard.

He moved within twenty feet, keeping to the shadow just shy of the wrack line. His hands were empty, but she knew better than to trust that. When he spoke, it was with the bored cadence of someone reading a shopping list.

"You took the wrong side, Detective."

Leilani spat a clot of blood onto the ground. "Yours didn't pay enough."

Alika cocked his head, as if considering the line for flavor. "They never do," he said. "But that's not why you're here, is it?"

Her feet were planted, knees slightly bent, the way her father had taught her, ready for a sucker punch, or a bullet. "No. I'm here because of my family."

He made a show of rolling his eyes. "Your father was a joke. A man with a cause, but no stomach to finish what he started."

She let the insult land. She'd heard worse, from men with smaller hearts and bigger axes to grind.

Alika took a step forward. His foot slipped on a chunk of coral, but he recovered, unhurried. "You think you fixed anything tonight?" He gestured at the water, at the half buried footprints and the chaos of the last hour. "You only delayed it. There's always another body. Another wave."

She kept her mouth shut, knowing now that words wouldn't buy her anything.

He closed to ten feet. The sunlight caught the glint of a blade, thin, short, black handle. She'd missed it until now, too fixated on his face. She assumed his pistol was empty as well. He saw her see it, and his lips peeled back from his teeth.

"It could have been different," he said. "If you'd learned from your old man. Instead, you inherited his weakness. His inability to pick the right side when it mattered."

She squared her jaw, ignoring the ache in her cheek. "You don't know anything about him. Or me."

"Oh, but I do," Alika said, his voice a purr. "I know more than you ever did."

She caught the tell, shoulders tensing, knees flexing just enough to signal his next move. When he lunged, she was already diving left, rolling behind a stand of saltgrass and into the lee of a big basalt boulder. The knife whistled through the air and missed her ribs by inches. She landed hard, grit burning her palms, but scrambled upright and bolted for the waterline.

He was fast. Faster than she would have guessed. His hand caught her by the braid, yanked her backward so hard her teeth clicked.

She elbowed him in the gut, hard, but he just grunted, twisted her around, and slammed her up against the cold wet stone. The knife pressed against the underside of her jaw, the tip cold and almost delicate.

"You know what happens next," he whispered. "You always did."

She waited for the blade to open her throat, or for him to change his mind. Neither happened.

Instead, another voice, thin and cracked, echoed off the rocks. "Alika!"

They turned. Down the beach, behind a crooked pillar of volcanic rock, stood Edward Kealoha. He looked weary, his shoulders slumped, but his eyes were bright and locked on Alika.

"Let her go," Edward said.

Alika didn't blink. "Go home, Eddie. This doesn't concern you."

Edward advanced, skirting the wrack line. "It concerns me," he said, his voice low. "If you're determined to finish the job, do it with me."

Alika sneered, knife not wavering. "I told you, your part is over."

But Leilani saw the flicker. Alika's eyes darted to Edward's hands. She used the moment to slam her heel down on the top of Alika's foot and twisted free. The blade nicked her jawline, but she was already stumbling away, a thin stream of blood rolling down her throat.

Edward closed the gap between them. He fished something from his pocket, a flash drive, bright and white in the sunlight, and tossed it at Alika's feet.

"That's everything," Edward said, each syllable

cracked and desperate. "The names. The money. Every call, every order you gave me. You want it? Take it."

Alika glanced down. The drive sat in a wet dent in the sand. He looked back at Edward, and back to Leilani, who was now crouched and bloody, but very much alive and angry.

"You sold me out," Alika said. There was a real hurt in his tone, a betrayal bigger than murder.

Edward's hands curled into fists. "I did what I had to. I thought we were protecting something, this place, our people. I never wanted." He broke off, voice shattering, "I never wanted anyone to die."

Alika laughed, sharp and mean. "That's the problem with you Kealohas. Never any conviction. Always waiting for someone else to clean up the mess."

He stooped, grabbed the drive, and snapped it in two with his thumb and forefinger. He turned on Edward, who stepped back a half-step.

"You think that's it?" Alika hissed. "You think they'll stop because you gave them what they want?"

Edward shook his head, shoulders folding inward. "No. But maybe she will."

Leilani, blood dripping down her neck, stood. She looked around for a weapon. "You're done,

Alika. You're not gonna disappear this time." She grabbed a piece of driftwood and held it like a bat.

She studied him, and there was fear on his face. Not of her, but of what he'd become.

He made a sound, almost a sob, but not quite. He rushed at her again, knife high.

Edward threw himself into Alika's path, taking the blade in the chest. The sound it made was more sickening than anything Leilani had heard at a crime scene.

Alika recoiled, shock on his face. The knife sliding free with a wet pop. Edward crumpled to his knees, one hand pressed to the wound.

Leilani didn't hesitate. She slammed Alika with the driftwood, knocking him face first into the sand. They wrestled for the knife, but her training and his exhaustion tipped the balance. She got his wrist, bent it back until the blade dropped, cuffing his hands behind his back with the cuffs from her belt.

Alika thrashed, howling, but she pinned him with a knee and let him scream.

She turned to Edward, who was slumped against the boulder, blood soaking his shirt. His eyes were glazed, and he tried to smile.

"Sorry, Lei," he said, voice soft. "I should have come sooner."

She ran and kneeled beside him, pressed her jacket against the wound. His blood was hot against her fingers.

"It's okay," she said, but she wasn't sure who she was saying it to.

The tide rolled in, lapping at their knees. The water was cold, relentless, erasing the blood and footprints as it flowed.

Alika was quiet. The fight was gone from him. He gazed at the sky, mouth working, but no words came out.

Leilani sat with her uncle, holding his hand, as the moon climbed higher. The world had gotten smaller. The three of them, and the ocean.

Above the surf, a siren called out, growing louder with each cycle.

She believed it was for them. Edward looked at her. "I called them," he whispered.

She should have said something comforting, some last benediction to a dying man. Instead, Leilani pressed her jacket tighter to Edward's chest, blood turning the gray windbreaker into a gory Rorschach, and stared at the slack, disbelieving mask that used to be her uncle's face.

Edward kept trying to talk. At first it was the same old apology, looped and cracked, lips feathered with red foam. As the world came roaring back, the apology shifted, became a confession, not of crimes, but of motives and doubts.

"I thought we could steer it," he mumbled, more to himself than to her. "If we kept a hand on the rudder. The stream, the people, the whole thing. But it was already gone, Lei. They let us believe we could matter."

She didn't answer. The words were too big, and the pain in her arms too sharp. Her palm was braced on his wound, sensing the pulse flutter and fade, and watched the moon paint stripes across his hair.

Alika was on his knees in the sand, wrists bound behind him. The fury in his eyes was undimmed. If anything, it was magnified by his defeat, a hunger so bright it seemed to burn the air.

"You're a disgrace," he hissed at Edward, voice carrying over the hiss of the surf. "All those years pretending you were different. In the end, you're like all the others. Weak."

Edward tried to sit up but failed. He looked at Leilani with desperation. "Don't let him." He coughed, the blood bubbling on his tongue. "Don't let him win, Lei. Promise me."

She nodded, the gesture automatic and meaningless. "He's done," she said, but it sounded like a lie.

Alika bared his teeth, spat sand. "No one's ever done, Detective. You think this is over? I planted seeds you won't see for ten years."

He shifted, bringing his legs under him as if to stand, but Leilani ran at him and kicked him in the side. He fell over in the water and winced.

"Stay down," she ordered, and the voice she heard was not her own but her father's, hard, flat, carved from the same old stone that had made a hundred bad men reconsider their life choices.

Alika laughed. "You going to beat me to death, Kealoha? That's not your way."

"No. But I'm going to bury you, and every bastard you ever made in your image."

The words hung there, bitter as the salt in her mouth.

Edward's breathing grew shallow. He groped at her sleeve, clutching it with blood-slicked fingers. "You can't fix it, Lei. You have to survive it. Don't." He trailed off, gaze flicking between her and the moon. "Don't let the ocean take you, too."

She wanted to say I won't, but she didn't know if it was true.

A shift in the sand, the faint scrape of movement. Alika, testing his bonds, measuring his odds as the surf inched up the slope.

"You don't get it, do you?" he said, his voice almost gentle now. "All your rules, all your history. This island only cares about one thing, the next tide. Everything else is flotsam. The story repeats. The names change, but the winners and losers stay the same."

Leilani stared him down and felt not fear, but pity. He was a fossil, dangerous, yes, but already doomed by the new current.

Edward shifted again, this time managing to half-rise. The effort cost him; blood poured faster now, soaking Leilani's hands. He fixed Alika with a glare that was pure Kealoha, sharp in death.

"No more blood," Edward said. "No more."

Alika's smile died. He looked not like a predator, but like a man who'd realized his own extinction.

The moment broke when Alika lurched for Edward, body moving with the savage, heedless force of a wild dog. Leilani dove forward, tackled Alika at the hips, and drove him backward into the churning shallows. They hit hard, water exploding in a spray that stung her eyes and filled her mouth with brine.

He was stronger than she expected, shoulders hard as rebar, thighs like concrete. He twisted, tried to bring his hands to her neck, but the cuffs held. Instead, he slammed his head forward, catching her across the brow.

The world snapped to white. She tasted copper. She lost track of up and down. The ocean rolled them, dragging them a few yards out before smashing them against the shore again.

Her head hurt, she had sand in her eyes and ears, and Alika's boot was driving towards her ribs. She curled, let the kick slide off her, and swung her leg wide, tripping him. He hit the ground hard; the cuffs making his landing awkward. She crawled onto his back, shoved his face into the wet sand, and rode out the struggle until he stopped moving.

The ocean was at full tide now, water slapping up around their waists. The sky had gone gray, clouds smothering the sun.

She looked back to shore, to where Edward was still upright, hunched but alive.

He watched her with a look that was pure relief, mixed with something older, more complicated.

"You, okay?" she called, voice cracked.

Edward tried to answer. He held up a thumb, bloody, but upright.

She dragged Alika farther up the beach, out of reach of the waves. He was gasping, sand caked in his hair and his face, but the fire was gone from his eyes.

Leilani searched his pockets, found nothing

but the broken flash drive and a battered pack of cigarettes. She crushed the drive under her heel and ground it into the sand.

"Your game's over," she told him.

He grinned, showing red teeth.

She left him on the sand and crawled back to Edward, who was now lying flat, his arms folded over his chest. His eyes were wide and clear.

"Lei," he whispered, "promise me something."

She tried to smile. "Anything."

"When it's your turn, pick the ocean. Don't let them pick for you."

She squeezed his hand hard.

The sirens arrived, painting the sky blue and white. In the distance, she heard her mother's voice. Or it could have been the wind. She drifted on it, before the world rushed in to claim her again.

Leilani braced her palm on Edward's wound, the sick heat of blood pulsing between her fingers, and locked her arm to keep the pressure steady.

He tried to lift his head. "They'll bury it," he said, voice no louder than a thought. "The evidence. They'll come for you."

"No one's burying anything," she said.

Edward's eyelids fluttered. "Get the lockbox. In

the lawyer's office. Not mine. He kept it for me, for." His breath hitched. "For insurance."

She nodded and leaned closer so he could see her face. "Where?"

A wet cough. "Chun's Reef. Office above the surf shop. Safe behind the diplomas. Combo is your dad's badge number, backwards."

She memorized it and repeated it back. "Badge number. Backwards. Got it."

His hand gripped her wrist, surprising in its strength. "Don't let them say he lost. He only lost because he loved too much." The hand loosened, fell away. "You're better than both of us," he whispered.

She wanted to shake him, to shout, but her training wouldn't let her. She kept pressure, measured his pulse, and told him, soft, but certain. "Stay with me, Uncle. You're not done yet."

Alika, a few yards away, cackled. With his face pressed into the sand and the cuffs biting into his wrists, he couldn't resist the last word.

"They'll forget you," he called. "All of you. It'll be as if none of it ever happened."

She ignored him. The paramedics sprinted down the sand, one with a trauma kit, the other dragging a gurney fitted with orange webbing. The first dropped to his knees beside Leilani, took in the wound, and got to work. Gauze, compression, IV. The other set about checking Alika, who tried to spit at him and got a face full of salt water instead.

Two patrol officers followed, guns out, eyes bugged wide at the mess on the beach. "Detective," one called. "Who's the primary?"

She gestured at Edward, her voice thick with something that wasn't tears. "He is. Get the suspect to the car. Don't let him out of sight."

The officer hauled Alika upright, half carrying and half dragging him. Alika sang as he was dragged away, a low, off-key chant, half in pidgin and half in Hawaiian. She couldn't make out the words, but the rhythm of it lingered after he disappeared into the flashing lights.

The medics worked on Edward, voices clinical and fast, but she saw in their eyes that the math wasn't good. Too much blood lost, too deep a wound.

"Can you save him?" she asked.

The older medic looked at her, not unkindly. "He might make it to Queens, but you need to be prepared, Detective."

She sat beside Edward, the sand cold through her jeans, and held his hand until the medics loaded him onto the gurney. He was unconscious when they reached him, but she could feel, in the last squeeze of his fingers, that he had meant what he said.

After the ambulance doors slammed and the siren faded, she walked to the shore. She stood in the surf, letting the water numb her ankles, her knees, the bruises, and cuts she'd gathered in the last hour.

She looked back at the crime scene. The sand was already erasing the footprints; the tide rising to smooth the violence out of existence. The only evidence left was the smear of red on the boulder, and that would be gone by dawn.

She listened for the voice of her father, some whisper of approval, or reproach, but there was only the ocean, endless and uncaring.

She took one last walk along the wrack line, eyes scanning for anything the tide had not claimed. She found the broken flash drive and the sharp glint of the knife in the half-light.

She bagged them out of habit and put them in the trunk of her Explorer.

The lot was emptying, blue lights still strobing in the rearview as she drove away.

Tomorrow morning, she would go to the lawyer's office at Chun's Reef, and she would find whatever it was her uncle had left behind. She would keep her promise. She would pick the ocean on her own terms.

But for now, she drove with the windows down, letting the salt and blood and old pain ride the wind.

When she reached home, the sky was graying. Kai was sleeping on the couch, a backpack hugged to his chest. He woke as she entered, rubbed his eyes, and asked, "Did you win, Mom?"

She smiled at him, her future, her clean slate, and answered, "Yeah. I won."

He smiled, rolled over, and drifted back to sleep.

She watched him for a while, before sitting on the porch, letting the dawn do its slow, indifferent work.

It would be a long time before the story was finished.

But she had survived it, for now.

And tomorrow, there would be something new.

# CHAPTER SEVENTEEN

## *Justice and Consequences*

She showed up before sunrise, keys jangling, bitter coffee in a paper cup, hair still wet from a two-minute shower and face unsoftened by sleep. The headquarter's bullpen looked nothing like TV, half-lit, taped up with signs from three elections ago, the long table mapped with salt stains and the kinds of scratch marks you only get from decades of bored or angry cops. She set the coffee next to the terminal, booted up the feeds, and paged through the city's arteries as if she could push the next twenty-four hours into compliance.

The morning's first round of raids wasn't scheduled for forty minutes, but she had stopped believing in schedules a long time ago. The command line blinked, cycling through live bodycam footage from every squad converging on the targets, city hall, two private security offices, the glass-and-steel shell of the developer's headquarters. The entire operation was balanced on a timer, the kind that counted down with digital ruthlessness. She watched the dots move across the map, a slow invasion force.

Kaipo checked in on the hour, voice scratchy from lack of sleep. "Command's green. No leaks on the council side. We've got assets on every exit. You're good to go."

Leilani flexed her left hand; the knuckles were raw from the last fight. "Copy that. Tell Flores and the others not to wait for backup. The councilwoman has three phones. Grab all of them."

"Heard. And Detective."

"What."

The pause was brief. "Don't second guess it. You did the right thing."

She didn't answer, killed the call and double checked the address sheet. Her father's badge sat in the pen cup, metal dulled with years, and she tapped it once for luck before clicking open the next folder.

Every raid needed a narrative, or else it was violence in the service of nothing. Theirs had a story, environmental crime, but it was corruption at the root. A web of land swaps and shell companies and bribes laundered through consulting gigs and family charities. She traced the money in her mind, dollar by dollar, routed through Delaware, to Singapore, to a private foundation in Honolulu with her uncle's name on the trustee list. It was so neat she almost respected it.

A new alert pinged. The SWAT team was in position at the developer's headquarters. She patched in the feed, the sound off, and watched as they breached the glass doors. Inside, the lobby was all water features and lava rock; the walls hung with blown-up photos of old Hawaii, glossy and curated for maximum investor nostalgia. The developer himself, a man with three names and a face made for press releases, came down the stairs in a sweat-wicking golf shirt, hands raised, still barking orders to his executive assistant as they snapped the cuffs around his wrists.

Leilani watched the body cam shake as the officers moved room to room, emptying drawers, sweeping up binders, bagging servers and laptops. Someone in a suit tried to object, but was muzzled with a dry recitation of the search warrant. She recognized the voice, Matsumoto, a steady hand, not prone to theater. The developer's face went from outrage to blank resignation in under a minute. She caught the moment his eyes locked on the warrant, reading his own name on the subject line. The man had thought himself untouchable, insulated by donations and dinners and the sheer inertia of power.

Another feed, city hall. The chief of staff for the mayor was already at her desk, typing madly, her phone clamped to her ear as two officers waited politely by the cubicle partition. When she looked up, the expression was one Leilani had catalogued since childhood. Disgust and disbelief, followed by the flash of calculation as she weighed whether screaming or compliance would play better for the cameras. In the end, it was neither. The chief sighed, stood, and let herself be led out past the wall of smirking legislative aides. The body cam caught them all, one or two hiding laughter, more than a few with eyes gone glassy with fear. The contagion was spreading.

She paged through the other targets. The developer's legal team went down with less fight. No one ever arrested a lawyer, so it was all bathrobes and slippers and spouses filming on iPhones, threatening lawsuits. The police department's own corruption, the ones who had helped rig evidence or bury complaints, got the courtesy of an internal affairs escort. One of them, a sergeant she'd once called to cover a suicide scene, wept as they put him in the car.

Through it all, the updates kept rolling in, each one colder and more certain than the last. Handcuffs, inventory, loaded boxes, evidence tags. The city was being peeled like a fruit, each layer more rotten than the one before.

At 8:27, a squad hit the construction site. The resort project was still a maze of mud and half-poured foundation. Heavy machinery locked down after the initial protests had drawn too much attention. The security guards went quietly. One of the foremen tried to run; they tackled him in the open and dragged him through a puddle so deep his slacks nearly peeled off. The news vans were there, hovering at the police tape, filming every grimace and slow-motion perp walk. Protesters from the old stream clean up stood with phones out, live-streaming their vindication. A woman with a lei of ti leaves did a slow, solemn dance, tears streaming down her face.

Back at headquarters, the war room was filled with officers, some she trusted, but most waited for orders or donuts. She moved from screen to screen, assigning cleanup crews, fielding questions, holding the nerves of the operation together. Every so often, she would check the phone, hoping for a word from Malia, or Isaac or her mother.

Nothing from Malia. Not yet.

At 10:03, the forensic team reported in. They had recovered the hard drives from the developer's penthouse suite, plus two locked briefcases from his private security detail.

The detectives lined up the contents on a butcher-paper table, drives, phones, folders labeled Strategic Alliances, handwritten ledgers in a script that looked suspiciously like the developer's own. In one folder was a thick, rubber-banded stack of cashier's checks, each for ten thousand dollars, each endorsed by a different city council member. Some of the names surprised her. Most didn't.

She was there when they cracked the first briefcase. Inside, nestled in black foam, was a thumb drive and a burner phone. The drive files were password locked, but the tech in the corner was already smiling. "These idiots always use the same trick," he said. "Birthdays or dead dogs. I'll have it open in an hour."

Back at her desk, the reports kept coming. News outlets blared headlines; the governor called to congratulate her, or at least to claim credit for the sweep. She ignored the calls, retreated to the evidence room, and started going through the piles herself, document by document, page by page.

It was never the big gestures that undid the powerful, but the paper trail, the careless email, the backdated invoice, the list of payments so arrogantly typed that it almost seemed personal. She made notes, tagged the folders, built her case with the meticulous fury that had been the only real inheritance her father ever left her.

When Kaipo checked in that afternoon, he said only, "You made the news, Lei. They're calling it the biggest anti-corruption sting in state history."

She didn't respond.

"Hey," he said. "You saved Malia. You saved all of us."

She sat in silence; the phone pressed to her ear, the pulse slowing, the adrenaline replaced by something colder and heavier.

"I wanted to save everyone," she said, voice flat.

"You did what you could. That's all we ever do."

Her thoughts turned to her father, her mother, and her uncle dying on the sand. She sensed the ocean endlessly washing away what the city tried to build.

"Yeah," she said. "That's all we ever do."

She hung up and buried herself in paperwork as the office fell quiet around her.

Night came on, slow and blue. Outside, sirens sang down the empty streets, but the sound was almost peaceful.

Leilani sat alone in the command center, reading every line, chasing the truth as far as it would let her. She'd lost count of the hours, lost count of how many times her hands shook and she forced them to stillness.

The island was changing. Maybe for the better, maybe only for now.

But at least she could say, with certainty, that for one night, the tide was on her side.

The holding ward was nothing like the TV dramas, no frantic nurses, no family huddled in corners with desperate prayers. It was a repurposed conference room with three gurneys, one nurse in teal scrubs, and the rattle of the HVAC fighting an endless war with Honolulu humidity. Someone had drawn the shades, but light still seeped through the cracks, painting slow moving bars on the linoleum.

Leilani signed in at the desk, badge clipped to her belt, and gave her name to the nurse, who looked her over with a practiced skepticism before waving her inside. The room smelled of rubbing alcohol and overripe fruit, as if someone had tried to mask one with the other and failed at both. Malia was perched on her cot, knees drawn up, the blanket cocooned around her shoulders so tight she looked shrink-wrapped. She held a paper cup in both hands, knuckles blanched, and looked at the floor.

Her wrists were a mess of bruises, the angry red blooms peeking out from under the blanket. A butterfly bandage ran across her left cheekbone, clinging to skin gone sickly with shock. Her lip was swollen, split at the corner, and her eyes, always big, always hungry for a joke, were now shrunken, rimmed in purple. She was the only one in the room, unless you counted the security camera blinking above the door.

Leilani stopped a few feet away, not wanting to startle her. "Hey," she said.

Malia flinched. Her hands squeezed the cup tighter, trembling so hard a little water splashed onto the blanket. She didn't look up.

"It's me," Leilani added. She dropped her hands to her sides, made her posture small, non-threatening. "You're safe. They're not coming back."

Still nothing. Leilani looked at the nurse, who hovered by the wall, pretending to check a chart but watching for fireworks.

She crouched, so they were eye level. "You remember me?" she asked, softer still.

Malia's eyes flickered. She nodded.

The blanket fell open an inch, and Leilani saw the track marks of restraint, thin, linear abrasions on the inside of each wrist, crusted over with iodine. She wanted to touch her, to squeeze her hand the way her mother had always done after a bad dream, but the gap between them seemed unbridgeable.

"Do you want to talk?" Leilani offered. "Or I can sit here."

A twitch, the beginnings of a shrug. Malia swallowed, and the movement of her throat looked painful. "They said" Her voice was a husk, hollowed by days of terror and dehydration. "They said if you didn't stop."

Leilani's jaw clenched. "I stopped them," she lied, but it was the only mercy she could offer.

Malia stared at her own feet, toes wriggling under the blanket. "It wasn't meant to be like this," she whispered. "I wanted." The rest got lost in the churn of the AC.

"None of it was your fault," Leilani said, more forcefully than intended. She calmed her voice. "You did everything right. You survived."

Malia made a sound that could have been a laugh, but there was no humor in it. "They made me watch. Said I had to see what would happen to the others if I didn't do what they said."

Leilani's stomach turned. "You don't have to talk about it right now. But when you're ready."

"I'm not ready." The words came out sharp, final.

Silence spun out, broken only by the crinkle of Malia's fingers on the cup. The nurse shifted, making a note on her clipboard, and left them alone. From outside came the muffled beep of an ambulance reversing, the squeak of gurney wheels on tile.

Leilani tried to recalibrate, scanning for any way in. "Can I get you anything? Food, better coffee?"

Malia's shoulders had curled in so far they seemed to press against her sternum.

"They said you'd come," Malia said after a while, the phrase plucked from nowhere. "Said you'd never give up. But that it would cost you more."

"It was worth it," Leilani said, and meant it.

Malia's face twisted. Not quite a smile, not quite a sob. She looked up and met Leilani's gaze with a ferocity that was pure, undiluted family. "You don't know what it cost me," she whispered.

Leilani let that hang. "I want to help," she said. "Not only today. Whenever you need me."

Malia closed her eyes. Her grip loosened on the cup and she set it aside, hands flexing as if testing for an injury.

Quick as a cobra, she reached out and grabbed Leilani's hand.

The grip was shockingly strong; the nails biting into flesh. She held tight for a full ten seconds, breathing fast through her nose, before she let go.

"Thank you," she whispered, and retreated into herself, folding the blanket back up to her chin.

Leilani rubbed her hand, fingers tingling from the pressure. "You're not alone," she said. "You never will be."

But Malia's eyes had gone glassy, focused on some point past Leilani's shoulder, and it was clear the work of repair would take months, maybe years.

When Leilani left the room, the nurse caught her in the hallway. "She's tough," the nurse said, admiration and warning in equal parts.

"Yeah," Leilani replied. "We both are."

The nurse nodded, and Leilani walked out into the pale, bruised light of late afternoon, the air outside thick with the threat of rain.

She sat in her car with her hands on the wheel, letting the adrenaline drain away, leaving her hollow but somehow moving forward.

Tomorrow would be for the aftermath, the slow rebuilding.

Tonight, it was enough to have saved one person from the wreckage.

The next morning, Leilani drove west, past the neighborhoods whose streams ran sluggish with red dirt, past the strip malls already baking in the sun, all the way to what was once old ranch land and would have been, by now, the first row of timeshare condominiums, if things had gone differently.

She parked on the shoulder, well behind the double row of city barricades and blinking sheriff's cruisers. The resort site lay beyond the chain link, a low wound in the greenery, but today the wound was being stitched shut by people who looked like her, who sounded like the past.

There must have been a hundred of them, protesters, hula troupes, kupuna in wide hats and Sunday shirts, and a half dozen television crews orbiting the action like remoras. Every so often a news van's PA system would sputter a snippet of pidgin or the drone of a city official's apology, but the real story was happening at the ground level, on hands and knees, with ti leaves and kukui nut leis and little flags of tapa cloth stabbed deep into the scraped red earth.

Leilani sat with the engine off, window halfway down, letting the voices drift in, laughter, ululations, the harsh sweet yips of victory. No one seemed to notice her battered Explorer, or the woman inside it with a split lip and an arm full of stitches and a badge she'd left in the center console. She watched as a group of teenage boys, shirts off, skin gleaming with sweat and marker, threaded a length of handwoven lauhala through the gap in the fence, binding it shut. A city worker in a day-glo vest tried to shoo them off, gave up and let them work.

Beyond the tape, the heavy equipment was frozen. Backhoes, dozers, the pitted yellow arm of a pile driver looming over the site like a deposed king. Someone had festooned the blade of a bulldozer with ti fronds and a string of battered plumeria, and a keiki in a blue princess dress clambered up onto the tracks to drape a lei over the exhaust stack.

It would all be back to normal soon, Leilani knew. Crews would come, haul away the trash, grind the scrawl off the cinderblock with acid and brushes. But for this one day, the place was ungoverned, claimed by people who had been told for generations to wait their turn, to let others decide what was sacred and what was fungible.

A woman in a lavender dress, she recognized her from the activist interviews, always quoted last, always calm, poured a jug of water onto the dirt. A hula halau lined up behind her, girls and women and one old man, all barefoot, all with hair caught in the wind. They chanted slowly at first, swelling into the song that flattened the reporters into sudden silence. The wind whipped the edges of the sound, sent it spiraling out toward the highway and the strip malls and the ocean, as if announcing to anyone who would listen. Here, for once, we won.

Leilani watched, unable to move, chest tight with something close to pride and closer to grief. She wanted to call her father, to tell him it wasn't all wasted, that the old ways still meant something, that you could sometimes drag the past into the present and have it not bite you in the end.

Instead, she stayed in the car. Watched. Let the song roll through her, the lines of girls swaying in unison, the old man weeping in plain view of the cameras and not caring who saw.

A police cruiser idled up the shoulder, slowed as it passed her. The officer inside, a captain, decorated, every bar and chevron gleaming, met her eyes and gave a nod, not of authority but of permission. The cruiser eased on, leaving her undisturbed.

In the distance, a makeshift podium had been thrown together. A folding table with a sheet of plywood balanced on top, and behind it, two city council members and a nervous developer whose suit was already defeated by the humidity. The developer tried to speak, but the crowd drowned him with a round of sharp, practiced chanting. The councilwoman waited, her hands raised, and, when the noise dimmed, announced in clear, tremulous English.

"Effective immediately, all construction at this

site is halted. Permits are revoked. There will be a full archaeological review, in cooperation with." She gestured at the crowd, at the lavender-dressed woman, at the old men and women in the front row. "With the community."

The crowd didn't cheer, not quite. They exhaled, long and tired, the sound of people unlearning decades of disappointment in real time.

Leilani leaned back, pressing her head against the seat, letting her body slump into the borrowed gravity of the moment. She saw a drone pass overhead, blinking green, capturing everything for an audience that would watch tonight and forget by tomorrow. But the people would not forget. They never did.

An old woman with hair pulled tight into a white knot limped up to the crowd. Her skirt was dusted with dirt, her slippers caked in mud, but she walked with the rigid bearing of someone who had once commanded a room with only her voice. She peered through the windshield of the Explorer, squinting past the glare. She raised a hand, two fingers held upright. The gesture was not quite a shaka, not quite a salute, but it carried with it a shared history and mutual recognition.

Leilani returned the sign, and the woman nodded once, a benediction or a challenge.

That was all. The elder turned and went

back to the crowd, vanishing into the shifting currents of the morning, swallowed by song and laughter and the first notes of a makeshift conch shell trumpet.

Leilani started the car, put it in gear, and let it idle, watching the people as they danced and prayed and wove the day's victory into a story they could carry home. She waited until the last of the TV crews had packed up, until the first of the cleanup teams had gathered near the tape, before she pulled away from the curb.

She drove slowly, savoring the weightless drift of exhaustion that followed a job that finished right. She would go home, shower, bandage what was left, and sleep for twelve straight hours.

Or not. There was one more visit she needed to make.

She signaled, merged back onto the highway, and drove toward the city, the air salty in her throat, the ache in her arms no worse than the ache of memory.

She wondered if the old woman at the lot had recognized her as a cop, or as a daughter of the man who'd tried, years ago, to save this land in courtrooms and council chambers and backroom deals.

It didn't matter. She thought either answer was enough.

And that was its own reward.

She parked in the shade of the ER loading dock, found a bank of quarter-run vending machines, and stared at the bright plastic glow for a full minute before going in. Even now, after everything, the smell of isopropyl and canned soup and old fear in the hospital corridors made her want to turn and run.

She signed in at the desk and answered the routine questions. "Are you family?" "Does he have a living will?" "Is there anyone you want us to call?"—with the flat affect she saved for interviews with hostile witnesses. The nurse at the intake window looked at the split on her lip, the bruises on her arms, and made a note without comment.

"Second floor, west," the nurse said. "He's awake."

Leilani found the room without effort. It was the same room where she'd spent the last days with her father. The same low hum of the HVAC, the same off-brand art of the Koʻolau in the rain, and the same soft hiss of machines measuring the vital signs of men who had already lost the war.

Edward Kealoha lay propped in the narrow hospital bed, his face the color of steamed rice, his hair wild and sweat-plastered. The dressing on his chest was thick, fresh, and bright white at the edges where the blood hadn't soaked through. Electrodes traced a constellation across his ribs; the monitor beeped, a little fast, but steady.

He looked up as she entered, surprise flickering through the narcotic haze. He grinned, and it was all the old Edward, the trickster uncle who used to swap out her school lunch for sushi and napkins full of rainbow sprinkles.

"You made it," he said. The words were dry as dust, but they held.

She positioned the file folders and a battered legal pad on the chair by his bed. "Got your message," she said. "Didn't expect it to come by way of attempted murder, but I guess you never do things the easy way."

He laughed and coughed, holding his side with a wince. "Never did. Ask your dad."

The name hung in the air like a prayer. She waited, letting the silence do the work.

Edward reached over, hand trembling, and lifted the envelope from the rolling table. He extended it to her, fingers white-knuckled. "For you," he said. "And for him. If you want it."

She took it, careful not to brush his skin, and turned it over. No address, no stamp, only her name in the same heavy block print he'd used on every birthday card since she could remember.

"What's in it?" she asked, though she already knew.

He gestured at the chair. "Sit. You might want to."

She did. The envelope was heavier than expected. Inside, a bunch of letters, some on legal letterhead, others handwritten, one or two photographs yellowed at the edges.

She flipped through the top one. A signed confession from a city councilman, dated years ago, detailing the scheme to divert conservation funds, to buy off environmental studies, to launder the land into shell companies. The name was not Edward's, but the web of signatures led back to him, and to her father.

She turned to the next, a letter from her father, dated two weeks before he died. It was written in the small, careful script he'd used for recipes and camping lists.

I know I will not make it to the end of this. They want me gone, but I won't go quietly. If you are reading this, you are the only one I trust.

The rest was redacted, names blacked out by years of re-copying, but the point was clear. Her father had never been a traitor. He'd died because he refused to be.

Leilani read the page until her eyes blurred.

Edward watched her, something between

pride and sorrow in the lines of his mouth.

"I tried to keep it away from you," he said. "All these years. I thought, if you never knew, you'd be safe. Or at least free."

She glared at him, hard. "So, you lied. To me, to Mom, to everyone."

He nodded, slow. "I did. I told myself it was for the right reason, but I don't know anymore. I didn't want you to turn into him."

She let the accusation land, tasted it, found it true and not. "You're not him," she said. "Neither am I."

"No," he said, "but you're the only one left with enough backbone to do what he started."

They sat in the soft whine of the monitors, the envelope open between them, the weight of a whole family's lies balancing on the vinyl chair.

"Is this enough?" she asked. "To stop it?"

Edward smiled, weak and unrepentant. "There's no stopping it. There's only surviving it."

She nodded. "I can do that."

He closed his eyes. When he opened them again, they were sharp and lucid. "You need to forgive him, Lei. It's the only way you'll ever make it out clean."

She stood, gathered the letters, and tucked

them into her jacket.

"I already did," she said, and left the room before he could see her not believe it.

In the corridor, she stopped at the water fountain and splashed her face. It was still morning, but the sun was high now, and the day was already hotter than any so far this year.

As she started for the exit, she passed her mother in the hall, hair still damp from the shower, a scarf knotted at her throat. Naalei stopped, glared at her, and in her gaze was all the anger and forgiveness of a woman who had loved too hard, lost too much.

They didn't say a word. They didn't have to.

Leilani nodded, and her mother nodded back. It was the closest thing to peace either of them would get.

She stepped outside, squinting against the light, and let herself feel the possibility of something better, not for herself, but for Kai, and for whatever future might be built on the bones of what her father and uncle had left behind.

She climbed into the Explorer, set the envelope on the dash, and drove.

There was still so much to do.

But for now, the road ahead seemed open.

And that, too, was enough.

# CHAPTER EIGHTEEN

## *Healing Wounds*

**M**orning was still a rumor, nothing but gray haze bleeding up from the mountain's shoulder. The only sounds in the clearing behind Naalei's cottage were the cackle of distant hens and the low, stubborn scrape of Leilani's own breath as she lugged a pair of canvas bags down the uneven slope. The grass was cold, soft as rabbit fur, and her feet left no mark on it. She could pretend that she was moving backward in time, back before the city and the case and the ocean of damage she'd ferried home with her.

She kneeled by the oldest mango tree, fingers already numb, and unpacked. Ti leaf mats, folded square and still damp from the night's dew; four stubby kukui nut lamps, already half burned from prior attempts. A battered Thermos and the mini Tupperware with salt and limu; and the basket Naalei had woven with strips of red hala, which this morning held nothing but a glass jar of water, three sprigs of fresh lāʻau, and a tangled length of raffia. Everything she needed for the ceremony, except the confidence to pull it off.

She worked the mats into a ring, knees protesting, measuring the space between each kukui lamp with the side of her hand. North, East, South, West, like her mother had drilled into her as a girl. Each lamp she buried a finger deep into the dirt, firm enough to hold against the wind, filling the shallow depressions with salt. At the center, she placed the altar. An upside down fruit crate, draped with a bolt of old tapa cloth, the glass jar at its heart and the medicinal greens fanned around it like offerings to a small, persistent god.

When she finished, she wiped the sweat from her brow and sat cross-legged in the circle. Her wrist twinged as she did; she rolled the sleeve back, checked the scar, pink and stubborn, letting the sleeve fall. No blood, no drama. Not today.

Naalei appeared after dawn. Her arrival was as it always had been, soundless, stately, as if the earth made way for her. She wore a faded muʻumuʻu the color of papaya flesh. Her hair was braided and wrapped with a lei of brittle, fragrant maile. Under one arm she cradled her pahu, the old drum shining with oil and use, its lacing snug and taut. She paused at the grass, surveying the setup. She gave a single, almost imperceptible nod.

"Beautiful, Lei," she said. "You remembered the lamps."

Leilani shrugged. "Like you taught me."

Naalei set the drum down and stretched her arms, joints popping in the hush. She moved to inspect the altar, touching each object with careful fingers. She took in the jar, the salt, the greens and the circle of mats. Her gaze drifted to Leilani's arm.

"Healing?" she asked, voice pitched so it wouldn't echo.

"Almost." Leilani flexed her hand, opened and closed her fist. "Good as new, if I don't get shot again."

A snort, half amusement, half censure. "Don't say that," Naalei murmured, but the ritual of it made Leilani smile.

They stood together neither looking at the other, both looking at the altar. The sky was turning blue now, thin and watery, and somewhere a rooster declared himself king of the island.

"It won't be easy," Naalei whispered. "Family never is, after this much." She left the word unspoken.

"Yeah," Leilani said, as silence filled the space.

The first to arrive was Kai. He wore jeans and a ratty hoodie; the hood pulled over his hair despite the lack of chill, and in his arms he carried a bucket of beach rocks, smooth, dark, each one glistening with the last of their morning rinse. He grinned at the sight of Leilani, but didn't approach, instead dropping to his knees and setting about arranging the stones in a winding pattern that traced the outer edge of the circle.

"Uncle Ed said you can't have a ceremony without rocks," he said, tongue poking from the corner of his mouth as he worked. "He said it's in the genes."

Naalei arched a brow but did not correct him. "He's not wrong."

Leilani watched her son, her chest tightening in a way that wasn't pain but was close enough. She wondered if he remembered the last time all of them had been in one place, and if so, which version of her he remembered, the cop, the mother, the stranger with the badge and the borrowed grief.

She was still watching him when Malia arrived.

Malia stepped into the clearing like she was entering enemy territory. Her hair was pulled tight, her dress severe, all black angles, and she kept her hands balled into fists at her sides. She didn't look at Leilani or Naalei, only at the circle, the mats, the lamps.

"Is it okay if I?" she asked, already scanning for a place to sit that wouldn't require her to touch or graze anyone else.

"Wherever you like, cousin," Naalei said, gentle. "The circle's for all of us."

Malia settled on the mat closest to the altar, knees drawn up, body rigid as an exposed nerve. For a few minutes she watched the jar of water, blinking hard. She wiped her eyes with the heel of her hand and fixed her gaze on the grass.

The air thickened. The tension was a thing alive, curling between them like the smoke from the kukui lamps, but no one tried to break it.

It was Kai who offered the only greeting. "Hey, Malia," he said, voice soft and brave. "Will you help me with the rocks?"

"Not right now," she whispered.

The last to arrive was Edward. He came slowly, hunched over a cane that looked borrowed from a stranger, his face still gray from the hospital but his eyes alert, measuring every detail of the scene. He wore a button-down shirt, wrinkled, and jeans that bagged at the knee, and his hair was uncombed, sticking up at odd angles.

He stopped at the mats, catching his breath. "This looks official," he said, almost managing a smile.

Leilani stood to meet him, offering an arm. He took it, but lightly, as if afraid he'd break something. They walked the perimeter together before settling at the mat beside Kai, who shuffled his bucket closer to share the rocks.

The circle was complete now. Leilani could feel it, a tightness at the base of her skull, the way the old ones described a net drawing closed.

Naalei took her place at the altar. She ran her palm over the drum, fingers poised at the edge. She looked at each of them. Leilani, Kai, Malia and Edward, measuring what they carried, what they had not yet let go.

"Thank you for coming," she said. "We have work to do."

Leilani sat, drawing her knees up, and looked at the faces around the circle. The set of Malia's jaw, the twitch in Edward's grip on the cane, the uncertain hope in Kai's eyes, and in her mother's face, a kind of fierce joy, made sharper by all that had come before.

In the center, the altar gleamed. The salt, the water, the greens. Each one ready to be transformed, to do the work.

She drew in a breath, and the circle held.

Naalei waited for the silence to settle. She spoke in a voice both familiar and foreign, a register older than the family, older than her own years. "The circle isn't a shape," she began. "It's a net. It holds what we cannot carry alone." She paused, letting the words drift out and back, before motioning for everyone to find their place on the lauhala mats.

Kai finished his arrangement of stones. He started around the circle, distributing them, one to Edward, one to Leilani, one to Malia, and, after a pause, one to Naalei herself. Each stone was painted with a crude symbol, spirals, birds, and what looked like a volcano, done in the bright, cheap acrylics of a craft kit.

When he offered the stone to Malia, he held it out with both hands, the way Leilani's father had taught him to give things he cared about. "I made this for you," Kai said. "It's a wave, because you came back." He hesitated. "The wave always comes back. That's what the book said."

Malia looked at the stone, her face closed tight. "Thank you," she said. She held the stone in her lap, her fingers rubbing the paint until a blue streak appeared on her thumb.

Leilani could see the change, a small shift in Malia's posture, the way her shoulders dropped a fraction, the way her eyes didn't return to the ground. She caught Naalei's look across the circle, a flicker of approval hidden under the mask of ceremony.

Naalei raised the conch shell, cradling it against her lips. "Before we begin, we let the ancestors know." Her inhale was slow, precise. When she blew into the shell, the sound was less a note than a vibration, a tremor that shivered through the clearing and seemed to startle the birds into momentary stillness. It echoed off the mango tree, fading into a hush.

She set the shell down, pressed her hands to the pahu, and began a slow, steady beat, two quick, one long, repeated. "I will chant. When I have finished, you will each speak. Truth only, or silence. Both are sacred."

Leilani watched her mother as she started the oli, her voice low and rhythmic, anchored by the drum. She had never been able to translate these words. Old Hawaiian was not her fluency, but the shape of the chant was like a wind winding up the valley, gathering force and speed and bursting free at the ridgeline.

When the chant ended, Naalei dipped her fingers into the bowl of salt water and passed it left, to Kai. "Cleanse and release," she instructed, and Kai did as he was told. He passed the bowl to Edward, who paused as if weighing the bowl itself. His hands were shaking, but he steadied them enough to dip them, wiping the brine on his wrists.

He glanced at Leilani. "Salt stings, but it also

keeps things fresh," he said, the ghost of an old uncle joke in his tone. She smiled, and the mask of fear and regret slipped from his face.

Leilani took the bowl. The water was cold, the salt already separating out. She stuck her thumb into the liquid, tracing the line of her old scar. It tingled but did not burn.

When the bowl reached Malia, she looked uncertain, almost afraid to touch it. But she did, and the relief on her face when nothing bad happened was so raw it almost hurt to watch. She set the bowl gently on the mat, so it wouldn't tip.

Naalei nodded, turned to Kai. "You first," she said. "Say only what's true."

Kai grinned, frowned, and shrugged. "I like when everyone's here. I miss when we used to eat pancakes together. I wish Grandpa was here, too."

Leilani's throat constricted. She looked at Naalei, whose eyes were shut, as if hearing another voice beneath the boy's.

Edward was next. He coughed and straightened his spine as if for an old parole hearing. "I never meant for any of this to happen. I tried to fix it. All of it. But I think I made it worse. I'm sorry, too," Edward said. "To all of you. Especially you, Malia." He didn't look up, just let his head hang, and the only sound was the drum, slow and bare.

Leilani saw Malia's hand move. She reached across the mat, fingers trembling, and hovered over Edward's, not quite touching. Risking everything, set her hand atop his.

He looked up. His face crumpled, a dam bursting behind his eyes, but he covered her hand with his own and held tight.

The backs of her Leilani's eyes burned. Something she refused to let slip free.

Malia stared at her stone, the blue swirl now smudged almost to gray, and rolled it in her palm as if testing its weight.

"I didn't think anyone would come for me," she said. The words were so quiet that Leilani thought she'd imagined them. "I kept waiting for it to be over, or for them to say it was a mistake and let me go." Her face twisted hard with old anger. "But it was never a mistake. They wanted to break me, and I think they did. A little." Her words hung, fragile and defiant. "But I'm still here."

She flicked a glance at Leilani, as if the eye contact itself was an act of violence. Leilani didn't expect to be called next, but Naalei's eyes found hers, steady and unyielding. "You, Lei."

Her mind went to her father's last letter, of the badge in her pocket, of every line of duty and family obligation that had twisted her into someone she wasn't sure she recognized. "I tried to protect you all, but I'm not sure I knew how," she said. The words were flat, almost apologetic. "I'm sorry for what I did and what I didn't do. I spent my whole life thinking I could hold the world together by force of will," she said. "That if I kept the rules, did everything by the book, it would keep you all safe." She let her voice ride the drum's rhythm. "But the book is a lie, or at least, it only tells the part of the story that fits in a report."

She looked at Malia, at the bruises still faint on her cousin's cheek, and at Kai, who watched her with a growing, solemn pride.

"I didn't save everyone," she said. "Sometimes I didn't try. I'm sorry for that, but I'm also grateful. Because all the ugly, all the hard parts, that's what made this possible. Us, here." She forced herself to breathe. "I'll do better next time. I promise."

The drumbeat continued, the sound working its way into her ribs, synchronizing with the thump of her heart.

When the round was complete, Naalei lifted the conch again and blew, a short burst, this time, more exhale than song. She reached for the saltwater bowl, raised it high, and poured it onto the ground at the altar's base.

"Finished," she said. "What was, is done."

They sat in the aftermath, the new light slicing through the trees and striping the mats with pale, moving bands. Kai grinned, picking out rocks from the grass and tossing them underhand into the old mango roots. Edward leaned on his cane, staring at the altar as if it might offer absolution. Malia rubbed the blue wave stone in her palm, the paint smudged onto her skin.

Leilani watched them, seeing with sudden clarity the fractures and repairs in each face, her son's simple hope, her cousin's wounded pride, her uncle's battered conscience, and her mother's old, complicated love, each one held in place by the net of the circle.

Naalei gave no further instructions. She chanted, a new oli, her voice higher, tighter, the words rising over the drum. It was not a song of triumph, nor a lullaby. It was the old chant of forgiveness, the kind that never used the word but let the shape of the breath do the work.

Kai joined first, humming. Trying to copy the sounds. Leilani followed, voice rough, her accent a patchwork of modern and old. Malia and Edward joined, too, until the whole family was wrapped in the same threadbare song, voices vibrating through the clearing.

It wasn't beautiful, but it was real.

When the chant ended, the world seemed sharper. The sun had shifted, throwing long rays that cut the circle into stripes of shadow and gold. The altar's jar caught the light, sending small, pale rainbows onto Naalei's hands.

She stood and retrieved a covered dish from the basket, a simple mound of roasted breadfruit sprinkled with sea salt and a drizzle of coconut oil. She broke it by hand, passing pieces around the circle. No prayer, no fanfare. Only the gesture of sharing.

Leilani bit into her piece. It was warm, smoky, and sweet. She let the taste dissolve, and was, unexpectedly, hungry. Not just for food, but for everything she'd starved herself from. Her mother's laugh, the sight of Kai's smile, the simple permission to exist without an agenda.

When the food made its second circuit, Kai piped up. "What did the breadfruit say to the salt?"

Naalei raised an eyebrow. "I'm almost afraid to ask."

"Nothing," Kai deadpanned, "it's breadfruit, Grandma."

For the first time in what seemed like a year, real laughter burst through the circle. Naalei's was loudest, edged with tears she didn't bother to hide. Malia laughed, a dry, reluctant snort, but it was more than anyone had hoped for.

Leilani let herself join, the sound awkward and foreign at first, until it filled her mouth and her chest. She wondered if the future could be more than survival.

The meal wound down. The sun crested the trees, and the lamps guttered out, their last smoke curling up and away.

Leilani watched her family. Edward's frame was lighter, his voice no longer trapped in his chest. Malia looking around, her gaze not flinching from others'. Her mother's hands folded, finally still, in her lap. And Kai, smudged with blue paint, but grinning, already plotting his next joke.

It was fragile, temporary, but it was enough. She understood now what her father had meant. The ocean always remembers its own.

The ceremony had not made them whole, but it had made them possible again.

And that was everything.

# CHAPTER NINETEEN

## *New Horizons*

There was no grandeur in the police department's ops room; only the hard lines of concrete and cinderblock, the buzz of ballasts, the persistent chill from an ancient air conditioner fighting the realities of a June morning in Honolulu. Still, someone had tried. Folding chairs were aligned with near-military precision, every one filled by the pressed-blue forms of HPD patrol and detective squads. Command staff clustered in the front rows, brass on their collars outshining the gold foil on the city crest hung at the head of the room. Up on the low riser, a battered oak podium stood flanked by the national and state flags, their colors leached to near monotone by years of sunlight and cleaning chemicals. The room vibrated with anticipation and the scent of warm bodies in polyester uniforms.

Leilani stood near the crowd, her class A uniform freshly dry cleaned, every insignia and hash mark exactly where the department manual dictated, but the jacket tight at the shoulders in a way that made her itch. Her last fitment had been two years and half a dozen scars ago; now, the left sleeve tugged with every micro movement. She had already noticed, with a mix of embarrassment and resignation, that the new ribbons and citations on her breast pocket made the fabric lay uneven.

The invitation had said 9 a.m. sharp, but the Chief was running late. Officers in the back row whispered bets about whether it was a traffic jam, an emergency call or a show of power. There was an odd hush to the chatter. Respectful, but not in the worshipful way she remembered from old timer retirements or high-profile memorials. More like a collective breath held by people who, for a single morning, could forget that the department's usual decorum included subtext, rivalry and a low grade suspicion that everything could collapse in a scandal at any second.

When the Chief appeared, the room snapped to attention so abruptly the metal chairs synchronized in their scraping. Chief Higa was short, thick-necked, and wore a smile like it was a burden. She adjusted the microphone, sweeping her gaze over the assembled officers, pausing a fraction too long when her eyes met Leilani's.

"Thank you all for being here," Higa began, her voice a practiced blend of benevolent authority and hidden fatigue. "Today we're not only honoring an officer. We're honoring the spirit of this department, and the city it serves."

The words were almost touching, if you didn't know how many of the officers present had bet cash on whether Higa would last another year in the post. But she continued, hitting all the expected notes, the cost of duty, the changing face of law enforcement, the critical need for community trust.

"Some of you knew Detective Kealoha before this year," Higa said, and the corners of the room tensed, as if the collective history of Leilani's family might make itself known in a single, embarrassing outburst. "But none of us knew how far she'd go to protect this community. The last month has tested every one of us. The violence in Kahaluʻu, the threats against our own, the attack at Laniakea, and the case that tied it all together, the murder at the old banyan grove." A ripple of recognition; the words had been all over the press for weeks, but the reality in the room was sharper. "It was Detective Kealoha who solved the case. Who saved a life, and, in a way, saved us all from a city that could have lost itself to fear."

Leilani blushed. It was not pride, not humility. It was a low, spiny discomfort at being the center of so much public attention, when so much of the work, so much of the pain, was invisible. Her mind wandered, against her will, to the moment she'd first seen Malia after the rescue, or the way Edward had squeezed her hand from his hospital bed, or how Kai had asked, "Did you win, Mom?" as if that were the metric by which you could measure trauma.

Higa gestured, and an aide brought up a velvet lined tray, upon which sat a commendation medal, a city seal in heavy, starched blue ribbon. The Chief cleared her throat. "Detective Leilani Kealoha, please come forward."

She moved through the gauntlet of stares, her heart jack hammering, her uniform chafing at the underarms. The crowd made space for her, but their eyes never left her face, searching for something. Confirmation of a rumor, or weakness, or the rare sight of one of their own made into a symbol. At the foot of the dais she squared up, feet at shoulder width, and force her shoulders down from their usual high-and-tight parade rest.

The Chief pinned the medal to her lapel, the metal cold through the layers of cloth and thread. Higa's hands lingered at her shoulder, almost a squeeze, before dropping away. "You did what had to be done," she whispered. "This city owes you its thanks."

There was a beat, a half second where nothing happened. The room erupted in applause. It was not the brittle, perfunctory clapping of a command meeting. It was a raw, uneven, thunderous noise, back row patrol clapping with open palms, brass at the front with slow, measured approval, and a few young officers hollering in ways that would have earned a glare on any other day.

Leilani nodded and smiled at the camera. Out of the corner of her eye, she caught a movement at the room's side door. A tall man with dark hair, neatly pressed slacks, and a new suit jacket over what looked like the same shirt he'd been shot in three weeks ago.

Isaac Torres, right arm now moving freely, the scar on his shoulder all but erased under a fresh tan. He hovered in the doorway, hands loose at his sides, not wanting to interrupt. Their eyes met, and the room faded, the flares of the press camera, the rattle of applause, and the fluorescent hum. In his gaze, she saw the whole bloody arc of the case. The chase, the near misses, the stubbornness that almost got them both killed, and the stubbornness that made them finish the job, anyway. There was respect in it, but also something softer, almost pitying. She looked away first.

The ceremony wound through the rest of the citations and retirements. They handed out awards for valor, for community outreach, and for five decades of unbroken service. There were speeches from the mayor and the union rep and a councilwoman who referenced the "ohana of law enforcement" three times in as many minutes. Each honoree shook hands with the Chief, posed with their plaque, prior to slipping back into the anonymous sea of blue and black.

When it was over, Leilani ducked out of the phalanx of well-wishers and made for the bathroom. She ran cold water over her wrists, letting it bead on her knuckles. She used a paper towel to scrub at the smudge of makeup the department had insisted on for media optics. She looked in the mirror. The hair, the eyes, the jaw, all her father's. The faint white scar, visible under the sleeve, caught the light, and she rubbed it, as if checking for some deeper wound.

The medal was heavy, almost fraudulent, pinned over her heart. She wondered if she'd ever get used to it, or if it would always be a thing borrowed from someone more worthy.

Back in the hallway, the ops room was already emptying. Officers ducked out with coffee in hand, headed to their beats or to the donut boxes that someone had wheeled out near the stairwell. The Command staff lingered by the doors, talking in hushed, conspiratorial clusters. No one was looking at her now, but she sensed a greater awareness of herself than at any other time in her life.

She took a slow walk along the corridor, where the floor-to-ceiling glass gave onto a partial view of the city, the sun burning off the night haze, distant mountains already glinting with promise or threat. In that moment, she wanted nothing more than to drive home, lose herself in the day's routine, and pretend she was another civilian whose only battle was against traffic or grocery bills.

Instead, she waited. For what, she wasn't sure.

A voice interrupted her thoughts, low and amused. "That was quite a show, Kealoha."

She didn't turn, but the reflection in the glass showed him, anyway. Torres, shoulder unbandaged, tie askew, eyes carrying the same tiredness that had burrowed its way into her own bones.

"You made it," she said, not trusting her voice to be steady.

He grinned, but there was a hollowness to it. "Didn't want to miss your big day." He held up a coffee cup as if toasting. "You looked good up there. Very regulation."

"Don't get used to it," she shot back, but with less venom than before.

They stood side by side, watching the city through the window. The silence between them was not awkward, but alive, filled with the things they'd never said, about the case, about what it had cost, about what came next.

Torres nodded at her medal. "Heavy, huh?"

She shrugged. "Better than a bullet."

He laughed. "Depends on the bullet."

She snorted. "It's gonna end up in a drawer with the others. My mother will take it out for guests, tell them I caught Ted Bundy. Or that I saved the governor's life with my bare hands."

He grinned. "Let her have her narrative."

"I'd prefer she let me sleep past five in the morning, but I guess every parent has their priorities."

A memory flickered. Torres taking the shot for her at the catwalk. The panic in his voice when he realized she was bleeding, too. She reached up, almost unconsciously, to touch the scar again. He noticed, and his eyes softened.

"You're not going to let this change you, are you?" he said, the words so gentle they almost stung.

"Not if I can help it."

He nodded, accepting the answer. "Good. Because if there's ever another mess like this, I want you watching my back."

She allowed herself a smile, small but

unguarded. "Same, Torres."

He looked as if he wanted to say something more, but the hallway filled with officers again, their voices echoing off the linoleum and steel. Torres stepped away, blending into the flow, but she felt the heat of his gaze linger on her as he went.

She stood there watching the city; the medal pressing a memory into her shoulder. When the sun was full on the glass, and the chatter had faded, she straightened her jacket, squared the insignia, and walked back through the heart of the department, past the awards, past the stares, into whatever the day would demand.

If there was pride in her step, it was tempered by exhaustion and a hard, bright understanding of what it meant to be the hero in someone else's story.

She would carry it for as long as she had to.

She found the break room by smell, burned coffee, something sweet and synthetic lurking under the bitter. It was empty, save for a couple of mismatched mugs in the sink and the fridge humming behind a poster warning against fridge pirates. The ceiling tiles sported a constellation of water stains; the Formica table at the center bore a spiral of scars from generations of restless cop hands. Leilani set her back to the door and melted into the cheap plastic chair, feeling the ache of the ceremony settle in her bones.

A moment later, Torres slipped in, moving with the loose, unhurried gait of someone who'd already mapped all the escape routes. He carried a mug, plain white, with a single blue fingerprint pressed into the ceramic, and watched her with an amused, slightly wolfish expression.

"I figured I'd find you hiding," he said. "Is that coffee legal?"

She shrugged. "Compared to the stuff at the FBI field office, it's artisanal."

He laughed, slid into the chair across from her, and propped his feet on the table, heedless of the scuff marks. His hair was shorter than before, tapered military neat around the ears; his face, still banded with fading tan lines, looked younger now that the constant threat of death had been dialed back to background radiation.

For a minute, there was only the distant whine of dispatch radios, the ticking of an ancient wall clock, and the faint, uncomfortable knowledge that the room was too small to hide anything, including silence. Torres toyed with his mug, spinning it slowly.

"I saw you talking to the Chief," he said. "You guys bury the hatchet?"

She hesitated. "Depends which hatchet. She's

got plenty." She met his eyes and found no judgment there. "She thanked me for not dying on her watch. And for not dragging the department through another PR disaster. Very heartfelt."

"She likes you," Torres said. "In her way."

Leilani took a sip from her own mug, grimaced at the heat. "You ever get the feeling this place eats its own?" she asked. "That no matter what you do, you're patching holes until the next leak springs?"

He nodded. "That's every agency I've ever worked. At least here, the holes are honest. In DC, they plug them with bodies."

She smiled, not quite believing him, but grateful for the effort. "So, what now? You ride the wave back to Quantico? Or are you sticking around for the inevitable lessons learned debrief?"

He set the mug down and leaned forward. He looked uncertain, almost vulnerable.

"Actually, I'm thinking of staying," he said. "There's a lot here that makes sense. Good weather, bad coffee, better company." He paused, letting the compliment hang. "And I don't love DC anymore. Haven't for a while."

She felt her cheeks go hot, a reaction she'd thought long since extinguished. She masked it with a sideways glance at the bulletin board, where a wanted poster for a cat burglar had been amended by someone to give the suspect a mustache and a cape.

"You'd hate it by Christmas," she said. "The rain, the traffic, the politics."

He shrugged. "At least here, politics come with palm trees. And the beach."

He let his gaze settle on her, softer now. "Besides, I never enjoyed being a tourist."

They sat in that awkward, promising space, the air heavy with the unspoken. As if on cue, he reached across the table, fingers grazing the sleeve of her jacket.

"Is your arm okay?" he asked, eyes narrowing with concern.

"Healed," she said. "Mostly."

He ran a thumb along the scar under her jacket, not pressing, tracing. "Does it still hurt?"

She forced a laugh. "Hurts less than paperwork. Or press conferences."

He left his hand there for a heartbeat too long, withdrew it, flexing his fingers like he'd picked up a static shock.

"I guess we both got out lucky," he said, voice lower now. "Could have ended a hundred ways. None of them as neat as this."

"Nothing about it was neat. I almost lost everything." She closed her eyes, remembering Kai's voice, the fear on her mother's face, and the cold click of her father's badge as she tucked it into her pocket before the final confrontation. "I don't know how to go back to normal."

He leaned back, studied her. "You don't. You start from where you are. Build something better."

She opened her eyes, surprised at the bluntness. "That simple?"

He smiled, rueful. "Not at all. But it's a theory."

She turned the medal over in her hand, feeling the roughness of the engraving. "My kid wants me to quit," she said. "Every time I drop him off, he asks if I'm coming home. Sometimes I don't know what to tell him."

Torres nodded. "He's smart. He knows the odds."

Torres tapped his mug. "What do you want, Leilani? If you could write your own ending?"

She almost laughed at the audacity of it but stopped. She'd never asked herself that, not since the case had started, maybe not since her father died. She tried every answer she could think of. Transfer to vice, move to Maui, retire and teach surf lessons. None fit.

"I want to matter," she said. "But I want my son

to feel safe, too. I don't know if you get both."

Torres nodded, eyes dark and steady. "You get as close as you can, and you take the rest on faith."

He saw her, not as a partner or a rival, but as if seeing the story of her, the battered spine and the battered heart. "You're the bravest person I know," he said, and there was no irony in it.

She swallowed, looked down, trying to remember the last time someone had said something like that to her without wanting anything in return.

"Careful," she said, smiling to cover the tremor in her voice. "I might believe you."

He laughed, and this time the sound was easy, familiar. "You should."

They sat for a while, neither speaking, letting the new rhythm of silence stretch and contract.

Torres checked his watch and stood. "You owe me lunch," he said. "That was the deal if we both survived."

She arched an eyebrow. "You're not going to try to expense it?"

He winked. "I'll expense the drinks."

He reached for the door. "Seriously, Kealoha. I'm not going anywhere. If you need anything, if you'd like to talk, call me."

She nodded, not trusting herself to speak.

He left, closing the door behind him. The air seemed emptier without him, but not lonely. Open.

She leaned back in the chair, let her mind drift. Outside, the office was alive again, phones ringing, officers shouting, the city still demanding everything it could.

She smiled, finished her coffee, and made a silent promise to try, at least, to take the next day for herself.

She'd earned that much. And maybe more.

Late light caught the high canopies, molten orange trickling through the green and lichen, dripping long bands of shadow onto the old footpaths of the banyan grove. For years, the place had served as a backdrop for missing posters, for search parties and the blue-on-white of HPD crime scene tape. Now, in the easy hush of a Friday evening, the only thing marking the entrance was a new sign, carved by hand, the grain of the wood still raised and pale against the fresh-cut letters: WAIKANALOA HERITAGE SITE — CULTURAL PROTECTED AREA.

Leilani parked in the shallow gravel turnout, killed the engine, and let her hands rest on the steering wheel. In the sudden quiet, the residue of the work week, the sting of the commendation, the emotional static of the break room, fell away, leaving a faint ache in her jaw and shoulders. She stretched her fingers, flexed the old scar on her arm, and stepped into the lull of birdsong and salt air.

The transformation was as complete as a resurrection. The battered chain link fence had been replaced by a row of polished ohia posts, their tops painted with bands of bright red. Discreet wire mesh trailed between them, low enough that a child could see over but high enough to keep out the careless or the malicious. At the foot of the path, a tidy, roofed kiosk held laminated info cards and battered field guides to native plants.

She walked slowly, every step sinking into the thin layer of leaf litter that had already recolonized the ground. The air was heavy with ginger, and beneath it, the cold vegetal loam of living root. The last time she'd come here, it was to search for bones and DNA, to pace the perimeter with evidence bags and nitrile gloves, all the while tracking the progress of a murder investigation that had already doomed three families and nearly drowned hers.

Now, there was nothing to investigate. Only to bear witness.

The path curved inward, away from the street, into the heart of the grove where the banyans grew in a kind of planned chaos, trunks twisting and multiplying, aerial roots probing the ground in slow, relentless droves. At intervals, small wooden plaques had been planted, some with the names of donors, others with the Hawaiian or Latin names of the trees. She paused at one near the center, fingers tracing the sun warmed edge.

A few yards away, a group of three moved into the dappled shade, their voices low and not for show. All wore the faded T-shirts of former protest movements, inked with slogans now blurred by too many washes. One man, broad shouldered, his hair gone salt and pepper, looked up and caught her gaze. He hesitated before lifting a hand in greeting.

She returned the gesture, standing still as they closed the gap. Up close, she recognized two of the faces, members of Sonny Alana's old core team, now gone respectable in cargo shorts and hiking shoes. They stopped a polite distance away, shifting their weight from foot to foot.

"Heard you might come by," the man said. His voice was rougher than she remembered, but the eyes were steady. "We wanted to say thanks. And to show you what we've done."

She took them in, noting the ease with which they deferred to her, still not sure if she was a friend or cop, or if there was a difference anymore.

"I came to see the trees," she said, but softened

it with a smile. "But I'm glad you're here."

The third member of the group, a woman, hair shorn close, a lei of maile strung loose around her wrist, stepped forward. She offered the lei to Leilani, the leaves fresh and green.

"We made this for you," she said. "For bringing it back."

Leilani hesitated, after which she bowed her head, letting the woman settle the lei around her neck. The scent, sharp, astringent, flared up and brought with it an unexpected twist of memory. Her father, hands in the dirt, teaching her how to wind ti leaves together for the last May Day before he died. She bit the inside of her lip and nodded.

The man cleared his throat. "We're trying to get the whole stream corridor certified. Keep the developers out. Sonny would've." He stopped but didn't flinch. "He would've wanted you to see it like this."

Leilani looked up at the tangled webs of banyan roots, the lattice of branch and light. She imagined the future that had almost slipped away, the land bulldozed, the water poisoned, her own name scrubbed from the story. The ache that had lived under her ribs since the case broke receded, not vanishing but leeching away into the soft, loamy ground.

The activists lingered for a few more minutes,

telling her about the grant money, about the work crews that came every weekend, about the kids from the middle school who'd painted all the new signs by hand. None of them mentioned the murders, or the blood that had once darkened the roots. There was no need; the place had already metabolized its grief, turning it into mulch, into new green growth.

When they left, it was with a handshake and a shy, awkward thank you. Leilani watched their retreat before she made her own slow way to the center of the grove, where a clearing had been swept of debris and ringed with the smoothed stones of the original ahu. She sat on the low bench set against the largest banyan, letting her back sink into the cool bark. The sun was dropping fast, painting the ground in shifting patterns.

She closed her eyes and listened to the sough of leaves, to the shriek of a distant myna, to the drone of traffic out beyond the canopy, faint, but present, as it always would be.

For a while, she existed. No ceremony, no badge, no report to file. A woman alone in the late sun, breathing in the life she had nearly lost.

A breeze kicked up, scattering a handful of yellowed leaves at her feet. She watched them spiral, land, become part of the whole.

She inspected her hands, the skin a patchwork

of old wounds and new healing, and felt a sense of completion.

She held her palm against the bench, rough with age, and looked up through the maze of branches to the blank, infinite blue above. She wondered, as the last light faded, if Sonny Alana had ever sat here, dreaming of how the world could be different. Or if her father had. Or if she, herself, could ever belong to a world that was this quiet, this generous.

She thought of Torres, of the break room, of the simple, stubborn hope in his voice. She thought of her mother, and her son, and all the hard, necessary truths they'd spoken in the circle.

She let her shoulders drop, her breath deepen and smiled.

The world had taken its share, but it had given back, too. In the end, it was enough.

As the shadows drew in, Leilani rose, touched the bark of the banyan, and made her way toward the road, the scent of maile and memory following her out of the grove and into whatever came next.

# CHAPTER TWENTY

## *Shadows Linger*

D awn was a thin blue promise on the horizon as Leilani Kealoha double checked the surf leash around her son's ankle, tucking the excess cord into the waxed groove of his battered board. Laniakea at this hour was empty, no pro's film crews, no groms with carbon-fiber toothpicks, only the rawness of the waves and the restless churn of her own nerves. She watched as Kai dashed ahead, his silhouette ragged against the paler sky, arms akimbo and sand spraying behind his bare heels.

"Race you to the break!" Kai called over his shoulder, never waiting for an answer. In the low light, his grin was visible, a white strike of mischief in a face too much like his father's.

Leilani jogged after him, her surfboard clamped under one arm, and tried to let herself feel the moment, the way her mother's mindfulness app kept insisting she should. The sand was cold and thick between her toes, the salt in the air cut sharper than any aftershave. The ocean's breath was rhythmic, a living thing, and for once her pulse matched it instead of resisting.

"Mom, hurry!" Kai wheeled around, impatience in every limb. "We'll miss the glass!"

She almost laughed. He'd picked up the old timer lingo from watching too many surf documentaries, and now every uncrowded morning was glass, every tiny run of decent swell a secret spot. He'd started keeping a notebook, too, taping in printed-out wave charts and scribbling little arrows to show how he thought the currents would bend by ten, by noon, and when school let out.

"Chill, Kaimana," she called back, using the name she reserved for days like this, the ones when he woke up smiling. "You know the ocean waits for nobody."

Kai dropped to one knee and started dragging his fingers through the sand, hunting for puka shells. She slowed her pace, letting him be a kid. Letting herself be the mother she'd promised, one day ago, to never stop trying to be.

She caught up with him at the waterline; the surf hissing up over their toes before sneaking away, cold and predatory. Kai had a handful of shells and a fragment of what looked like a coral tooth, which he slipped into the pocket of his board shorts with the ritual seriousness of a young priest.

"Ready?" he asked, all business.

"Ready," she said, and kneeled to check his leash again, partly out of caution, partly out of compulsion.

Kai rolled his eyes, but the move was reflex, not rebellion. "I'm not gonna wipe out."

"Everyone wipes out," she replied. "It's genetic."

He snorted, then turned his attention to his board, inspecting it for dings. She did the same, running her hand over the rail, checking the wax. This one had once been her brother's, glassed heavy and yellowed with age. It rode low and stiff, but she trusted it more than any of the pop-out tech the kids used now.

She watched Kai's fingers as he traced the sun faded logo. His nails were short, bitten. The cuticle on his right thumb was torn. He'd probably picked it raw during yesterday's spelling test, if the ink stain on his knuckle was any clue. The sight made her throat tighten, which was absurd, but there it was.

Kai was first into the water, board cocked under his chest, shoulders working as he paddled out through the slow break. She followed, letting the cold wake up her arms, pushing out into the deeper blue, keeping her son in the corner of her vision.

They cleared the foam in three sets. The water was glassy, like Kai said, the dawn wind enough to brush their faces. The beach behind them was a featureless ribbon. No parked cars yet, no beachcombers, only a wandering dog and a cluster of birds picking at last night's drift. Above, the sky was turning from navy to gold, and in the slant of the new light every ripple glowed.

Kai lined up for the outside, all business now. He kneeled, watched the sets, and threw a look over his shoulder. "Next one's yours!" he called.

She grinned, felt the sudden and uncharacteristic urge to show off. When the wave lifted her, she popped up, knees bent, eyes forward, letting the board carry her through the bowl. It wasn't a big ride, but it was fast and clean, and the spray off the lip felt like proof that something in her body still worked the way it was supposed to. She rode it almost all the way to shore, bailed in the shallows, turning in time to see Kai go for the next set.

He caught the wave perfectly, crouched low and let the nose hover above the surface as he carved, slow and sure. He wiped out spectacularly, tumbling over himself, but when he surfaced he was laughing, face wild with the joy that had been missing from her life, and his, for months.

She swam out to meet him. "Nice, dude," she said, bumping her fist into his. "I didn't know you had it in you."

He beamed. "I'm gonna be better than you soon."

She ruffled his hair, ignoring the wet protest. "Impossible."

They paddled together, riding the lull and letting the sea decide what would come next. Kai had a million questions. Did she remember that one storm last year, when the current sucked all the sand off the reef? Was it true what the TV said, that sharks mostly bite white boards? Could he, maybe, if he got good enough, enter the winter contest next year?

She fielded the questions, dodging the ones that touched too close to the heart. Every so often, she'd glance back at the shore to check for hazards or rogue sets, but for the most part, she allowed the moment to fill the cracks that work and worry had left inside her.

They took the inside waves first, small, forgiving, the kind that built confidence and let Kai show off without risking a trip to urgent care. He paddled hard, braced his knees, and when the wave picked him up, he popped up with a gawkiness that was all elbows and wild balance. Sometimes he made it, sometimes he didn't, but each time he emerged from the whitewater with a shout, eyes bright, and hair slicked to his forehead.

Leilani hung back, letting him lead, calling out pointers only when he looked ready to listen. She studied the mechanics of his body: the sharp turn of his hips when he steered, the flex of his knees as he crouched, the way he bit his lip in concentration before committing to a run. At the end of one ride, he spun the board out and landed flat, sending a geyser of spray into the morning air. It caught the light and made a halo around him that was gone as soon as it formed.

"You see that?" he hollered, voice ragged from the salt.

"I saw," she called back, letting herself laugh. "But next time, try not to drink the whole Pacific, yeah?"

He blew a raspberry, then ducked under the next set, surfacing a few yards closer to her. They bobbed together, arms draped over their boards, the ocean settling into a lull that made conversation easy.

"You think they're gonna let me surf in the contest?" Kai asked, breathless but hopeful.

"If you keep your grades up," she said, knowing it was both a promise and a bribe. "And if you stop using your homework as a napkin."

He snorted but didn't argue.

A bigger set rolled in, and Kai paddled hard, getting ahead of the break. Leilani shadowed him, hung back, letting him take the lead. He caught the wave right at the crest, managed a shaky turn, and as he reached the bottom, pulled off a clumsy but determined attempt at a cutback. The move was raw, all momentum, and no finesse, and she thought he might eat it hard.

But he held on. Recovered. Rode it out, whooping as he coasted toward the shallows.

She clapped, letting the next wave carry her, catching the tail end and riding it in tandem. They were side by side, slicing the surface, and when she glanced over, Kai's mouth was open in a wild, animal grin, that reminded her why none of the casework, none of the grief, could ever matter more than this.

They ran it back for an hour, taking turns and pushing each other, swapping boards for a set to see if it made a difference. It did, but only because Kai said her old lady board made him look slow. When the crowd thickened, a couple of teenagers with fresh gear, a couple of retirees in matching rash guards, Leilani signaled for a break, steering them toward the rocks.

Between rides, they lay on their boards, bellies down, heads pillowed on crossed arms. Kai hummed some song under his breath, off-key but familiar. She looked over at him, this small miracle she'd been allowed to keep, and knew with terrifying clarity that nothing in her life mattered as much as this.

After a while, she said, "Would you like to go in?"

"Not yet," he said, eyes on the horizon. "Let's float for a while."

They did.

The sun had almost cleared the trees when they paddled back to shore, arms spent, legs numb. Kai carried his board with exaggerated care, avoiding the sharp rocks, and set it on the sand like it was made of glass.

Leilani shook the water from her hair. She looked out at the surf, scanning for threats. None presented. For this one morning, at least, everything was as it should be.

"Best morning ever," Kai declared, face upturned to the warming sky.

She wanted to say me too, but squeezed his shoulder, letting the gesture say what words couldn't.

Behind them, the city was waking up, the distant rush of traffic a reminder that the world would not pause, not for anyone. But here, in the hush and the hush alone, they had made a space for themselves.

Leilani breathed deep, the salt burning in her nose, and she let herself believe that peace was possible.

Kai was the first to speak. "You ever get scared, Mom? Like, not in the ocean. But, you know, about work stuff?"

She let the question hang, tasted the truth before saying it. "Yeah. All the time. But I try not to let it show."

"Uncle Ed says you're the bravest person he knows."

She laughed, but it came out softer than she meant. "Your uncle exaggerates."

"Nah," Kai said, propping himself up on his elbows. "You are. Grandma says so. She said you went after that bad guy when nobody else wanted to help."

Leilani stared at her feet, digging her toes into the cooling sand. "I was doing my job," she said. "Sometimes it's not about being brave. Sometimes it's all about showing up, even when you're tired. When you'd rather stay home and surf."

Kai shrugged. "I bet you were still scared."

She nodded. "Yeah. But that's how you know you're doing something important."

He looked out at the waves, thoughtful. "I think I'd be a good detective. I already figured out who was stealing the muffins at school."

"Oh, yeah?" she said, smiling for real now. "Who was it?"

He leaned in, stage whispered, "Mr. Aiona, the janitor. He puts them in his thermos when nobody's looking."

She feigned shock. "You should tell the principal."

He smiled. "Nah. He's cool. He gives me extra towels when I have P.E."

They lapsed into comfortable quiet, letting the sounds of the morning fill the space. The rush of the surf, the distant calls of birds, the thump of someone's radio farther down the sand. She could have stayed there forever, absorbing the simple, relentless presence of her son.

Eventually, he sat up, dusted himself off, and said, "You wanna go again? The wind's coming up. Might get choppy soon."

After looking at her watch, she did the mental math on how much time they had before the city called her back. "One more set," she agreed, rising to her feet.

They waded back into the water, boards at their hips, and paddled out past the chop. The waves were messier now, but they worked with what they had, taking quick drops and cutting across the face before the wind could tear it to pieces.

On his last ride, Kai caught the wave late, almost wiped out, but hung on, carving a line that was more luck than skill. When he beached the board, he turned to her and lifted both arms overhead, victorious.

"Best wipeout ever!" he yelled, laughing so hard he fell over again.

She caught up with him, wrapped him in a hug that left them both dripping and sticky with salt. He squirmed but didn't pull away.

They stood there, the sun on their backs, watching the waves collapse in on each other.

"Let's do this again," Kai said, voice muffled against her shoulder.

"Yeah," she said. "Let's."

For a few minutes more, they watched. Mother and son. Detective and apprentice. Both quietly certain that, for today at least, nothing could touch them.

The world could wait.

By the time the sun was high enough to turn the water into polished glass, the beach had filled. Pickup trucks and battered Subarus lined the roadside, and the first of the weekend surfers arrived in packs, lugging boards and coolers, barking greetings to friends as if the world were on permanent vacation. Leilani and Kai staked out a spot on the slope above the wrack line, spreading their threadbare towels and shaking salt from their ears.

Kai plopped onto his back, still humming from the last set, arms pillowed under his head. He chattered about the waves, about how he'd almost stuck the landing, about how next time he was going to win the heat at school. She let him talk, let the stream of words wash over her, half-listening and half somewhere else, a place where the future was not guaranteed, and every scrap of normalcy had to be guarded like stolen goods.

Her phone buzzed against her thigh, once, twice. The vibration was subtle, but enough to slice through the early morning stupor. She'd left it zipped in the waterproof pouch attached to her bag, a habit carried over from days when the only threats were water damage and the occasional sand invasion.

She let it buzz a third time before unzipping the pouch and flipping the phone into her palm. She glanced at the screen, hoping for nothing more than a calendar notification or a text from her mother. What she saw instead was a number she didn't recognize, with a local area code. No name, no context. A single line of text.

*ALIKA WAS THE BEGINNING. THE REAL MASTERMIND SENDS REGARDS.*

She stared at it, letting the words sink past the armor she'd built over the past few weeks. Her first reaction was anger, hot and immediate, a spike that made her jaw clamp shut and her grip on the phone go white-knuckled. The second was calculation. Who would send a message like this, and why now?

She scanned the beach, shifting her weight so she could see both the parking area and the paths leading down from the bluff. Most of the newcomers were kids, or old-timers too battered to get caught up in city drama. She looked around the benches under the hau trees. The benches where the regulars sometimes stashed coolers and watched the surf. No eyes on her, no one lingering too long.

Kai had gone quiet, watching a group of boys his age mess around with a soccer ball near the tidepools. She tried to slip the phone away without him noticing, but he caught the movement, eyes narrowing with the sharp intuition only children possessed.

"Work stuff?" he asked.

"Yeah," she said, faking a smile. "Nothing I can't handle."

He sat up, digging his heels into the sand. "You sure? You look like you're gonna punch someone."

She forced a laugh, ruffled his hair, and set the

phone face down on the towel. "The usual. Bad guys with nothing better to do."

"Is it about the case?" he asked. "The one from before?"

She hesitated. "Sort of. But it's over now. We're cleaning up."

He absorbed that. Satisfied, he flopped back onto the towel. "Okay," he said, "As long as you don't have to work today."

"I won't," she promised, and almost believed it.

A shadow fell across the towels. She looked up to see a boy from Kai's class, towel draped over his shoulder, face sunburned and smiling. "Kai! You coming to play or what?"

"Yeah!" Kai jumped up, grabbing his board and the spare rash guard from the bag. He turned back to Leilani, eyes bright. "You wanna come watch?"

"In a minute," she said. "Go have fun."

He sprinted off, leaving a spray of sand in his wake.

She waited until he was out of earshot before she opened her phone again, staring at the message. She noted the number, ran it through her memory, but it didn't ping. She flicked over to her contacts, compared area codes, looking for a match to any of her recent cases. Nothing. The brevity of the message, the lack of taunt or threat, unsettled her more than any long-winded rant. Whoever sent this knew her. Knew how to say enough to unbalance her, to remind her that peace was a mirage, always receding.

She thumbed in a reply, kept it short.

Who is this?

She waited, staring at the screen as if her will alone could force a response. Nothing came. After a minute, she powered the phone off, set it back in the pouch, and tried to shake the dread from her bones.

She packed up the towels, the sunscreen, and the bag of half melted mochi snacks. She stashed Kai's sandals and rinsed her board, all the while scanning the crowd for anything that didn't fit. But it was a Saturday, a beach, and for all the city's undercurrents, nothing jumped out.

When Kai returned, flushed and sweating from his game, she let him drink half the water bottle in a single pull before suggesting they head home.

"Already?" he complained, but the protest was weak, the exhaustion catching up with him. He didn't notice the way she gripped the boards a little tighter, or the way she walked closer to the road, watching the shadows between cars.

They loaded up, boards rattling in the back, and pulled onto the highway as the first of the noon traffic snaked past. Kai was asleep before they hit the second stoplight, sand crusted in his eyebrows, mouth open in a soft snore. Leilani drove with one hand on the wheel, the other drumming the dashboard, replaying the message in her mind and assembling the mosaic of possibilities.

As they hit their street, she'd made three mental lists. People who hated her enough to send a threat, people who had the resources to do it, and people who wanted her scared but not dead. The overlap was larger than she'd like to admit.

She parked in the driveway, killed the engine, and let the car tick and settle. She didn't want to wake Kai, so she sat next to him, letting the silence fill in the cracks that fear had made.

He woke on his own, blinking at the sudden stillness. "Are we home?"

"Yeah," she said, brushing sand from his cheek. "We made it."

He smiled and bolted for the front door, already planning out his day.

She followed, slower, letting the sun wash over her as she walked. At the door, she paused, turned back to scan the street. No strange cars, no unfamiliar faces. But the feeling didn't fade.

She stepped inside, dropped her keys in the

bowl by the door, and went straight to her bedroom. She pulled out the old evidence box, the one she'd promised herself she would burn, but never did. She opened it, sifting through the files, the pictures, the broken badge from the first case that had ever scared her. She pulled out her father's notebook, thumbed through the pages until she found the one with his handwriting underlined twice.

The ocean always brings the truth back.

She closed the box, sat on the bed, and let her mind settle.

Whatever this was, she'd handle it. Like always.

But for now, she let herself have the afternoon. Let Kai have his cartoons and his snack and his nap. Let the world turn and wait for the next wave.

It would come, and she'd be ready.

That was the job.

Later, after dinner, she took Kai out to the patio, watched him practice tricks on his skateboard, his feet scuffed and bloody, but his determination unshaken. He fell a dozen times, got up and tried again. She watched, pride and fear mingling in her chest, and knew she'd do the same.

When the sun set and the sky went purple, she

made them hot chocolate and let Kai stay up late. She lingered over the taste, the quiet, the simple fact of being alive.

She sat at the kitchen table long after he'd gone to bed, staring at the phone, waiting for it to buzz.

When it did, the message was shorter than the first.

*SOMEONE WHO KNOWS.*

She laughed, the sound equal parts dread and defiance. She turned off the phone, set it down, and walked outside. The moon was up, painting the world silver and sharp.

She stood in the yard, the grass cold under her feet, and stared out at the horizon. Somewhere out there, the next case was waiting. She felt fear and subsequently released it. And when she stepped back inside, she felt, if not peace, at least a kind of armor.

It would have to do.

# Acknowledgements

A special thank you to my daughter Christina J. Morgan, my unofficial collaborator.

Thanks to my editor, Laura Dragonette, whose efforts helped turn my manuscript into a polished novel. Her help is greatly appreciated. Any mistakes the reader may find are solely the responsibility of the author.

Special thanks to my daughter Stephanie Morgan, my beta reader. Stephanie has read every novel in its rough stages and rarely gets to see the completed product. Her insight and critique have been critical in making sure the stories make sense.

Also, I would like to thank my family for their encouragement. I have been telling them stories since they were little, and I always told them that someone should be writing this stuff down. I decided to write it down myself.

I want to thank my closest friend, Trish Moakler-Herud. She has been encouraging me for years to write my stories down. I hope this will make her proud.

A special thanks to my late wife, Jane. She pushed me for years to become a writer, and my biggest regret is that she didn't live long enough to see it happen. I love her with all my heart and miss her every day. I think she would be pleased.

Finally, thanks to the readers. Without you, none of this would be important.

# About the Author

**2019 Pacific Book Awards Best Mystery Finalist** . . . *Crime Delayed*

**2020 Pacific Book Awards Best Mystery Winner** . . . *Crime Denied*

**2020 Chanticleer International Book Awards: 1st Place Blue Ribbon, CLUE Book Awards for Suspense, Thriller Fiction** . . . *Crime Denied*

**2021 Chanticleer International Book Awards Finalist, CLUE Book Awards for Suspense, Thriller Fiction** . . . *Crime Conspiracy*

**2021 Chanticleer International Book Awards Finalist, Book Series, CLUE Book Awards for Suspense, Thriller Fiction** . . . Crime Series, The Buck Taylor Novels

**2022 Chanticleer International Book Awards Finalist, CLUE Book Awards for Suspense, Thriller Fiction** . . . *Crime Exploded*

**2022 Chanticleer International Book Awards Finalist, CLUE Book Awards for Suspense, Thriller Fiction** . . . *Crime Spree*

**2023 Chanticleer International Book Awards Finalist, CLUE Book Awards for Suspense, Thriller Fiction** . . . *Crime Scene*

**2023 Chanticleer International Book Awards Series Finalist, Mystery & Mayhem Book Awards...** *Crime Series*

Chuck Morgan attended Seton Hall University

and Regis College and spent thirty-five years as a construction project manager. He is an avid outdoorsman, an Eagle Scout and a licensed private pilot. He enjoys camping, hiking, mountain biking and fly-fishing.

He is the author of the Crime series, featuring Colorado Bureau of Investigation Agent Buck Taylor. The series includes *Crime Interrupted, Crime Delayed, Crime Unsolved, Crime Exposed, Crime Denied, Crime Conspiracy, Crime Unknown, Crime Exploded, Crime Spree, Crime Family, Crime Scene, and Crime Victims.*

He is also the author of *Her Name Was Jane*, a memoir about his late wife's nine-year battle with breast cancer. He has three children and four grandchildren. He resides in Lone Tree, Colorado.

# Other Books by the Author

Dear Reader, thank you for reading this novel. Please enjoy the other books in this series and follow Colorado Bureau of Investigation Agent Buck Taylor and his team as they investigate new and sometimes unusual crimes in the Colorado mountains. Each novel is a separate story, and they can be read in any order, but you might find it more enjoyable to read them in order.

Happy Reading,

Chuck Morgan

*"Crime Interrupted: A Buck Taylor Novel by Chuck Morgan is a gripping, edge-of-the-seat novel. Right from page one, the action kicks off and never stops, gaining pace as each chapter passes." Reviewed by Anne-Marie Reynolds for Readers' Favorite.*

Finalist . . . 2019 Pacific Book Awards Best Mystery

*"This crime novel reads like a great thriller. The writing is atmospheric, laced with vivid descriptions that capture the setting in great detail while allowing readers to follow the intensity of the action and the emotional and psychological depth of the story." Reviewed by Divine Zape for Readers' Favorite.*

*"Professionally written in the style of a best-selling crime novelist, such as Tom Clancy, Crime Unsolved: A Buck Taylor Novel by Chuck Morgan is a spellbinding suspense novel with an environmental flair. Intriguing subplots of fraud, survivalist paranoia and murder weave their way through the fabric of the plot, creating a dynamic story. This is an action-filled, stimulating tale which contains fascinating details that are relevant in our present climate." Reviewed by Susan Sewell for Readers' Favorite.*

"*Chuck Morgan has a unique gift for plot, one that makes Crime Exposed: A Buck Taylor Novel a hard-to-put-down book. From the start, readers know what happens to Barb, but they become curious as they follow the investigation, wondering if the characters will find out what happened to her. The descriptions are filled with clarity, and they offer readers great images. The prose is elegant, and it captures both the emotional and psychological elements of the novel clearly while offering vivid descriptions of scenes and characters. This is a fast-paced thriller with memorable characters and a criminal investigation that is so real readers will believe it could happen." Reviewed by Romuald Dzemo for Readers' Favorite.*

**Winner . . . 2020 Pacific Book Awards Best**

## Mystery

**2020 Chanticleer International Book Awards: 1st Place Blue Ribbon, CLUE Book Awards for Suspense, Thriller Fiction**

*"It's really progressive to see a female serial killer portrayed with such intelligent writing and depth of character, and the cat and mouse chase dynamic is thrown off nicely by the switching of genders. What results is a really enjoyable thriller and crime mystery novel, and overall Crime Denied is certain to please fans of both hard-boiled detective tales and action/adventure crime novels." Reviewed by K.C. Finn for Readers' Favorite.*

**2021 Chanticleer International Book Awards Finalist, CLUE Book Awards for Suspense, Thriller Fiction . . . *Crime Conspiracy***

*"This makes for a truly dynamic story where anything is possible, and a hero you can root for even when it looks like all is lost." Reviewed by K.C. Finn for Readers' Favorite.*

*"This is a book you can't put down, which will entertain you on many levels, and at times make your skin crawl; the kind of book that remains in your*

*thoughts long after you finish reading." Reviewed by Steven Robson for Readers' Favorite.*

**"I read Crime Unknown in one sitting. The plot is intense and the main character, Agent Buck Taylor, is a hero like no other.** *This book has everything a thriller needs to be and more. I thought I knew the story at the beginning. Buck will solve a tricky murder case, I thought. But Chuck Morgan adds a twist to this story that expands it and makes it one of the most enjoyable books I've read in this genre. I loved that the lead was such an awesome well-rounded fellow but that he also had a support team who were just as important to the story." Reviewed by Maureen Dangarembizi for Readers' Favorite.*

**"Crime Unknown is a thoroughly enjoyable read and I would not hesitate to recommend this book to fans of the crime genre and those looking for a gateway in."** *Reviewed by K.C. Finn for Readers' Favorite.*

**2022 Chanticleer International Book Awards Finalist, CLUE Book Awards for Suspense, Thriller Fiction . . .** *Crime Exploded*

*"Action-packed and fast-paced, I was sucked into the story the moment I opened the novel.* The author built the story to perfection. Chuck Morgan gave just the right amount of suspense, mystery and action to keep readers' attention on Buck and his team. There was never a dull moment in the story. The narrative ran smoothly until the end; it followed the development of the story and the pace set by the characters. I enjoyed the twists and turns. What I loved more than anything else in the plot was how calculating Buck was. He was smart; he didn't let the FBI discourage him and kept his head in the game. The action gave me an adrenaline rush. Absolutely brilliant!" Reviewed by Rabia Tanveer for Readers' Favorite.

**2022 Chanticleer International Book Awards Finalist, CLUE Book Awards for Suspense, Thriller Fiction . . .** *Crime Spree*

*"It is one of the best crime novels I have read in a long while, with real characters developed in a way to let you get to know them intimately, understand them, and appreciate their strengths and weaknesses. The plot is tight, exciting, and tense, with plenty of action, and it will grip you from the start. The bizarre storyline is enthralling, written in descriptive prose that lands you right in the middle of the action. Forget sleep; once you pick this book up, you won't want to put it down until it's finished. Fantastic story, and highly recommended for fans of high-octane crime thrillers." Reviewed by Anne-Marie Reynolds for Readers' Favorite.*

*"Crime Family is the tenth book in the Buck Taylor series. Chuck Morgan had me hooked from the first page until the end.* There was never a dull moment with all the action; one chapter flowed into the next. The story was fast-paced and kept me on the edge of my seat. I kept turning the pages to find out what would happen next. I was intrigued, and with all the twists and turns, I could not predict what was looming. The characters were well-developed. Each had a background description, and it was fun getting to know some of them. The story was excellently written with a fitting ending." Reviewed by Alma Boucher for Readers' Favorite.*

*"Crime Scene is a must-read for lovers of mystery sleuth and murder tales with a touch of conspiracy."* Reader's Favorite review.*

*"Crime Scene has a carefully designed intrigue that deepens with every unforeseeable turn of events, and a dynamic narrative."* Reader's Favorite review.*

*"This is a great book. Holds your attention and you don't want to put it down. I would recommend this book to anyone who loves a good crime novel."* Amazon review.*

*"Spellbinding, gripping, powerful, and relevant are just a few words that come to mind after turning the*

*last page of Crime Scene: A Buck Taylor Novel, book 11, by Chuck Morgan." Amazon Review.*

"**A riveting plot and good pacing keep the reader in suspense as Buck Taylor and his team establish evidence beyond a reasonable doubt.** *The author sustains interest by skillfully showing the art and intuition involved in crime investigation and the science behind it, as well as the elements that can delay or confound it. There are a lot of quirky characters in the novel and the author gives them mannerisms, voices and descriptions that make them distinctive and realistic. The details and descriptions of the work and everyday life of the players are both pleasantly appealing and revolting, depending on the scenario. What's most captivating and intriguing about the character development is the backstory of the unhinged characters and how the author uses them as part of the perplexing trail of a horrendous crime. Themes of sadism, cruelty, grief, forensics, police procedures, and even a little bit of romance can be found in this installment of the Buck Taylor series. Highly recommended for crime story fans who especially enjoy the information as well as the twists, turns, and the untangling of intricate and cold case crime sprees." Reviewed by Carmen Tenorio for Readers' Favorite.*